A Strange TWIST of FATE

Romantic Mystery

Debra Erfert

Debra Erfert

A Strange TWIST of FATE
© 2017 Debra Erfert
All rights reserved.

No part of this publication may be reproduced, scanned, uploaded, distributed, stored in a retrieval system or transmitted in any form or by any means, electronic or mechanical, including photocopying, recording, or otherwise, without written permission from the publisher.

This is a work of fiction. Names, descriptions, entities, and incidents included in this story are products of the author's imagination. Any resemblance to actual persons, events, and entities is entirely coincidental.

Book Edition: March, 2017
Book ISBN-13: 978-0-9968597-6-9
ISBN-10: 0-9968597-6-4

Cover Design by D. Robert Pease,
walkingstickbooks.com
Edited by Andrea Pearson

Published by
Stone Horse Press, LLC

A Strange Twist of Fate

Also by Debra "DJ" Erfert

Changes of the Heart
Relative Evil
Window of Time
Window of Death
A Deadly Glimpse (Novella)
Window of Secrets, Mission: Oasis de Huacachina (Novella)
Royals of Monterra: It Takes a Sleuth (Kindle Worlds Novella)

Debra Erfert

Dedication

For Mike, my love.

A Strange Twist of Fate

One

Anna Eddington considered her options as she fingered the tiny plastic baggie of white powder in the pocket of her sweatshirt. She could put her car into drive and leave the dark street where she had been waiting for close to thirty minutes. Or she could stay and meet with a man she knew had committed several felonies in a desperate need to buy another hit of cocaine. But a sense of urgency drove Anna to that dangerous place. After nearly a year of trying to find the person responsible for killing Greg, she still had no solid leads. Tonight could change things—if she had enough guts to go through with the deal.

Seeing the thin figure of the man she'd lured to the spot outside the small bar on Van Buren Street in Phoenix sent her heart racing. Even in the low light, Anna recognized his scraggly face from the mug shot stapled to the file. The case her husband had prosecuted ended over two years ago, but the man hadn't changed. He still wore facial hair, growing in rough patches. His greasy, longish blond hair was poking out from under a black knit beanie. Being early March, the night was cool. He had on several layers of clothing, including a dirty hooded sweatshirt jacket not unlike the one she wore. Anna's smelled like lavender, but from his grungy look, she assumed his didn't. He'd spent all of six months sentenced to Phoenix's county jail for pushing down an old woman and then stealing her handbag. Bystanders caught him red-handed, yet he got out quicker than common sense dictated.

Razor, the man's nickname Anna read in Greg's case file, bobbed his head around, no doubt looking for her. After a deep breath to bolster her courage, she pulled the hood up over her head and got out of the car. That movement got Razor's attention. Fear pierced her heart, but she had to believe he knew something about the crash. She suspected that someone Greg sent to prison, or was about to prosecute, intentionally killed her husband. Nothing else made any sense. Maybe Razor heard who had sent Greg's Cherokee off Interstate 17 and down into the Bloody Basin canyon.

A moment of panic made Anna stop short of where he stood. His squinted eyes were bloodshot. Had she made a mistake coming?

"Did you bring it?" Razor asked, stepping closer.

She brought out the baggie, her hand shaking slightly. He reached for it, but Anna moved it around her back.

"No, not until you answer a couple of questions for me. That was the deal."

Razor had several teeth missing when he smiled. He pulled a box cutter from his pocket, sliding it open with a touch of his thumb.

A bright light blinded her.

"Stop—police!"

Razor pivoted and ran away.

"No, wait, come back!" Anna shouted—pleaded. The next instant, she was shoved up against the brick wall of the bar, face first, her shoulders pinned.

"You're under arrest for the sale of narcotics," a man's gruff voice said in her ear.

"No!" Anna screamed. "Let me go. It's not real. I swear!"

"Sure, lady," the cop said as he forced her arm behind her back.

"I can explain—please let me explain." Anna stopped pleading when she remembered what her dad always told her. Never try telling anything to a beat cop. They won't care, and all that could happen was you'd incriminate yourself. She needed to be careful and wait until she could call her dad for help.

"Do you have an ID?"

"It's in my car." The cop pulled her away from the wall, pausing only to pick up the small baggie from the sidewalk before

A Strange Twist of Fate

leading her across the street, back toward her Impala. "How do you know that's my car?"

"I was watching you."

Anna cringed at how tightly he held her arm. It hurt. "Why?"

"Your car is out of place on this street. I knew you were up to something, but I thought you were the buyer, not the seller."

"But I *told* you . . ." Anna shut her mouth, knowing it was useless. His only goal was to make an arrest.

~*~

There were only so many excuses Detective Lee Adams could find for not going home. It was nearly 10:00 p.m., yet he couldn't help but look around his office again, trying to see something else to clean or organize. Or maybe he could even delve deeper on another case—anything to keep from going back to a depressingly empty apartment. He caught sight of the overused couch. Sleeping there again would save him the reminder that his divorce was close to final. He'd slept there on too many occasions when he had serious cases to complete even while he was married, so it wouldn't be out of the ordinary.

"I need to make a phone call!"

An angry woman's voice gave Lee the temporary reprieve he needed to take his mind off his sleeping situation. The report room was quiet, adding to the loud volume of the woman's voice. Lee stopped at his doorway in time to see Bobby Zimbroskie pulling her by the arm toward him. She had on tight blue jeans, a loose-fitting T-shirt, and a sweatshirt jacket. Her ponytail held back blonde hair, but several thick strands hung loosely in her face. She looked so young—midtwenties at best. A scratch on her cheek had bled down to her chin. The areas under her eyes were streaked in black. Her mascara had run. She looked as if she'd been crying. He'd seen it on his wife's face like that only once, not too long before she told him she was divorcing him.

The woman looked straight into Lee's eyes and pleaded, "Please, call Judge Jackson Wright for me." Zimbroskie's rough

Debra Erfert

treatment nearly tripped her on their way farther through the report room to his usual writing station at the end of a long, narrow table.

Lee followed them. "Take it easy with her, Bobby."

Zimbroskie glanced over his shoulder with a scowl on his brow. "She's not cooperating." He sat her down in a hardwood chair at the end of the table.

Lee noticed the woman's hands were cuffed behind her back, and the chair's wooden arms bit into her elbows. He could tell by the way she acted that she wasn't intoxicated. Her pupils looked normal, so no drugs.

"What did she do?" Lee asked.

The cop held up a baggie filled with white powder and dropped it on the table. "I hooked her trying to sell cocaine."

"I told you—it isn't real," the woman said, her voice low and tired sounding.

"I'm Detective Lee Adams. What's your name, ma'am?" he asked, keeping his gaze on the brown-eyed woman.

"Julianna Wright Eddington," she said, staring hard at Lee.

Lee blinked several times as the name *Wright* sunk into his tired brain. "Holy . . ." He glanced at Zimbroskie, who didn't skip a beat as he typed on the desktop computer, probably starting his arrest report. As Lee dug in his pocket for his handcuff key, he asked, "Bobby, did you field-test the contents of that baggie?"

"Not yet." Zimbroskie tossed a woman's handbag beside the baggie. "I'll get to it. But I caught her in the act of haggling with a greasy-haired scumbag tweeker."

Mrs. Eddington looked up at Lee again. "Would you please call my dad?"

"Lean forward." Lee reached down between the chair and her back and unlocked her cuffs. "Let's wait a few minutes and get this cleared up without you using the judge's name to get you out of trouble." Zimbroskie's head jerked up, as if he'd just connected the name. He wasn't known as one of the best and brightest, but he was on top enough to see a drug buy. Or he had been voyeuristically watching the woman and stumbled onto her attempt.

A Strange Twist of Fate

"Yeah, her dad's Judge Jack Wright," Lee confirmed to the startled beat cop. He also remembered reading that Mrs. Eddington's husband died a year ago. She was widowed at twenty-four years old—much too young to have lost a husband.

"Hammer Jack," Zimbroskie whispered. He shifted his eyes to Mrs. Eddington. "Your dad is going to be mad as hell when he finds out you're snagged for drug sales."

"Did you actually see the exchange?" Lee asked.

Zimbroskie sat back. "Not exactly. I stopped it just before. And it was a good thing, too. That scum pulled a box cutter on her."

"So you don't have sales." Lee touched Mrs. Eddington's arm. "Let's go to my office to see if you even have possession." He pointed to his door. "It's over there," he told her. "Bring your field-test kit, Bobby."

She tried to stand up, but she faltered. Lee grasped her shoulders, just to help her get up. When she straightened her back, he let her go. He picked up her handbag and led the way to his office. "Please, take a seat next to my desk, Mrs. Eddington." Before he sat down, he opened a first-aid kit hung on the wall near the doorway and took out several things the wounded woman needed—a few packs of antiseptic towelettes and a small bandage. He set them on the edge of his desk closer to where she sat down. She stared like she didn't know what to do with them.

"Your cheek is bleeding," Lee said quietly.

She touched her face with her fingers. It must've been hurting. She had known which one to inspect. Her eyes began to shimmer, and she sniffed a couple of times. Lee opened an antiseptic packet and handed her the towelette. When she looked around, he asked, "What is it?"

"I need a mirror." She motioned to under his arm. "I have one in my purse."

Lee set the bag down on his desk and asked, "Bobby, did you search this?"

"You bet."

"He also searched me," she added very quietly.

Debra Erfert

Lee swung his eyes around to Bobby again. "Is that right?"

"Yeah—sure I did."

"Couldn't you get a female officer to meet you at the scene?" Lee asked.

With a shrug, he leaned his shoulder against the doorjamb. "It was only a cursory search for weapons. It's not like I did a strip search right there on the street."

Lee let out a heavy breath and made a mental note to report the policy breach to the sergeant. But what was done was done. He would make sure the woman's rights were protected from this moment on. He handed her the purse. While she found her mirror, he took the test kit and baggie from Zimbroskie's hand and began the testing. It wasn't hard. All it took was a tiny sample of the white powder dropped into a flat plastic vial of special liquid. After Lee had broken an even smaller glass bubble inside, he shook it. If the powder were a drug, then the liquid would change colors. The color chart on the side would tell him which drug it was. If it turned blue, it was positive for cocaine. Pink would prove it to be an opioid drug like morphine or heroin. If the powder turned the fluid brown, then she had meth. Not surprisingly, it stayed clear. Lee held the test up for Zimbroskie to see.

"It's clean," Lee said. He tossed the test-kit vial into the trash and watched Mrs. Eddington dab at the blood on her face. The towelette got dirty very quickly, and he opened another one, knowing she might go through a couple.

"I'll kick her loose," Zimbroskie said, pushing up from the doorjamb.

"No, I'll take care of her," Lee told him. "You just close out the case you opened on her."

Zimbroskie stared at Mrs. Eddington for several moments as she continued to wipe the blood off her wounded face with the towelette Lee had opened for her. "Sure." He turned and stormed back into the patrol room.

Lee stepped to the door and watched the patrol officer for a few moments. Zimbroskie's demeanor had changed slightly. He

A Strange Twist of Fate

dropped down hard in his chair and started stabbing at the computer keys. Lee could see that he was angry about something ... maybe because Lee had horned in on his bust? Or debunked it?

Lee pulled a chair away from the wall and positioned it in front of the woman. He noticed that she'd cleaned the makeup off from under her pretty brown eyes, as well as getting the rest of the blood off her face. He took the bandage from his desk and tore open the package.

"Hold still." He carefully placed the bandage over the scratch. Using only his index fingers, he gently smoothed down the sticky ends before throwing away the plastic coverings in the trash can.

"Thank you," Mrs. Eddington whispered.

He picked up the baggie and studied the powder inside. "You know, selling something that even resembles drugs is still a felony if you were trying to pass it off as such."

Mrs. Eddington licked her lips and swallowed a couple of times before she replied. "It's powdered sugar, and I wasn't selling it."

"Then what were you doing with it?"

Her eyes darted to his desk phone. She had wanted to call her father earlier, but there wasn't a need to bring him in now. He lifted the phone closer to her, to give her that option if she still wanted it. She returned her gaze to him.

"I—I was going to trade it for information."

"What did you want to know from a dangerous, strung-out drug addict?"

She touched her cheek again. "It doesn't matter now. I'll never be able to ask him. He'll never trust me enough to meet with me again." She tossed the bloody towelettes into the trash can. "I've lost my last chance."

He waited a few moments before asking, "At what?"

Mrs. Eddington took in a gasping breath, biting back tears and shaking her head.

"Did you drive a car to the meeting?" Lee asked.

She nodded.

Debra Erfert

He stood up and grabbed his jacket off the back of his desk chair. "I'll give you a ride home."

"What?" Mrs. Eddington asked, standing up. "No, I don't need—I saw the tow truck take my car away. Can't I get it out of the impound tonight?"

Lee shook his head. "It's nearly ten thirty. They won't open until morning." He could see the tears glisten in her eyes again. "If you want, I can pick you up and bring you back—help you through the process. Or do you want me to call your dad?"

She looked startled when he mentioned her dad. It took another moment before she said, "There's no need to get him involved now. I'll accept your offer."

Lee had no choice now but to leave his office and head to his apartment—alone, after he dropped off a very lucky woman at her home. She may not have known it, but Zimbroskie probably saved her life when he arrested her. A junkie in need of a hit would be willing to use a weapon to get it. He had a box cutter? That sounded familiar. Lee might've seen an assault report that involved a weapon like that within the past few weeks.

He locked his office after they stepped out into the patrol room. Zimbroskie watched them leave out the back door, to where Lee had his private vehicle parked.

Mrs. Eddington was noticeably quiet while he opened her door. She didn't speak a word until he pulled his car to a stop at the edge of the parking lot.

"Which way?"

She let out a heavy sigh. "I live in Scottsdale."

He nodded and turned north. He knew the way to the affluent city, and truthfully, he wasn't surprised she lived there. Lee remembered what had happened to City of Phoenix Assistant Prosecutor Greg Eddington a year ago. He'd seen pictures of the prosecutor and his wife in the online newspaper shortly after his car crash. He'd had a promising career ahead of him. The crash was suspicious, but the highway patrol had no leads. There was an investigation, although he didn't hear where it went—if anywhere.

A Strange Twist of Fate

Lee looked over at Greg's widow. She kept her head turned away from him, staring out into the darkness. He wondered what she was doing tonight on a dangerous street normally occupied by prostitutes and strung-out losers. She said she wanted information. Now Lee was curious about what she would've asked that crackhead if she hadn't been arrested. She was right. She probably wouldn't have another chance to ask him any questions, but maybe Lee could for her.

"What's your address?"

"East Gainey Ranch Road." She finally turned to look at him. "Do you know where that is?"

"I do." Lee glanced at her. "I started out as a patrol officer in Scottsdale about ten years ago."

She nodded, then fell back into the quietness she'd been in for the past twenty minutes, resuming her staring out the window as if she would miss something important if she stopped looking. He headed east. Another fifteen minutes later, he pulled onto her wide street. He'd forgotten how huge the houses were on her cul-de-sac—and expensive.

"Second house on the right," she said, just above a whisper.

The single-story, sprawling ranch-style house had stacked stone accents along the lower half of its exterior and sat back a good distance from the street. Lee stopped at the sidewalk in front of the curved driveway and killed the engine. Just as he reached for his door handle, she spoke up.

"The porch light is off."

"Do you remember turning it on before you left?" he asked.

"I'm sure I did." She turned and stared at him.

"The light bulb could've burned out."

"I suppose."

"I'll walk up with you." He got out and went around to her door, but she'd already opened it and was starting to get out. He followed her only a few steps up the driveway before she stopped.

"I'm positive I closed the courtyard gate," she told him.

Debra Erfert

Lee could see the short wrought-iron gate standing ajar. Putting that together with the missing light, his internal alarm rang loudly. He took Mrs. Eddington's elbow and moved her back to his car. Once inside, he backed up far enough that they weren't in view of the front window any longer in case a perp heard his car drive up. He took out his cell phone.

"I'm calling this in, Mrs. Eddington." Her eyes were wide, but she didn't argue with him. He touched 911 and waited for only a moment before hearing a woman's voice.

"Scottsdale police, fire, what is your emergency?"

"This is Phoenix Police Detective Lee Adams. I need officers at 3546 East Gainey Ranch Road for a possible burglary in progress. I have the homeowner safe in my private car—a 2010 black Buick, parked next door."

"Yes, Detective. Right away. Do you want to stay on the line?"

"No, it's not necessary. Thank you." Lee pressed End but held on to the phone.

"You think I have a burglar?"

"I don't know, but telling that to the dispatcher will get help faster than saying we have suspicious circumstances."

Mrs. Eddington relaxed and sat back. "Oh, you don't really think this is all that serious?"

Lee leaned over the steering wheel, keeping his eyes on the dark house. "I don't like to take chances."

"But sometimes taking chances is a necessary evil," she said quietly.

"Like what you did tonight?"

She didn't respond.

It took another couple of minutes before Lee saw two cars with their headlights off slowly roll around the corner. When the streetlight hit them, he could see that they were patrol units. They stopped parallel but across the street from him.

"Stay here," Lee told her. "I'll explain what's happened." He paused before getting out. "Do you have dogs in the backyard?"

"No, no dogs. I'm alone."

A Strange Twist of Fate

He gazed at the woman for several moments after that admission. His heart tugged knowing she didn't have someone to go home to. He knew what that felt like.

With her gaze on the dark house, she said, "Just so you know, there are motion-detecting lights around the sides and back of the house."

"OK. This shouldn't take long. Hold tight and keep the doors locked." Lee got out and met up with the two officers, briefed them on the situation, and then followed them into the courtyard carrying his .40-caliber Glock he took out of his holster. They moved in the darkness up to the front door, and only then did Officer Sanchez use a small flashlight to check the lock. It was secure. When they reached the side yard, Lee got an uncomfortable feeling.

"The homeowner said there are security lights." His eyes were adjusted to the darkness enough to see a light fixture protruding from under the eaves. "That one didn't come on."

"Like the front porch light," Officer Newman said quietly.

Systematically, they checked around the whole house, wriggling doorknobs and pushing against windows in darkness. Nothing moved beneath their hands, but that didn't mean someone hadn't gotten inside and was waiting for her to come home.

"I'll go get the homeowner's keys," Lee told Officer Newman. "We'll need to clear the interior before we let her in."

"We need to ask her about that," Officer Sanchez said. He pointed at the patio lawn chair pushed up against the side of the house under a small window, clearly out of place. The other matching outdoor furniture was positioned around a cozy fire pit farther in the backyard.

"Yeah." Lee walked back to his car, and as she saw him approach, she got out.

"Is everything OK?" she asked, looking at the officers coming up behind him.

"We couldn't find anything open, but the lights didn't come on."

"Any of them?"

Debra Erfert

"No, ma'am," Officer Sanchez said.

"We'll find out why before we take off, but we need to clear the inside." Leaving her alone felt wrong. "We did find something else."

Mrs. Eddington pulled her sweatshirt jacket tighter across her chest and looked toward the front of her house. "What?"

"A patio chair was pushed up against the house under a window."

"That isn't right. Did someone get into the house from there?"

"We found some scratches on the frame, but all your windows are locked. May I have your house key?" Lee asked.

"That can't be a coincidence," Mrs. Eddington told him, holding out her key ring to Lee.

"Do you have an alarm system?"

She shrugged. "I do, but when I try to arm it, the base's voice tells me that I have an open window. I haven't called the company to fix it." She shuddered. "I wasn't in a hurry because we have a security service that patrols our neighborhood. I thought that would be enough. I guess I should make that call."

"Yes, ma'am," Lee said.

"Should I wait in your car again, Detective?"

"No, I'll stay out here with you while the officers go inside and do their jobs." Lee gave the keys to Sanchez. "It shouldn't take long."

"OK."

Newman and Sanchez went to the front of the house and disappeared through the door.

"Are you cold?" he asked when she crossed her arms over her chest.

"A little. And I'm worried."

She had a right to be worried. Someone had been on the property, but for what purpose? Robbery? Or for something even more insidious? She was alone, and anyone who had read a newspaper about her husband could piece that together—if they

A Strange Twist of Fate

had enough intelligence. "It shouldn't take too long. These guys are well trained. And then you can get yourself a hot cup of coffee."

Mrs. Eddington took a sudden breath—and then sneezed once, then twice.

"Are you ill?" Lee asked, touching her shoulder.

She pointed at the trees planted along the side of her property. "Allergies."

There were at least ten or more citrus trees in a row near the wall. They were all in blossom and smelled sweet.

"What can I say—I love the fruit," Mrs. Eddington said when she caught him staring at the trees. "This way, I have fresh juice anytime I want it."

"Even when getting what you want causes you pain?"

"If I think it's worth the trouble, then, yeah."

Lee didn't think they were talking just about the fruit. He thought he caught a glimpse of a stubborn personality under her cautious shell.

One at a time, each window they could see had light coming from behind the blinds. Moments after the garage light blinked on, Sanchez came out and made his way to them.

"It's clear. If you'll come inside, you can check to see if anything is out of place," the officer said to Mrs. Eddington.

Lee stayed a step behind the widow up the driveway. He was anxious to see what the house looked like inside. From the outside, it easily was ten times bigger than his apartment. It even dwarfed his house—the one that his soon-to-be ex-wife still occupied.

When they passed the garage, his curiosity about seeing what cars were parked inside had him looking in through its window. Plastic tubs of various sizes had been stacked on shelves lining one wall. Two refrigerators sat next to each other near a door, and a small car wrapped in white canvas sitting on a utility trailer took up a single bay. He couldn't tell its make, but it was low and small.

Mrs. Eddington caught him looking—again. She headed for the courtyard without commenting.

Debra Erfert

With the lights shining from every window of the house, Lee was sure that would make Mrs. Eddington feel safer after they left. He knew it would make him feel better about leaving her ... alone.

A Strange Twist of Fate

Two

Anna watched the detective walk down the driveway. It was odd, the way he looked back a couple of times, almost like he expected her to stop him. He didn't need to worry about her. She didn't find anything touched. It didn't look like anyone got inside. Although they did discover all the security lights had been loosened. Not just one, but all four, just like the porch light. A sudden sensation of loneliness began to build in her chest when his figure disappeared into the darkness. It wasn't like tonight would be any different than every other night over the last year. She had her coping mechanisms solidly in place. Dependable routines were what saved her sanity after Greg died.

With Detective Lee Adams's business card in her hand, she checked the door lock again before marching to the kitchen and straight to the freezer. Tucked inside were several quarts of premium ice cream. After such a stressful adventure, she needed chocolate fudge and peanut butter, and lots of it. Tonight, she wouldn't even use a bowl. She yanked off the lid in a surge of pent-up, angry energy, took a large spoon from the utensil drawer, and strode back and forth alongside the breakfast bar as she ate. It took a few bites of the icy creaminess before her shoulders began to relax. The next spoonful slowly melted in her mouth as she stopped her anxious pacing. She savored the blend of rich chocolate and peanut butter while she stared at the little white card on the counter.

The detective wanted her to call him if she needed anything more tonight. He also told her he'd be back around nine in the morning to take her to the police impound yard to get her car released. That was an offer she'd readily accepted. He might have some pull on getting the service charge dropped. After all, it was an unjustified arrest, and her car would've never been towed if the cop had followed procedure and did that field drug test. But he also managed to stop her from being robbed of her little packet of powdered sugar. Razor had pulled a box cutter so fast she didn't have time to react.

Someone had come to her house, and it freaked Anna out. Over the last eleven months since the highway patrol closed out Greg's case, she'd asked a lot of questions of too many people, it seemed. Had she rattled someone enough for them to come after her—or at least try to break into her house to see . . . something? Could that someone have known she was keeping a scrapbook of information on what she'd learned since starting her investigation of Greg's death?

Anna plunged the spoon into the ice cream, then left it on the counter before heading into the dining area to the antique sideboard behind the table. Where tablecloths and linen napkins would've been kept a century ago, she had her home office stored. Covering the top of the chest, she had her most important pictures framed and arranged in chronological order from left to right. Seeing Greg's smiling face and the happier times they'd had went a long way toward helping her hold to her goal, especially whenever she hit another dead end. He deserved to have his death resolved, not just closed and forgotten. Anna would find his killer, and if he or she were coming after her, then she'd be ready.

She lugged a big binder off the sideboard's bottom shelf and carried it across the room, over to the hope chest positioned in front of the couch. Her main scrapbook held not only copies of old police reports of the cases that Greg prosecuted, in chronological order, of course, but also mug shots and the outcome of each case. Shortly after he'd died, Anna had taken his personal laptop from the second bedroom, which he'd turned into his office, and had printed out all of his files, including his closed cases. Knowing his password made that easy. It was the same as hers. The county office didn't know about her pilfering. She'd kept that a secret from everybody.

A Strange Twist of Fate

Anna wrote her own notes, too, after she'd gone back and questioned as many people involved in each case as she could, looking for any lingering grievance against Greg, thus any implied motive. She'd had some close calls with angry family members who didn't appreciate her hints that their criminal relative could also be a murderer.

Greg had also sent more than a half dozen murderers to prison in his three years in the Phoenix prosecutors' office. The two years before then, he was one of a handful of Maricopa County public defenders, and not very many of his clients were innocent, but he negotiated plea bargains that kept them from serving long sentences. She didn't rule out one of them not being happy with the sentence and holding a grudge against him.

In the beginning, she'd started with those cases, but like Razor, some had still been in jail, and she didn't question all of their relatives while they were still serving time. She'd need to go back over those files again to check on new releases.

Anna opened the binder to where she had it bookmarked. Razor's picture stared up at her. If, by chance, he was the one who tried to get inside her house, not taking the proper precautions would be stupid. She got up and retrieved the ice cream from the counter, along with the detective's business card, and took them to the coffee table. She then went to her bedroom.

Kneeling next to her side of the mattress, she reached under the bed with her right hand and pushed a button on top of a metal box suspended from the frame, then placed her four fingers on a cool, contoured pad, using her prints to unlock it. A low, subtle beep was followed by the sound of a door falling open. Without looking, Anna grasped Greg's Walther PPK .380-caliber handgun from the biometric safe. She reached in again and took out the extra magazine, too. She needed to be ready in case that someone came back and tried again—and actually made it inside.

Sitting on the couch, Anna put the gun and mag on the table next to the binder, then picked up the carton of ice cream as she kicked off her tennis shoes. Her routine would continue, although each time her thoughts drifted back to the detective and the way he stared at her, the ice cream seemed to lose some of its deliciousness. She must've looked dreadful to him.

With her finger and thumb, she unbuttoned her jeans with a pop, then sat back until she was comfortably leaning against the soft cushion and her feet were up next to the binder. Her waistband had grown too tight, and they were relatively new jeans. It's not like she didn't know she had a problem with her weight—her mother practically wouldn't let her forget it. Lately, she made sure she found something else to do when her parents' dinner invitation came.

Truth be told . . . her mother might be right. She hoped she wouldn't need to buy another pair of pants in yet another larger size. Obviously her eating habits had taken a dive for the worse. She pulled the rubber band out of her hair, letting down her ponytail.

Funny, she hadn't thought about how she looked in a long time. Why would she care, really? Anna was a woman on a mission, and being fashionable and trim didn't factor into how well she did her investigation. But becoming an out-of-control overeater of her beloved ice cream and fast food didn't help, either, especially if it impacted her health or potentially clouded her judgment.

She set the half-empty carton down on the floor and dropped the spoon inside of it. Figuring out a new routine shouldn't be too difficult. Instead of downing a quart of ice cream every night, she'd . . . eat something healthier.

Starting tomorrow.

To go along with that new goal, she'd get back into the routine of morning runs. She used to be a runner in high school—seven years ago. Those two small changes would be enough to stop her from growing out of her new clothes. Anna groaned as she pulled the soft zebra-print throw cover over her legs and slid down far enough to rest her head on the pillow. She figured the next few days were going to be very physically painful, although it couldn't be worse than the emotional pain she'd endured for the past year.

A Strange Twist of Fate

Anna reached out to the hope chest, touching the grip of her gun and adjusting it for a quick retrieval—just in case her intruder returned to stop her from finding Greg's killer.

~*~

Lee turned down the police radio of his undercover cruiser as he drove to Scottsdale. He was ahead of schedule in picking up the widow. She expected him closer to nine, but he'd been so antsy to get back to her that he left way earlier than he should have. Plagued with tumultuous thoughts of last night's events, Lee had tossed and turned more than he'd slept. In his head, he played out different hideous scenarios for why all the lights around her house had been loosened, and all of them ended with Mrs. Eddington being in serious trouble.

Lee knew what it felt like to be alone, but he couldn't imagine what life was like for her, losing her husband so suddenly. Where could she turn now? Her parents? From everything he'd heard about Hammer Jack Wright, he was as stern as they came. Just from the few court cases Lee personally had dealt with, he knew the judge to be a fair man who followed the letter of the law and almost never deviated from it.

As he turned the corner onto Gainey Boulevard, a tall woman jogging immediately caught his attention. Earlier that morning it had been cool, but the sun had heated up the air enough Lee didn't need his dress jacket any longer. The woman had on sweatpants and a long-sleeved sweatshirt—completely overdressed for a run in warm weather. Her blonde hair was pulled back in a ponytail. There was something wrong with her stride—it was out of rhythm. Lee's pulse quickened. He recognized the woman. He slowed down, matching her sluggish pace, and lowered the passenger window.

"Mrs. Eddington?" Lee asked as he leaned over the seat. "Are you all right?" Taking one look at her pink, sweaty face and the grimace wrinkling her pretty forehead, he knew the answer. He flicked on his dashboard lights and stopped in the bike lane. By the time Lee rushed around the front of the car, she had reached out with one hand and propped herself up against the trunk of a convenient tree. The walking path had few people on it. Most were walking small dogs, and all were apparently oblivious to her condition.

"Detective Adams," Mrs. Eddington huffed breathlessly, "you're too early!"

Lee's steps faltered. He didn't expect a reprimand. "Are you injured?"

Her eyes were closed, and the hand that wasn't glued to the tree was pressed into the side of her abdomen. Sweat streamed down her face. The collar of her oversize sweatshirt was damp.

"No. I'm ... I've got a leg cramp. It's not that bad." Her breaths were coming in sharp gasps.

Lee dropped his gaze to her foot—the one she had suspended above the ground. "I'll give you a ride home," he told her, and he turned back to his car. After he'd opened the passenger door, he looked to see her still clutching the tree, her brown eyes on him.

"Give me a minute."

He got worried all over again. "Can you put your weight on your foot?" Lee asked, moving back over to her side. "May I help you?"

Mrs. Eddington blew out a heavy breath, sounding impatient. "I'm fine! It's just a stupid cramp." She put her foot down, then slowly limped her way over to the car. She sat down hard with an expulsion of air, and then Lee closed the door. After he got back inside, he turned off his dashboard lights and drove toward her home.

"Thank you," Mrs. Eddington said quietly, leaning over her knees. She had her hands on her lower leg, massaging her calf.

"It's not a problem." Lee kept glancing at her heavy clothes. She had to be sweating to death in them. "Were you out on a run this morning?"

Mrs. Eddington gazed up at him and lifted a single dark blonde eyebrow. Yeah, he knew it was a stupid question. "That was my intention." She sat back and sighed loudly. "It just didn't work out

A Strange Twist of Fate

that way." Then she muttered under her breath as she pulled at the sweatshirt's collar, "Stupid new routine."

Lee smiled. She, at least, had tried doing something he used to do on a regular basis. Exercise. From her heavy breathing, he guessed she was very much out of shape—not like he could tell by her loose-fitting clothes. They swallowed her up. She didn't say another word on their short drive. He pulled into the curved carport and killed the engine. Lee had every intention of helping her inside, but by the time he made it around to her door, she had already gotten out. The pained expression she wore earlier on the walking path still clung to her pretty face. Just as he was about to offer his arm as a support, she slowly limped her way up to the wrought-iron gate.

He followed, keeping a close pace behind her. Once inside the courtyard, she stopped in front of a small grouping of colorful potted plants and started to kneel. Instead, she squealed and grabbed her leg. Her cry instantly shot sympathetic pain throughout Lee's whole body. He'd had charley horses before, and they were never fun. Lee grasped her arm, keeping her from falling. A moment later, she regained her balance, and he let her go.

"Detective? Would you please get my key from under the small pot for me?" she asked breathlessly.

Lee tipped the pot and picked up the house key. She reached for it. He guessed she wouldn't let him help her open the door. Damn, she was a stubborn woman.

The savory scent of bacon had him salivating the moment he stepped into the foyer. He'd skipped breakfast.

"I need to shower before we go," Mrs. Eddington said. She nodded to a room off the foyer. "You can wait in the living room." She turned in the opposite direction and limped slowly down a hallway without giving him another glance. He didn't know how she could stand walking on a cramped leg. Yeah, she was stubborn.

Lee stood in the foyer until she disappeared into a bedroom and closed the door. He also heard a click. She'd locked the door. Huh! She didn't trust him. He thought he had an honest face. Lee stood

Debra Erfert

at the entrance of the formal living room. In the farthest corner, a black baby grand piano took up an impressive amount of space. The remainder of the room held an expensive-looking couch and two chairs upholstered in the same floral fabric that were strategically placed, facing a central low table. He didn't want to sit on the uncomfortable couch knowing that a woman could take an hour to shower and dress. At least Carolyn, his ex, almost always took that long.

Instead, Lee took a stroll around the high-ceiling family room that included the kitchen at one end with a dining area in between. It was impressively big. His home had an open concept like this, just not on the same scale. He liked the spacious feeling. A long breakfast bar with a black granite countertop separated the kitchen from the other two rooms. Even that room was large enough to handle several cooks at the same time.

Mrs. Eddington had the same type of sideboard cabinet his grandmother had in her house. He grinned, remembering that his grandmother hid bottles of liquor behind the tablecloths and napkins. He'd inherited it and the matching dining room set after she died a few years back. Now he wondered if he would lose those in the divorce, too.

Lee recognized Greg Eddington's smiling face in all of the photographs placed on top of the cabinet. Mrs. Eddington looked different. She was a beautiful woman, radiant in the arms of her late husband. Back then, she wore her hair down, around her shoulders, unlike the way she'd had it since he'd met her last night. He noticed her eyes right away. It seemed most blondes had either blue eyes or green, but Mrs. Eddington's were soft brown, the same shade as a Hershey's milk chocolate candy bar. Even without makeup, they were beautiful. He'd tried not to stare, at least noticeably, but he knew she caught him doing it once or twice. He just hoped she wasn't upset with him—although she did lock her door. That could be a clue to her feelings.

Lee approved of the big-screen television. It sat on a shelf next to a large river-rock fireplace. She had an overstuffed sofa facing

A Strange Twist of Fate

the TV and fireplace, with an antique blanket chest she was using as a coffee table in front of the sofa. The two wingback chairs, one on either side of the couch, made for a cozy setting in an otherwise large room. What piqued his curiosity was the thick scrapbook left open on the chest, and, interestingly enough, a Walther PPK semiautomatic handgun sat next to it.

"Fascinating," he said quietly. "A woman not afraid of guns." He noticed the pillow and blanket. It looked like she'd slept there last night. Lee sat on the couch and looked at the oversize pages of the binder. To say he was surprised at seeing a felony arrest report would be a colossal understatement.

"Holy crap," he muttered, reading the report. "Harold Bivens, a.k.a.: Razor. Felony arrest, robbery using a box cutter, October 18, 2014..." Lee took in a fast breath. "Mrs. Eddington, what are you doing?" He kept reading. This wasn't the crime he'd remembered recently coming through the station, but it sounded so close the same man might've done it. "Assistant Prosecutor Greg Eddington agreed to a plea bargain." He tapped a handwritten note paper-clipped to the side. The script was clearly feminine. Probably Mrs. Eddington's? And she was not happy with the six months Bivens served before the State of Arizona released him. He'd spent the minimum time required behind bars. The date, time, and meeting place told Lee that Mrs. Eddington had met with Razor last night. Bobby told him about the box cutter. "Holy crap."

Lee stared at the mug shot of a man whose age on paper was only twenty-eight. His haggard face belied that date. Underneath that report were other older reports belonging to the same man. Notes, in the same handwriting, were paper-clipped to each page, outlining the outcome of each case. She had Bivens's criminal history, plus more. She seemed to have some personal information as well. If it was correct, she had his mother's name and home and work addresses, and the same information on a woman who reportedly claimed to be Bivens's girlfriend. She also had the girlfriend's criminal history.

Debra Erfert

"Hmmm . . ." Lee tapped his fingers on the edge of the binder a few times before he opened it to the first page, taking care not to dislodge any of the notes she'd so carefully posted. The criminal report she had stapled onto the black insert dated back five years. Her note showed that Greg Eddington was Louis Mendivil's public defender.

"What are you doing?"

Lee jumped at the sound of Mrs. Eddington's tight voice. Ten minutes? She was a quick dresser. She swept around the sofa and grabbed the binder away from him, holding it tightly to her chest.

"I'm sorry," he said, standing up. "It was lying open. I—"

"You were supposed to be in the front room." Mrs. Eddington rushed to the sideboard and opened the door, revealing books, a computer, stacks of paper, pencils and pens, and even a printer.

"What are you doing with those?" Lee hung back and watched her hide the big binder of criminal information from him. Like putting it away would make him forget about seeing it.

"None of your business." She shoved the door closed and turned around. Her hair was in a ponytail, and she wore no makeup, but she'd changed from the ugly sweat clothes into curve-hugging blue jeans and another too-large T-shirt. The few moments she had been close to him, he'd detected the sweet scent of flowers drift off her skin.

"Was that the man you met last night?" Lee asked. "The one with the box cutter?"

Mrs. Eddington strode to a chair near the foyer and picked up a handbag. "I told you—it's none of your business." She looped the long strap over her head and hung the bag across her body as she headed for the blanket chest.

Lee couldn't let it drop, not after seeing the portfolio of cases she had accumulated. From just what he'd read, the notes were too extensive to be anything other than an in-depth investigation of— something. And since her husband's name was on the reports he saw, he guessed it was most likely connected somehow with his death. "I assume you've read *all* of Bivens's arrest reports."

A Strange Twist of Fate

"Of course I did," she snapped as she picked up the Walther and slipped it into the side of her handbag, zipping it closed. "I'm ready to go get my car now."

Lee stared at her bag. "Do you know how to shoot that?"

With the squint of her dark eyes, he knew questioning her was a mistake. "Do I need to call a taxi?"

Lee glanced back at the cabinet once again before striding to the front door. His heart pounded. He didn't know if he was angry with the woman or overly concerned. All he knew was his thoughts were racing. Most of all, he didn't know why he cared so much.

He leaned next to the open passenger door, waiting for her to make up her mind if she was coming with him or if she had decided to call that taxi. But she practically stormed over to his car without so much as a thank you before getting inside. Lee swung the door shut, trying to control his temper. He didn't know why things had gotten out of hand. He wasn't snooping. She had left the book in plain sight. If it had been a secret, she should've put it away before he'd arrived. She acted like she had a guilty conscience. Was she doing something wrong—possibly illegal? Where did she get all the reports? Clearly, she had been trying to get answers from Bivens, and in doing so had put herself into an extremely dangerous place—almost deadly.

Debra Erfert

Three

The drive to the police impound yard was frostily quiet. The only conversation came from the radio traffic, and that wasn't very interesting. Fridays were a toss-up, depending on certain conditions. The moon would be at its fullest tonight, and Lee knew from working the streets for the past ten years that the crazies would come out in force. He'd been dispatched to some of the oddest calls during a full moon.

Lee pulled in through the impound yard gate and parked near the small kiosk. He recognized Kevin Harrison, the officer who came out holding a clipboard. He'd worked with the retired detective for nearly six months before he transitioned over to the civilian position at the yard.

Mrs. Eddington had opened her door before Lee had even gotten out. No chance for him to be the gentleman—again.

"Detective Adams," Kevin said, reaching his hand out to Lee.

"Hi, how're you doing?" Lee asked, shaking Kevin's hand.

"Doing great," he said, glancing behind Lee at Mrs. Eddington. "How's Carolyn?"

Lee cringed at the question. Since the divorce papers had been served, he hadn't talked about his private life at work. It was a subject that he would have to get used to answering. "I'm not sure, Kevin. We're getting a divorce."

Harrison's weathered face frowned. "Oh, hell, Lee. I'm sorry. That's tough."

Shrugging, Lee looked over his shoulder. Mrs. Eddington stood close enough she'd heard his news. "Kevin, we towed Mrs. Eddington's car last night by mistake. We're here to spring it."

"By mistake, huh?" Harrison checked his clipboard. "Eddington . . ." A moment later he passed the clipboard to Lee.

A Strange Twist of Fate

"You'll need to sign here, Detective Adams, guaranteeing the tow was unrighteous, and then Mrs. Eddington will sign."

Lee took the pen and scribbled his name. He passed the clipboard to Mrs. Eddington, but she didn't sign right away.

"I'd like to see my car first," she said, looking off into the lot of vehicles. "It was in pristine condition before it was towed. It better still be that way."

"Sure," Harrison said with a sniff. "It's just a formality. It's parked in back. Follow me."

Lee didn't make a move until the widow was next to him. She still walked with a slight limp. "How's your leg doing, Mrs. Eddington?"

"Better, Detective." She finally gazed at him, even gave him a tentative smile. That little effort transformed her eyes from sullen to charmingly hopeful. "Thank you."

Seeing that change did something funny to his heart—it skipped just for a moment. It was a most welcome sensation he hadn't felt in a long time. "We don't have to rush, right? Give your muscle more of a chance to recuperate." Or maybe she was in a hurry. She looked at her watch. "May I ask you a question?"

"Yeah, I guess."

"Did you drink enough water this morning?"

That brought her to a standstill. Lee stopped as well. Her eyes were on his tie, but he didn't think she was admiring his ability to coordinate its color with his shirt that morning.

"I"—Mrs. Eddington licked her lips—"I wasn't thirsty. I guess I forgot." Her gaze went up to his eyes. "I'm very thirsty now that you brought it to my attention."

"A sports drink with electrolytes cut with water would be better for you."

Her brows scrunched together. "And you know this how?"

Lee grinned, dipping his head. "I went through the police academy here in Phoenix, and I had my share of leg cramps during PT. The electrolyte drink split with water was what was pushed on us. It's not something you tend to forget."

Debra Erfert

She nodded and started walking again, just at a slower pace. "I'll stop by the grocery store on my way home."

Lee stayed next to her, pleased that she didn't act upset with him any longer. He momentarily thought it strange that he should feel that way. He might've been able to think about it a little deeper if in the next instant she hadn't let out a sound reminiscent of a bear growl.

"What did you do to my car?" Mrs. Eddington rushed the last few feet to her white Impala.

It didn't take a seasoned detective to notice how uneven the car sat. When Lee got to the other side, next to the once again irate widow, he knew why her emotions had flipped.

"The tire is flat," Kevin said.

"It wasn't that way last night!" Staring at Kevin, Mrs. Eddington clutched her handbag like she was planning on whipping out her gun. And considering he had wanted her signature so quickly, Lee had to wonder if he knew about the damage. She started walking around the car, scrutinizing it.

Lee held out his hands toward the angry woman. If she made a move to her purse zipper, he was within reach to stop her. "It might've happened anyway," he rationalized, following her. "Flat tires happen."

When she got back around the car, next to Kevin, she slapped her hand on her thigh. "Do something," she demanded.

"I can have a man from the city shop come over and change it," Kevin told her.

Mrs. Eddington flung her arm toward the trunk. "But then I'll be driving on the donut spare, and I'll have the flat tire in the trunk." She glanced at her watch.

"Don't worry, Mrs. Eddington," Lee said. "We'll make good on the tire." Her reactions totally confused him. Last night she was reticent, seemingly helpless at times. That had made him want to protect her. But this morning she was on the edge of biting their heads off.

Kevin had already taken out his phone.

A Strange Twist of Fate

"How long will this take?" she asked, her fingers tapping her bag.

Kevin spoke into his phone. "Hi, Frank. Kevin Harrison . . . yeah, doing good. Hey, we have a problem with one of our tows . . . a flat tire." He crouched down and studied the tire. "No, I can't tell. You need to fix it or replace it. When do you think you can you get to it?" He paused and then said, "Around one?"

"I don't have time for this." Mrs. Eddington pulled out her phone from her jeans.

"Do you have an appointment?" Lee asked.

"Something like that." She started tapping on her phone.

"I can give you a ride," Lee told her. "When your car is repaired, I can come and bring you back."

"I need my car sooner than four hours." She pressed the phone to her ear when an audible voice was heard coming from it. "Hello, I have a flat tire, and I need it repaired. How soon can you come out?" She nodded. "And how much will it cost?" Her eyes jumped to Lee's before she turned away from him, and her voice lowered. "How much did you say?" Her shoulders fell. "No, no, never mind. Thank you." She stared at her phone for several moments.

"Why don't you use that car in your garage—the one under the tarp?" Lee asked softly. She looked up at him with her eyes moist. That wasn't what he expected.

"I can't. It's just a shell."

Lee stepped closer. "Look, I can get you where you need to be."

After she took another glance at her watch, she straightened her back and sniffed. "I'd appreciate a lift."

"I'll let Detective Adams know as soon as it's done," Kevin said as he stood up. "And I'm sorry this happened."

Mrs. Eddington nodded and then strode, limping slightly, back to Lee's car without saying another word. He quickly made sure Kevin had his cell number before joining her in his car.

Debra Erfert

Even before Lee turned over the engine, she said, "I need to be at East Broadway Road and South Fourteenth Street in twenty-five minutes."

"That's doable." But he didn't drive straight there. He pulled into the parking lot of the first convenience store he came to. He didn't hear any complaints as he got out. He made his purchases quickly. Back inside the car, Lee passed the orange sports drink and bottle of water to the dehydrated woman.

"I didn't know which flavor you like, so I bought you my favorite." Lee started the engine.

"You didn't need to do this," Mrs. Eddington said, cracking open the orange drink. "But I'm glad you did."

Lee didn't back up right away. Instead, he watched with beguiled interest as she drank down nearly half the bottle before coming up for air. She drank with her eyes closed, seemingly savoring every swallow. A trickle of fluid had escaped her lips, and she dabbed her chin with the back of her hand. He didn't want her to think that he was staring, so he put the car into reverse and continued on their way, but he could see with his peripheral view that she poured the water he bought her into the drink, mixing them together like he'd suggested earlier. That gave him a generous boost to his ego.

While she seemed to be in a better mood, Lee thought he'd bring up the meeting she had with the doper last night. He'd been more than curious about that since he'd seen the reports in her binder.

"Mrs. Eddington, you know, pulling a knife on someone is a crime." She stiffened noticeably, but he kept going. "I could have a warrant put out on Bivens, and then during questioning, I could ask him what it was you wanted to ask him." He could see her head turn toward him a little more. Her fingers went to her bottom lip, and she slowly stroked it. He looked closer at her. She was staring at the dashboard. Yes—she was giving it serious thought.

"Could I listen in on the interview?"

A Strange Twist of Fate

He glanced at her again. She stared at him instead of the car. "I can arrange that."

"Would he know I was there?"

"No, you'd be behind a two-way mirror."

She fiddled with her lip some more and then squinted at him. "Why would you do this?"

Why would he, indeed? He didn't want to make it sound like the only reason he wanted to haul the addict in was to keep her safe, which, essentially, it was. Even the thought of Bivens's being the reason for her outside lights being unscrewed bothered him more than he cared to admit. He then thought up a good excuse. "I saw a robbery report come through where the perp used a razor-knife box cutter. I'll go look it up and see if it fits Bivens. That would give me probable cause to bring him in and question him."

"OK. Do it if you can," she told him, with that slight grin gracing her lips again. There was also an excitement in her eyes that gave Lee an invigorating charge.

With her phone in her hand, she asked, "Do you need Razor's address? I have it in my notes. I can text it to you."

In a matter of a minute, Lee heard his phone ding once. That was his text notification. The widow was efficient if not tenacious. He listened quietly as she gave him a detailed physical description of Bivens, including the grungy hooded sweatshirt jacket he'd worn last night. Lee remembered she'd worn the very same kind, except hers had smelled like lavender, the same scent he'd noticed clinging to her skin this morning.

"Pull over here."

Lee slowed down. "But we're a block away from the address."

"I know. Please pull over."

He did as she asked. The asphalt parking lot of the abandoned business had cracked from years of intense desert heat and neglect. It sounded like popcorn beneath the cruiser's tires. "Is there a reason I can't drop you off at the door?"

Debra Erfert

Mrs. Eddington stared at his suit before looking intently into his eyes for several moments. "Frankly, Detective Adams, I don't want anyone to see me getting out of a police car."

He'd felt like she'd punched him. "Because I'm a cop? Would I embarrass you?" Lee looked down the street. The building on the corner had several women milling in front of it. They were dressed similar to her, in jeans and T-shirts. What could she be doing that being seen with the law was bad? Breaking the law, perhaps? The thought disturbed Lee terribly.

"If you could be back here around noon, I'd appreciate it," she said before hopping out. She'd slammed the door before he could ask another question. He sat and wallowed in his darkened mood and watched her glance over her shoulder at him as she approached the group of women. They hugged her before disappearing inside the building.

"OK, Mrs. Eddington," Lee said aloud. "What are you doing inside there that you don't want them to know about me? Or is it you don't want me to know what you're doing in there?" He drove back out onto the road and slowly passed by the door she'd entered, even as more poorly dressed women of varying ages went inside. "The Salvation Army? Not a disreputable place." He turned around and made another pass. The few windows were tinted dark enough he couldn't see through them. The clock on the dash reminded him that he only had an hour and a half to get that warrant and be back, or Lee had no doubt the widow would find another ride to her next destination.

A Strange Twist of Fate

Four

Anna went to the door and looked for Claudia to arrive for the class. After an hour, she was fairly sure Razor's girlfriend was a no-show. It would be a first since the beginning of the year. The self-defense classes, put on free by an ex-marine, were a huge draw. Anna had arranged it eight months ago after Maria Gonzalez had her jaw broken by an outraged husband out on probation, a man Greg had put behind bars. Maria was one of her first contacts after Greg's case had been closed. Getting the woman to confide in her hadn't been hard, especially when Anna brought over homemade soups during her recovery. Anna had helped her get a restraining order and a temporary home, complete with people who were more threatening than her deadbeat husband. The Angels in Black Leather, a motorcycle biker group, were only threatening to the abusive bad guys and were very protective of those in danger.

During the court case, the whole front row of the gallery had been filled with members of the Angels. Anna sat behind them. Every time Maria looked uncertain, her eyes would fall on the men and women wearing the black leather vests with white angel wings stitched on the front shoulders. She then lifted her chin and pushed forward. That gripping testimony sent her husband to prison for five years. Now Anna feared for Claudia's safety. That woman had helped her set up the meeting with Razor, Claudia's current boyfriend, and it went bad. Her being absent from their class might be a result of that. Or it just might be a coincidence. At least Anna hoped it was.

"Anna..."

She pulled her thoughts away from Claudia and gave her attention to retired US Marine Caesar Aguirre, who stood close behind her. He'd come every Friday on his lunch hour from his

Debra Erfert

second career as a baker, bringing his wife and their eighteen-year-old daughter to teach the small group of women to defend themselves.

"No matter how much you try, Anna, you can't control the universe," Caesar said quietly, with a touch of a smile.

"Life would be so much easier if I could."

He chuckled. "Tell me about it."

Anna returned her gaze out the glass door. "It's just not like Claudia to miss a class. I hope she's all right. She didn't call me."

"All right is a relative term when you live with a violent felon."

Anna had confided many of her investigative findings with the baker. Those secrets were what might've spurred his volunteering to help the handful of abused wives and girlfriends.

"Was this a mistake?"

Caesar placed his hand on her shoulder. "Was what a mistake?"

She gave the slightest nod to the women sitting on the padded floor mats, taking a break from the strenuous stretching and maneuvers he'd taught them over the past hour.

"Not a chance," he told her in a hushed voice. "You are a godsend to these women. They have hope and a chance of a future without pain because you cared enough to . . ." He shook his head.

"To interfere in their lives?" Anna finished the sentence for him when he floundered for the right words.

"Basically," he said, chuckling.

A faded orange Dodge Charger rolled slowly along the street. Anna could see the angry face of a man whom Greg had sent to county jail for two years. He'd been released almost three months ago. His mug shot mirrored that expression. "Christina"—she took a quick look at the dark-haired beauty lying on her back with her hands folded across her chest—"Frank just drove by."

Christina's eyes got wide.

"Doesn't he know you're here?" Maria asked softly.

Christina shook her head, getting up. "I told him I was going to my sister's house." She started breathing faster as she rushed to

A Strange Twist of Fate

her bag in the corner of the room with the other handbags and backpacks. "He's going to be pissed I lied!"

"Did you drive your car here?" Anna asked.

She nodded, her eyes straying to the back door. "I gotta go."

Anna strode to the lockers lining the far wall, took down her handbag sitting on top, and beat her to the door. "I'll walk you to your car," she said as she hung the strap over her shoulder.

"So will I," Maria told her. She squared her shoulders and headed their way.

Beth stood up and said, "I'm not afraid of a man."

"Hold on ladies," Caesar said, with his hand pushing against the back door, keeping it shut to stop them from leaving. "You can't be getting in his face. This isn't what I've taught you."

"We're not," Anna said. "But there's safety in numbers. And if it comes down to it, we're not letting Frank whoop on Christina."

"That's here," Angelina said softly, still sitting on the floor. "But what happens after she's back at her house and you aren't there to stop him from . . ." She lifted one shoulder and lowered her head.

Anna knew why the petite older woman was afraid. Mostly, she was speaking from experience as an abused spouse, with a husband still in jail after Greg got a solid ten-year attempted murder conviction. Anna would've thought that Angelina would be the first to try to talk Christina out of going back to the same hurtful place that she'd been in for much too long.

"Angel's right." Christina shouldered her bag. "I need to go out there by myself. If Frank feels like you're gangin' up on him," her voice dropped, "it'll be worse later." She stopped next to Anna. The smile on her lips quivered. "Don't worry. I can smooth things over with him."

"You'll call me if . . . ?" Anna hugged her, asking the same unfinished question she did all her friends. They had an open line to her in case they needed anything—anytime.

"I swear."

Debra Erfert

Anna squeezed once more before letting her loose, and then the young woman slipped out the back door—alone. After she rushed to the nearest window facing the parking area, Anna saw Frank getting out of his car. He'd blocked in Christina's compact Honda. While Anna couldn't hear what was said, the angry expression Frank had been wearing seemed to dissipate, if not completely then at least enough that he didn't look like was going to hit her. She had no doubt a few lies were being told to cover the lie that got her to the class in the first place. Christina got into his car instead of her own, and they drove away. He didn't burn out, squealing his tires, which Anna saw as a positive sign.

"I think I'm done for the day," Anna said, with her forehead leaning against the window.

"Where's your car?" Caesar asked from over her shoulder.

Oh, yeah. "Stuck in the police impound," she whispered so only the ex-marine could hear.

"You're joking."

"I wish I was." Anna turned around.

His fingers came close to touching the bandage on her cheek. "Were you arrested?"

A sigh escaped her lips before she could stop it. "Briefly. I have a ride coming in a few minutes, but I'll sit outside and wait for him."

Caesar grinned. "Him? Dare I hope you're finally dating?"

"No, it—it's too soon to even be thinking about that yet." She glanced at the women huddled together as they gathered their bags. It seemed they all thought the class was over. "A police detective gave me a ride here, and until I get my car back, I'm dependent on him to get around."

The grin didn't fade, and he wiggled his brows. "Is he single?"

"He's married." And then she remembered his hesitant confession to the impound officer. "At least until he signs his divorce papers. Besides, I have my investigation—I need to find out who killed Greg before I get involved again."

A Strange Twist of Fate

Leaning against the wall, he asked, "How is it coming along? Have you learned anything new since last week?"

Shaking her head, Anna admitted, "I still don't have a single definite lead—yet. I did find another pickup—one that came close to matching the description of the one that pushed Greg off the road—but it was a bust. No white transfer paint or damage on the right side. I still have contacts in each of the body shops in and around Phoenix who are specifically looking for that kind of damage. But so far, nothing." She sat on the windowsill. "I've nearly come to the end of Greg's case files. I'd hoped Razor might've heard something while he was locked up, someone who possibly had a hit out on Greg. The detective who helped me is going to collar him this afternoon, hopefully, and ask that question on my behalf."

"Seriously? A hit?" Caesar pushed up from the wall. "It's not like your husband was prosecuting the mob, or a high-profile politician running for president. His cases were small-time ones. Hiring someone to kill a man takes big money—"

"Or a big grudge," Anna said.

Caesar kept his voice near a whisper. "But a disinterested party won't kill someone for someone else's grudge—"

"Not without him having a personal interest in it." Anna stood up, grinning from the excitement building within her. "You're right."

"Oh no," he moaned. "You have an idea."

"Yes, I do," Anna said. "I really didn't investigate the families of those still incarcerated at the time of Greg's crash."

Caesar's gaze briefly landed on the group of women.

Anna whispered, "They were different, and you know it." She added, "But I've got to do some research before acting on my hunch."

"Anna?" Maria asked. "Do you need a ride home?"

Anna shook her head. "I have a ride coming."

Maria grinned and looked toward the window. "You mean that cute cop is coming back?"

37

Debra Erfert

Anna felt dismayed. She'd tried so hard to keep her friends from being negatively impacted by her involvement with the police, yet by the smiles and head nods they were giving her, they not only knew about the detective but weren't put out by his presence.

"He, like, drove by twice after you came inside," Mary Jane said. "He is good-looking, you know, for a cop."

She'd seen him too? Had they been talking about it without her knowing?

"What's his name?" Maria asked as she moved to the same window Anna had been looking out of a few minutes before. From there, they could see the place he'd parked when he dropped her off.

"Umm . . ." Anna shrugged, not keeping eye contact with anyone.

"Give it up, girl!" Mary Jane said with a laugh.

Caesar gave her a knowing look with a wriggle of his brows again.

"Fine." She'd tell them his name, but she most certainly wouldn't tell them how she met him. Besides being embarrassing, they would learn how deep her investigation was. She didn't want them to think that they had only been sought out for information, which was essentially the truth in the beginning, but after Anna had gotten to know them, as individuals, her motives had changed. "Detective Lee Adams."

"I know him," Angelina said quietly. "He investigated a break-in I had a few months ago. He was very knowledgeable and courteous. After he lifted some fingerprints, he took the trouble to clean off that black dust. It was very considerate. He's a nice man." She nodded. "I approve."

"Then I approve, too," Mary Jane said. "He'll be a good provider."

Anna opened her mouth to tell them that she wasn't dating him, but just as quickly she closed her lips. If she weren't dating him, then someone would surely ask why he dropped her off and was

A Strange Twist of Fate

picking her up. If she didn't lie, then she'd have to tell about her arrest. Anna didn't like to lie.

"I think that's your detective," Maria said, with her finger on the window.

Anna could see that he'd parked in the same place as before. He didn't bother getting out. It seemed he continued to honor her request to keep at a distance. She was impressed. "I shouldn't make him wait."

"Don't forget your bread," Colleen, Caesar's wife, said, rushing to the cardboard boxes stacked next to the wall. Caesar always brought a loaf of his specialty bread for each of the women, with the exception of Anna. She received not one loaf, but a dozen individually wrapped, handmade loaves that never made it to her home. She usually had them all given away within an hour after leaving class, and he knew it. Giving her so many extras was one way he helped feed some homeless in the neighborhood.

"Thanks, Colleen." Anna lifted the big box by the cutout handholds and hurried to the door before any of the women could ask to meet the detective. She knew they were curious about him, but she couldn't take the chance that one of them might ask how long they had been dating. And since they weren't dating, her white lie would come to light. "See you all next week," she said to everyone before escaping out the front door.

When she got close enough to see the detective's curious face through the windshield, he got out, opened the back door on his side, and then took the box from her hands.

"You were baking? That's why you didn't want me to know what you were doing—you are learning how to bake?" Detective Adams inhaled with his face inches above the aromatic loaves of bread.

"Not exactly." Anna didn't offer more of an explanation before heading to her side of the car as he set the box on the back seat. Even before he had the car in gear, she was already thinking about Harold, the Vietnam vet who spent most of his time on the street

Debra Erfert

deep inside a bottle of cheap whiskey. If he remembered to eat, it wasn't very often. "You got Razor's warrant?"

Detective Adams took out a folded paper from the inside of his suit coat. "I did. We'll go by now." He set the warrant down on the seat before lifting the microphone from the dashboard. "David seventeen to dispatch."

"David seventeen, go ahead."

"Please send two units to 12370 Cortez Avenue for backup on a warrant."

"Ten-four, David seventeen. Sending two units for backup."

As he hung the mic on the silver hook, the detective said, "After reading that report I was telling you about, I'm sure the perp is Bivens. I'll call the victim to come in and look at a photo lineup before this is done."

Anna nodded. It would be good for Claudia if Razor went to prison. She'd been clean for the past six months. Having a user back in the house could only lead her to addiction again. With only a few miles before they got to their address, Anna sent Claudia a text. It was a simple question. *You home?*

She waited with the phone in her hand for a return text. After several minutes of no response, that uncomfortable feeling she had during the class hit her again. Where could Claudia be? If she had gone to her mother's place in Tucson, Anna was sure she would've called for a ride since she didn't have a car.

"When we get there, Mrs. Eddington, I want you to stay in the car. Understand?"

"I understand." Anna nervously tapped the side of her phone, watching the detective's face as she said, "His girlfriend may be there. Her name is Claudia Ortega. She doesn't have any outstanding warrants, and she's not violent, so please be nice to her."

With a glance at her, he asked, "Do you know that she's there?"

Anna looked down at her phone. "No. I sent her a text, but she didn't respond."

A Strange Twist of Fate

His brows scrunched together. "Are you trying to warn her about Bivens's warrant?"

"I . . ." If Anna was honest, that was exactly what she had planned on doing. "I guess I was."

He let out a heavy-sounding breath. "That, Mrs. Eddington, can get us killed."

"But Claudia isn't like that."

"Domestic cases are the most unpredictable situations for a police officer—and the most dangerous." Adams glared at her with a frown on his lips. "What did you tell her?"

"I only asked if she was home," she said defensively.

"And that's it?"

"Yes," she said, snapping the word sharper than she'd intended.

He nodded. "OK, just don't contact her again."

Anna crossed her arms tightly over her chest and tapped her foot. All she did was try to help a friend—to find out why she didn't show up for class and maybe tell her to take a hike for a while—and she got her head bit off.

He must've seen her sulking because he added, "At least until after we have Bivens in custody."

"Fine." Anna drew in a sigh of a breath and muttered, "Just fine," not loud enough for him to hear, and stared out the window while they drove another couple of miles in silence. When he stopped a few apartments down from their address, she could see Razor's place. Each of the four identical apartments was a very small single-family home, all lined up next to one another. The exterior stucco looked in fair shape, for the most part, but none of the renters kept a green lawn. The only space between the apartments was the single-width driveway leading into the open carport. There was at least one car in two of the other driveways.

"I don't see Razor's car. He's not there."

"How do you know what he drives?"

Anna kept her eyes on the target house. "I've done my homework."

"Did you know his license is suspended?"

"I'm sure he doesn't care."

After a moment, he lifted the mic. "What kind of car does he have?"

"A '97 dark gray Chevy Cavalier with a dent in the driver's door and a broken left taillight."

"Huh!" He held the mic close to his mouth. "David seventeen to dispatch."

"David seventeen, go ahead."

"Release my backup, please. The target is not home."

"Ten-four, David seventeen."

Anna watched the detective hang up the mic before he leaned back. He looked like he was getting comfortable. That was a bad idea, considering his undercover car was as out of place in Razor's neighborhood as her car was last night. The scent of the bread wafting from the back seat tightened her stomach in hunger. She needed lunch—and soon. "Well, we can't sit here and wait for him. He'll spot us and run."

"I guess you're right. Where did you park when you did your surveillance?"

Anna never staked out Razor, although she'd done her fair share of surveillance on a number of other people she suspected might've killed Greg. "What makes you think I would do something like that?" The width of his smile intrigued her.

"I got a brief look at some of the handwritten notes in your investigation binder."

"And you read that I had staked out Razor?"

He didn't answer right away. He must've been waiting for her to admit it. She knew he was reading her book, but he couldn't have read notes that weren't there. Anna knew about the car from when Claudia drove it. She only wrote down the year, make, and model so she wouldn't forget it. Was he trying to bluff her? Anna tucked a few loose strands of hair behind her ear and waited for him to speak. What he said next would be very telling of his character.

A Strange Twist of Fate

Detective Adams started the car. "How about some lunch? My treat."

"Uh-huh." Anna crossed her arms over her chest. She noticed the detective's smile slackened a touch but didn't completely leave his lips. He'd avoided the issue. While not lying, he didn't admit the truth, either. Anna had used that same tactic on more occasions than she cared to admit.

Debra Erfert

Five

Anna let the detective open the doors for her, not only the car door but also the entrance to the fast-food burger restaurant he'd driven them to. She'd been too hard on him, not giving him a chance to be courteous when he'd tried on several occasions. Her stubborn streak sometimes came across as being mean, and he didn't deserve to be on the receiving end of that.

The ordering line moved quickly. It was a good thing. Anna was starving, but she didn't want to order more than he did. Falling back on a tactic from when she was dating, she stared up at the menu board and casually asked, "So, Detective Adams, what are you going to order?"

He cleared his throat, looking at the people in line. "Would you mind calling me Lee—even if it's only for the duration of our lunch?"

"I suppose I could." Anna inwardly frowned at his not wanting to be identified as a police officer in a crowd. She hoped it wasn't because of how she had treated him earlier. Looking at the counter help, she wondered if they would treat him differently if they knew he was a cop. Worse, perhaps? Anna had assumed the women at her class wouldn't care to associate with a cop after having to deal with them in such negative ways. But that hadn't been the case. For some reason, that gave her a great sense of relief.

"And my name is Julianna," she told him. His smile touched his blue eyes. She wondered if he wore that handsome tie because it brought out the brilliant color of his eyes so well. "You didn't answer my question."

His gaze went up to the menu board. "I'm half-starved. I skipped breakfast."

A Strange Twist of Fate

When it was their turn to order, Anna waited until Lee finished, and she ordered the exact same thing—another old dating trick. Not that they were on a date, although she liked the way he rested his hand on the back of her elbow, yet didn't push her toward any specific table. Carrying a numbered placard and her cold diet soda, Julianna led the way to a table near a window overlooking his parked car.

No matter how much Anna tried not to think about it, sitting across the table from Lee felt like a date. Every time she looked up at him, she caught him staring at her. He had done that a lot over the past two days. Trying hard, she quashed an impulse to push the stray strands of hair back from her face. Maybe if she talked about his work those feelings would change. As she tore the wrapper off from around her straw, she asked, "How long have you been a detective?"

"Nearly a year already." Lee grinned. "It's been a real learning experience—and a struggle at times. But in some ways, it's gone incredibly fast . . ." The smile on his lips relaxed, not quite turning into a frown. Julianna waited for him to finish his thought, but with the way his eyes seemed to lose focus, well, she didn't press him to continue.

"So . . . you knew the officer at the impound yard. Kevin?"

Lee pushed his straw through the lid of his soda. "Yes, Kevin Harrison was a detective when I was promoted. He taught me a lot in the six months we worked together."

"And he'll call you as soon as my car is ready, right?"

"No doubt about it." Lee bobbed his head to the side once as a corner of his mouth lifted in a grin. "But if he doesn't contact me by one, I'll find out why."

A young woman delivered their burgers and fries, setting the tray on the table between them, then left.

"I'm curious about something, Julianna." Lee carefully folded back his burger's wrapper.

"Actually, my friends call me Anna," she said with a shrug.

45

Debra Erfert

Lee smiled. "OK, Anna. Would you tell me what car you have parked in your garage?"

It might've been impolite when she laughed, but from the moment she saw him looking in through the garage window, she knew his curiosity about what lay hidden beneath the canvas would eat at him. "That is . . . was my husband's project car that he started shortly after we were married. Being a public defender, then a prosecutor, his schedule didn't give him much spare time. He only got as far as buying the body. It's a '67 Shelby Cobra."

Lee stopped moving his burger in midlift to his mouth. "You have a Shelby Cobra?"

"Not a whole one." Anna savored a delicious bite of her sandwich while admiring Lee's look of envy. Truth be told, Greg had had that same wide-eyed expression the first time he saw the car sitting in the seller's backyard. She never could understand the big draw of old cars, especially one sitting in pieces. Anna's phone beeped once as she got a text.

"Do you have plans for it?" Lee asked.

Anna took out her phone from her pocket. The text was from Claudia: *Im leaving Razor. Need a ride and a place to live. Can u help me?*

Anna quickly returned the text. *Yes. Where and when?*

"Anna?"

She looked up and gasped a soft breath. She'd promised not to contact Claudia. Anna got up and moved around the table and scooted onto the bench next to Lee, holding the phone to where he could read the messages.

"Is that Bivens's girlfriend?" Lee asked.

"Yes."

Claudia texted back: *Im @ circl k now.*

"That's just down the road from their place," Anna told him.

"Ask her if Bivens is at the apartment," Lee whispered.

Anna nodded. *Is Razor home?*

Y.

"I guess that would be yes," Lee said.

A Strange Twist of Fate

Anna was already standing up. "Come on. Let's go!"

"Now?" Lee had his hamburger in his hands. "It can wait five minutes."

Anna turned on her heel and strode away. She'd take a taxi, and Lee could choke on his lunch for all she cared. She sent Claudia another text as she pushed through the door.

I'll be there soon. Hang tight. She didn't wait for an answer before looking up a number for that taxi.

Lee brushed by her, heading for his cruiser. "Come on." He had his car keys in one hand and his soda in the other.

He obviously didn't choke if he could snap out those two words. The impatient tone of his voice didn't help to calm the irritation she felt over his sounding selfish. He would've rather eaten than help her friend. The only reason he wasn't still inside, comfy cozy and enjoying his lunch, was probably because he felt guilty, and guilt wasn't a good reason to do anything.

Lee had her door open when she got there. She could tell by the near frown on his lips that he was still put out. He wouldn't look at her, and he closed the door too hard. Since they only had a few minutes before they got to the Circle K, Anna had to get help quickly—Lee wouldn't be enough. And she knew just the person to text: Scarlet Craig, or Scar, as her fellow Angels in Black Leather bikers called her. She would call the others Anna needed. Yes, Scar would act immediately.

~*~

"Bivens's car still isn't there," Lee said as they rolled by Razor's place on the way to the Circle K six apartments down.

Had he left again? The thought of him going after Claudia frightened Anna.

When they turned into the parking lot, Anna felt immensely relieved to see Claudia standing near the ice freezer. "Please park around the side of the building."

"Sure."

At least he didn't argue with her. He drove around the outside of the parking lot, lowering the chances of Claudia seeing Anna inside his car. Lee parked in the farthest slot away from the front. If Claudia came around the corner, Anna wouldn't see her. Several cars were parked in between, obscuring her view.

"Ask her where Bivens went," Lee said, turning off the car.

"Oh, really? You think that didn't occur to me?" She got out of the car, letting the door slam for emphasis. When she rounded the corner, the roaring sounds of Harleys pulling into the parking lot vibrated the big windows. Anna needed to catch Claudia before she ran from the bikers.

Catching Claudia's frightened stare, Anna's heart dropped to her feet. She had matching dark bruises under both eyes. As Anna got closer, red marks became apparent on Claudia's cheek, and her bottom lip was swollen, too. She'd been beaten. Anna's anger flared.

"Claudia!" She gathered the shaking woman in her arms. "I'm sorry."

Claudia sobbed on Anna's shoulder. "I can't take it anymore. I'm so afraid of him."

Anna looked up and saw Lee standing a few feet away. He'd taken off his suit jacket and tie and rolled up his shirt sleeves, and with the way he was sipping on his soda and looking at his phone, he could just be a random customer hanging around. But she knew better. He needed information.

Holding her tighter, she asked, "What happened?"

"Razor killed Ginger," Claudia said, gasping. "He picked her up and threw her against the wall, and he killed her!" She cried harder still.

Lee's eyes went wide.

"He killed your Chihuahua?" Anna asked, making sure Lee understood that it was her dog and not a human. His subtle nod told her he got the message. "What about you? Did he do this to you?"

Claudia moved back, touching her face. "I yelled at him for—for doing that to Ginger, and he beat me up. I—I was afraid he would kill me, too. I can't handle staying with a user anymore."

"Is Razor still home?"

A Strange Twist of Fate

She nodded.

"But his car isn't there."

"I know. He told me it broke down last night, over on Van Buren."

Lee strode back toward his car. He must've heard enough to do his job, and he didn't plan on waiting for her to come along.

Anna waved at the two men by their bikes and one woman standing by a car, prompting the three to approach. "You shouldn't have to be afraid. These people can protect you." Claudia's frightened stare landed on the black-leather-clad bikers.

"Are they the same people who helped Maria?"

A great sense of relief filled Anna. Obviously Maria had talked to Claudia. Smiling, she said, "Yes, and they're here to help you if you want it."

Claudia's shoulders slumped, as if relieved. "I'm so glad."

Anna smiled at Scar. "This is Claudia Ortega, and she's requesting sanctuary with the Angels."

~*~

Talking Claudia into Scar's sedan had been far easier than Anna thought it would be. And she knew the woman was in safe hands. Razor would not be able to find her. It took all of five minutes to help change Claudia's future. Now if only she stayed the new course, like what Maria had done, she could have a chance at a decent life.

Anna walked down the sidewalk toward Razor's apartment, expecting to see a police car with him inside it. But no, she didn't even see Lee's car. Could he have parked around the corner, out of sight of the apartment? A troubling thought crept into her mind. What if in the few minutes it took her to take care of Claudia, Lee had been able to arrest Razor, stick him in the back of his car next to Anna's box of bread, and was on his way back to the police station—all without letting her know about it?

She came to a stop a couple of doors down. The front of Razor's apartment looked undisturbed. No one was there. Had she really missed everything? The thought left Anna feeling disappointed and somewhat perturbed at Lee for not calling her about it. The Circle K was probably the best place to wait for a taxi since that seemed to be the only ride back to the impound lot at the moment.

The sound of fast-moving shoes scuffing on concrete drew her attention. When Anna looked between the apartment and the abandoned house, she caught her breath.

Razor!

In the brief moment she thought about running back to the Circle K, he made up the distance between them.

"Where is she?" he asked through clenched teeth. Razor whipped out his box cutter. The sun glinted off the razor-blade knife pointed at her throat.

Anna couldn't run now, not without getting slashed. Razor exhaled hard in her face—the pungent order of his breath turned her stomach. What could she do? Scream? Then a thought hit her as if in a daydream—a single maneuver Caesar had taught. It was so clear. Anna dropped backward onto the concrete sidewalk—her elbow stopping her fall. Pain shot through her arm, but she didn't let that prevent her from swinging her legs, knocking Razor off his feet onto his side. He landed with a loud expulsion of breath.

"Anna!" Lee shouted from down the street.

Acting quickly, Anna kicked Razor's face once, twice. It stunned him long enough for her to roll away.

"Lee!" Anna yelled. With a burst of adrenaline in her veins, she sprung to her feet and jumped over Razor's legs. Lee and two officers ran toward her from down the block. She got in three steps before a horrendous pain seared through her lower leg. Anna screamed in agony, tumbling down onto the dirty street. She reached down and clutched her pain-filled calf, expecting to see Razor's blade embedded in her leg. But he was up and running back toward where he had come from—between the apartment and abandoned house. A horrendous leg cramp had taken her down, worse than earlier that morning.

A Strange Twist of Fate

As Lee stopped to help her, the two officers headed after Razor.

"Anna..." Lee sat her up. His brows were raised high over his wide eyes. "Are you hurt badly?"

She looked at her hand. It was scratched and bleeding. Oddly enough, she couldn't feel it. The pain in her leg dominated everything. "My leg." She moved her toes, and the pain flashed red-hot. She flinched and gasped. Lee wrapped his arm around her back, slid his other arm under her knees, and picked her up off the street. Anna held her breath and stayed very still, trying to make herself lighter while he carried her. With his quick stride, it seemed he didn't have any trouble. Although she was embarrassed by the extra weight she'd put on, she was impressed with his strength.

The car was parked around the corner with the patrol units lined up behind it. High-pitched sounds of sirens grew louder in the distance. The officers must've called in a foot pursuit, and their backup was coming code three. Anna's heart hadn't slowed down since she first saw Razor coming at her.

"I'm going to set you down. Hold on to my neck if you feel like you're falling," Lee told her with a voice so soft it caressed her skin. His gentle gaze made her heart melt.

Anna looped an arm around his neck, keeping him close. "Did you see what I did?"

"Yes." Lee got the door open.

While standing on one foot, she laughed. "I took down Razor almost without thinking about it!"

Lee helped her sit on the passenger seat. "I know. You did a fantastic job," he said, crouching beside her. He tenderly pushed back a few stray hairs clinging to her face.

"I wasn't scared."

Lee reached inside and got the mic.

"I mean, I was scared, totally, but I did what I needed to do." She couldn't stop smiling or slow her heart. Excitement—that was the amazing feeling coursing through her heart, although it didn't stop the pain in her leg. She kept a solid grip on her calf.

Debra Erfert

"You're amazing." Lee spoke into the mic, "David seventeen to dispatch."

"Razor had a box cutter, and I knew I couldn't run, so I threw myself down. He never expected me to kick his feet out from under him. I saw his eyes pop open wide as he fell." She laughed again.

"David seventeen, go ahead."

"Send rescue to my location for a female with cuts and an injured leg."

"Ten-four, David seventeen."

Anna gazed at her hand. "It's not that bad."

Lee tossed the mic to his seat, then reached over and firmly took hold of her hand, the one that kept her cramp from becoming too much to bear, and raised it high enough so she could see her bloody elbow.

"You're dripping on my upholstery," he said with his lips in a flat line. He held out a folded hanky and carefully pressed it on the biggest cut.

During class, they'd had a soft pad to fall on when they practiced. The rigidity of the concrete didn't give under her body. The compress stung, her leg was in agony, and she had a sneaking suspicion that tomorrow her whole body would be terribly sore from the fight and from her misguided run this morning.

"Taking down Razor felt totally great," Anna said as she held the hanky to her elbow. "I surprised myself being able to remember that maneuver. It was simple, really. Sometimes you practice, but that doesn't translate into reality, you know? Caesar will be so proud—"

"Caesar?" Lee asked quickly.

Anna looked over at Lee. He stared at her with an intensity she hadn't noticed before, with brows pushed close enough together that a groove had formed between them. "Uh-huh. He probably didn't anticipate me getting busted up like this."

Now his lips dipped into a frown. What did she say?

Lee took out his phone. "What's his number?"

"Whose number?" Anna asked.

A Strange Twist of Fate

"Caesar's. I'll call him for you."

Something had changed. She could feel it. But what, exactly, she didn't know.

"Why would I want to call him—right now?"

Lee looked upset with her, maybe confused. She could understand why, a little, considering she'd interfered in his arresting Razor. But it hadn't been intentional. Anna stared at his face—really stared. The subtle shaking of his head, the way his mouth hung open, the fire in his dark blue eyes.

He dropped his gaze. "If I was your boyfriend, I would want to be here for you, especially with you being hurt."

He not only didn't look into her eyes, but it also seemed he couldn't get enough of studying her injured elbow. Then a realization struck Anna. The detective almost sounded jealous. Could he be? From the very beginning he'd been protective of her, first with the insensitive patrol officer, then when they'd found out her house was tampered with. Even after Anna's anger about getting a flat tire had turned into rudeness directed at him, he'd hung in with her.

"Lee"—she waited until he looked up—"Caesar Aguirre, retired marine commander, is married and has a daughter in college. He comes to the Salvation Army building every Friday to teach a group of us women to defend ourselves." She nodded her head toward the back seat. "He also bakes a mean loaf of bread." She watched him stare at the box of plastic-wrapped loaves. In seconds, the edges of his ears tinged bright pink, but then his eyes returned to hers and lingered.

"I don't have a boyfriend," Anna said without looking away. Her news about Caesar dissolved the frown, and if she wasn't mistaken, his lips now had curved subtly upward.

Sirens took their attention away from their conversation. A fire truck was coming from down the street. In the next second, the siren cut off, but the lights kept flashing as they approached.

Debra Erfert

"Do you think the officers caught Razor yet?" Anna asked as the rescue truck pulled up next to the cruiser. "Shouldn't you be out there, too?"

"They're wearing body armor; I'm not." Lee reached around her to turn up the police radio. A single low tone beeped. "That tone means the channel is dedicated to an emergency. Most likely the foot pursuit." He let out a deep sigh. "Or it could mean they lost him and are now doing a search."

Anna leaned on the headrest. "It's my fault he got away. We've lost our chance to get him to talk."

"You're wrong. Bivens must've seen us drive by and got out then. Him seeing you on that sidewalk was a stroke of luck for us. It drew him out in the open. Don't beat yourself up—I mean worse than what you've already done." Lee grinned as he stood up.

He didn't seem upset with her.

Lee met the paramedics as they climbed down from their truck. He must've been briefing them on her condition, with the way the men looked over at her during that short discussion. Before they came, they took several big plastic cases from compartments built into the side of the truck. Lee stood back, watching.

The two paramedics fussed over her, cleaning her wounds and then bandaging them. They left her with instructions on how to ease her muscle cramp. She already knew how to do that. What Anna *didn't* know how to do was find Razor if he got away. He'd pulled a knife on her twice, and both times something prevented her from being seriously hurt—or even killed in a horrifically vile way. If the officers didn't catch him today, then he might try to find her again and take out his anger on her.

A Strange Twist of Fate

Six

Lee couldn't believe the expert moves Anna had put on Bivens, taking him down with a maneuver even he hadn't been taught in the police academy. Evidently, she didn't believe it, either, not with the way she kept retelling what happened over again. He hadn't heard her talk so continuously before. Not that he minded—he enjoyed it, actually. Her voice was slightly deeper than most women's, yet it wasn't raspy like a smoker's would be. No, it was smooth, sultry, with lilting moments. She barely paused between sentences while he drove them toward the impound lot. Anna said that Caesar taught them self-defense. Lee wanted to meet the retired marine and tell him he'd done a commendable job.

Bivens had slipped the dragnet perimeter that the officers set up. With a total of eleven uniformed cops, four sergeants, and one police dog, the ex-con had disappeared. Lee called in the warrant to dispatch, so every cop in the metropolitan area would be on the lookout for the suspect. Hopefully, the man would be in custody within the next twenty-four hours. At least Lee hoped for Anna's sake he would be.

"Oh, would you drive by East Broadway Road, near the Salvation Army building?" Anna asked as she reached into the back seat.

The loaf of bread in her hands made him wonder if she wanted to go find her self-defense instructor. He might get to thank Caesar sooner rather than later. In ten minutes, she had him pulling into an insurance company parking lot. The neighborhood wasn't the best.

"Are you going to bribe your insurance agent for better rates with that?" Lee asked, cracking a smile.

"Hardly. I'm making a delivery." Anna opened her door.

Debra Erfert

"How's your calf?" Lee's quick question stopped her from getting out. He watched her slowly extend her right leg and move her foot. When she flinched, he had his answer. He held out his hand. "Let me make the delivery for you."

Anna stared out her side of the car for several moments before looking at Lee. "Are you sure?"

"How hard can it be delivering bread to an insurance agent?" Lee said as she laid the loaf in his hand.

"I would guess probably pretty easy." Anna cocked her head to the side and grimaced. "But that's not where this is going."

Lee hesitated with his door open. "Where, then, exactly?"

Anna leaned closer to Lee, holding his gaze with a steadiness that suggested confidence. "You must do exactly what I say, or you'll scare him."

"Him? Him who?" Lee didn't dare look away from her and lose the emotional thread he felt with her. She moved in a little closer until a hand's width separated them.

"Behind the planter alongside the building is a Vietnam vet named Harold. That's the place he feels safe. He's mostly saturated in anything alcoholic, but his preference is whiskey." Anna frowned, shaking her head. "From what I understand, he believes staying drunk keeps the demons from taking his soul. He has PTSD, so don't make eye contact or any loud noises. Just set the bread on the edge of the planter near him, and tell him . . . tell Harold to remember to eat it. Hang there a moment to see if he says anything to you. OK?"

Lee took a moment to study the way the same loose strands of blonde hair fell around her face. They never seemed to stay in her ponytail. Thick, dark blonde lashes surrounded her warm brown eyes, making them look large and very alluring. The overly big T-shirt she wore most likely had belonged to her husband. To Lee, she seemed to be a down-to-earth kind of woman.

"I'll tell him—don't worry."

She smiled. "You better make your delivery."

"But don't look at him."

A Strange Twist of Fate

"That's right."

"I'll do my best." Lee got out and rounded the car, grateful he hadn't put his jacket or tie back on. The afternoon had grown warmer, and sweat prickled the back of his neck. He could see the eight-foot-long red brick planter alongside the building. Its height might've been a foot tall by two feet wide, but the evergreen bushes still growing in the container obscured anybody who might be hiding behind it. Lee smelled Harold before he saw him—the rank odors of the perpetually unwashed.

When he stepped closer, a moving head of wiry gray hair caught his attention. Evidently, Harold heard his approach. Lee kept his eyes down on the asphalt as he set the plastic-wrapped loaf of bread on the low wall of the planter nearest the man and took a step back. "Anna said to remember to eat your bread."

"Where is she?"

The softness of Harold's voice surprised Lee. His words hadn't been slurred, but through all the various repugnant odors emanating from behind the planter, Lee smelled alcohol, too.

"She's in my car."

"She under arrest?"

Even without his suit coat, he looked like a cop. "No. She has a leg cramp from jogging this morning." A rustling noise almost made him look behind the bushes at Harold. Instead, he used his peripheral vision and saw Harold's sunken black eyes above hollowed cheeks. His white hair puffed around a dark face.

"You sure she ain't in trouble?"

Lee turned and looked at Anna sitting inside his car. She gave a hesitant wave in their direction. He had to wonder if she had ever seen Harold. "She's a nice woman," Lee told him.

"She's a pain in the . . . backside."

Lee laughed.

"Tell her I saw a dark truck."

"A dark truck?" Lee shook his head.

"Aren't you hip to her investigation?"

Debra Erfert

"Some of it." Lee didn't exactly lie. He'd read several pages of her binder filled with files and her notes before she'd caught him.

"Then you know she's looking for the dark truck that killed her husband. I might've seen it in the alley. Two white dudes swiped the copper cable off that electric pole, and if I read them right, they didn't stop with that one. They were two bad dudes."

"Huh." Lee looked toward the alley, at the wooden pole the transient talked about.

"And you think that these men might've had something to do with Greg Eddington's crash?"

"Not a clue—what's your handle?"

"My handle? I'm Detective Lee Adams."

"Listen, Adams, you just tell Anna about the truck. I promised her I'd watch out for it. I promised!"

Lee heard the irritation in his voice. "I'll relay your message to Anna, Harold, but can you tell me anything else about the truck—anything that would make it stand out?"

"Now you're sounding like a cop." Lee froze. Oh, crap, he went too far. Anna didn't say anything about not asking questions. He heard plastic crinkling. It could be the bread wrapper he was opening, but there wouldn't be a way for Lee to smell the aroma of the bread over the stench of the camp. The moment Lee started to move to go back to his car, Harold said, "The truck was a late-model, dark blue Ford F-150 with a black metal cage over the top and bed that had a ladder laying over the driver's side. I thought I heard the sound of a ricochet. It took me a few moments to realize I wasn't under fire. It was the loud twang of metal snapping. Scared the hell outta me. That's how I knew they was up to no good."

Lee nodded. "Thank you, Harold." And as an afterthought, he added, "Enjoy your bread. It smelled delicious."

When he got back in the car, Anna asked a reasonable question. "What took you so long?"

"Your friend had possible information on a dark truck—"

Anna gasped loudly, taking out her phone. "What did he say?"

A Strange Twist of Fate

Lee explained what Harold had told him while he drove around the block to the dirt alleyway.

"Did he see a license plate?"

"He didn't tell me—and he would've told me if he had, right?"

"I'm sure."

Lee stopped next to a thick wooden electric pole that had several lines running from it down the alley. He didn't need to get out of his car to see that a cable was missing—the end of it was dangling near the transformer on top, and a piece of it was sticking up from the dirt. The braided copper cord had been cut away.

"What does that do?" Anna asked, leaning over him and looking out his window.

"That was a grounding wire in case of a lightning strike." Lee drove to the next pole with a transformer. "There were several cases like this last year in an older neighborhood where the utility lines are still above ground. New construction, like your home, has all the electric lines, cable lines, and such, embedded underground."

"What happens if it gets hit by lightning without that wire?"

"Uncontrolled power surges into the homes. It can blow every appliance that's not surge protected—and sometimes even protected ones." Lee stared at Anna, who still hadn't sat back on her side of the car. Her lavender fragrance was stronger with her so close. "During a thunderstorm last summer, lightning struck a Glendale neighborhood transformer. It blew up and caught fire. The power surges really did a job on the surrounding homes. There were several reports of smoke coming from plug outlets in the houses closest to that pole, and one confirmed house fire was directly related to the absence of the stolen grounding wire."

"So those copper cables are pretty important."

"And valuable. Copper is stolen for its worth. The thieves sell it as scrap. It's used in construction—anything from water and gas pipes to roofing material."

"And grounding electrical poles." Anna pointed her finger at the pole outside his door. "That one is vandalized, too."

"Yeah."

"So it was two guys driving a dark blue Ford F-150?"

"Right."

"And Harold couldn't see the passenger side to see if there was body damage?"

"No, he saw the truck on the driver's side."

Lee watched Anna tap like a madwoman on her phone's keypad, obviously making copious notes, probably adding every small detail he told her Harold had observed about the incident. The speed at which her two thumbs moved was faster than he could type with both hands on his computer keyboard. Her concentration intrigued him. Greg Eddington's career as a prosecutor was well known in law enforcement circles, but what had occupied his wife's time while he worked? Did she work too? It made sense.

"Did Harold give you a description of the men?"

"Huh?" Lee had to blink several times to pull his thoughts back to their conversation. He chuckled, and said, "White dudes."

"Which means they could be Hispanic or Anglo. You should report these thefts," Anna told him, as she continued to type, "and have APS come out and replace the cables before we have another storm—and another house fire where someone could be killed."

~*~

Lee had to admit—Anna was sharp. She saw the crime from all angles, and she knew what to do almost without pause.

On their drive back to the station they made another seven stops, giving out the rest of the bread—and in the process, gleaning one more tip about a possible crime from another transient. Although the act of donating the food was altruistic, Anna received something out of it too—information. It seemed she'd built up a network of snitches, and he had to wonder how far that network went.

By the time Lee pulled up next to the impound yard kiosk, Anna had barely taken her eyes off her phone, reading her notes, he assumed. She seemed enthusiastic about something—and that bothered him probably more than it should have. Lee had only

A Strange Twist of Fate

guessed that the big binder had to do with her investigating her husband's death, but Harold solidified it into fact. Greg Eddington sent criminals to prison, and apparently, Anna was questioning those same people. There wasn't any other way of looking at it—Anna put herself in danger with each contact. And now she had another tip—another lead to take her closer to solving a crime that left her husband dead. Lee needed to know what she was thinking—what she was planning—but he needed to ask carefully, or she could shut him out.

"Thanks for the ride and for your help," Anna said, opening her door.

"Wait."

Lee got out and rushed around the car, mentally formulating how he could weasel his way back into her investigation. He wanted to get another look at her binder. She'd stayed seated, and Lee crouched outside her open door. "We never did get to eat our lunch. How about I pick up some takeout and follow you home?"

"Oh . . ." Anna rubbed her right calf while slowly flexing her foot. "I was planning on soaking in a hot tub, but I am hungry." She gave Lee a smile that tripped his pulse. "That would be nice."

Lee tried to keep his smile from being too revealing about his motives—of his wanting to know more of her investigation—and wanting to hang around her just a little while longer.

"Good."

He held out his hands to her, and she took them. Lee wanted to be sure she could walk without too much pain. She limped a little, but he didn't think she'd cramp up while driving. Lee left her to sign off on the release form while he switched out his work car for his personal car. He found her idling near the parking lot exit, waiting for him. After a brief wave, she pulled out into traffic—and Lee had to use all his driving talents to keep up with her. The term "aggressive" sprung to his mind. "Skilled" was another word for the way she drove. If he didn't know better, Lee might've thought she was trying to lose him.

Debra Erfert

Seven

Anna drove quickly through town to the freeway, the fastest way to get home. She'd kept glancing in the rearview mirror at Lee. He'd done an admirable job in keeping pace with her in his old Buick. When he turned off to get their lunch, she knew she didn't have much time to get home and transfer her notes from her phone into her binder. She pulled into her garage and pushed the button, killing the engine. Anna loved her Impala. The keyless ignition made unlocking her car as easy as grasping the handle. Starting its engine took one touch. The keyless fob she carried in her handbag made the magic possible.

Anna rushed as fast as she dared, avoiding another leg cramp, to where she kept her binder hidden—in the antique sideboard. As soon as Lee told her about the two "white dudes" in the dark blue truck, her heart had leaped up to her throat. Caesar had put an idea in her head about how only a family member would be the one with enough motive to push Greg off the road, killing him, and Anna knew of only one such brother team who fit the criteria. They had a long history of criminal activity, where one or the other was in jail. In this last case, Wade Gaines, the younger brother, had been given a three-year stint for fighting in a bar and nearly beating in the head of his opponent after the man was on the floor unconscious.

She set the heavy binder on the dining table, not bothering to take it to the cedar chest, which was the usual place where she would update her investigation. She had no time to relax on the couch with a carton of ice cream, not with Lee on his way.

Jeremy, Wade's older brother by ten months, was employed in construction—off-the-books kind of employment. Greg called him a day laborer, where tax records weren't kept, and criminal history

A Strange Twist of Fate

didn't count against them, as long as they had their own tools and knew how to use them.

Anna opened the binder to *G* for *Gaines* and found Wade's arrest report. It had his address in the personal information section. She doubted he still lived at that same place, unless his girlfriend could've kept up the rent without his income. Anna had his mother's address written in her notes and also Jeremy's home address, which was really only an apartment in the back of the mother's main house. Wade wasn't due to get out for another . . . oh, crap! Wade Gaines should've been released before Valentine's Day, three weeks ago. The chances of Harold's "two white dudes" being the Gaines brothers just increased tenfold.

After she put two big sticky notes on the report, Anna got down to the business of transferring the information Lee had garnered from Harold, writing as fast as she could and still making it legible. Tonight would be a good time to do a stakeout on the most logical place to find the brothers—their mother's house. Anna flexed her foot, feeling the painful knot in her calf. Maybe she could do the surveillance tomorrow instead and take that bath tonight. Her phone camera didn't take such good pictures in the dark anyway.

"I thought that's what you would be doing," Lee said.

Anna jumped up, letting out a shriek as she turned around.

Lee stood near the entrance of the foyer, holding a paper bag and two sodas in a cardboard carrier. His eyes might've been wide open, looking all innocent, but his mouth, tweaked up in a grin, showed he knew he'd scared her.

"You left the garage door open. I thought . . ." Lee shrugged.

Anna pressed her hand to her chest. "You still could've knocked."

He nodded toward the table. "I didn't want to disturb your concentration." He stepped closer. "I figured you needed to get your notes down."

It was too late to close the binder now, especially with the way Lee was staring at the picture of her suspect.

Debra Erfert

"Is that who you think drives the truck?" Lee asked as he set the bags on the table.

Anna stared at his curious face. He'd proven over the past two days that she could trust him. Was that too quick? He seemed honorable. But he was still a cop, and the paperwork in her binder had been illegally obtained. Anna could go to jail for having it. She studied his eyes—they were kind, and she'd been alone too long. She hoped she wasn't letting down her guard just because of a handsome face. "What did Harold tell you about me?"

Lee opened the first bag. "That . . . you were investigating your husband's car crash." He sat down in the chair next to where she stood. "I remember reading about it, just after it happened. I thought it was an accident."

Anna dropped in the chair next to his. "If it had been an accident, then the driver of that dark truck had nothing to be afraid of. Instead of stopping after hitting Greg's car, he took off. Witnesses who did stop gave DPS only a vague description of a dark pickup truck. He intentionally rammed into Greg, making him crash down into that canyon."

Lee nodded, his eyes on the binder again. "And you've been doing a follow-up investigation after DPS closed out their case?"

"Um . . . yes."

"Who else knows about your investigation?"

"Very few."

"Harold?" Lee asked.

"Yes, he does."

"And your other contacts—the ones you take the bread to?"

"They know enough."

Lee pointed at the binder. "Who knows about that?"

Anna put her hands across the top. "No one."

"But me?"

"What exactly do you know about it?"

Lee rested his elbows on the table and leaned closer to her, staring intently into her eyes. "That you probably have every case your husband worked on—and every arrest report that came with

A Strange Twist of Fate

them—information that should've never left his office, let alone fallen into the hands of a civilian."

Anna's pulse jumped, beating up into her throat. Breathing became difficult. She felt lightheaded.

"I can't imagine how you managed to stay out of jail." Lee sat back and smiled. "You must have some very tactful approaches."

"What?" Anna took in a deep breath, then another. "You're not going to take this away from me? And arrest me?"

Lee pursed his lips, shaking his head. "I'm not even going to ask how you got them. As far as I know, your husband made a habit of making copies and had them lying around his home office. How would you know they had to go back to the district attorney's office?"

Anna covered her face with her hands, trying to keep from crying. From the very beginning, she knew she couldn't confide in her own mother—she had enough emotional problems of her own. Anna certainly couldn't tell her dad what she had been doing. With his high-level sense of ethics, he would've immediately taken away her binder and maybe even had her do community service as a punishment. She was sure he could do that. Hiding her investigation was second nature after nearly a year. But Lee had accepted her obsession almost without question. Relief seemed to drain from every part of her body, especially her heart. She felt a warm hand on her shoulder.

"Are you all right?" Lee's tender voice brought unavoidable tears to her eyes.

With a swipe of her unbandaged hand, she dried her cheeks and tried to smile. Her lips wouldn't cooperate very well. "I'm OK."

He reached over and used his thumb to gently wipe another stray tear. "You're tired. Maybe you should take a nap after you eat."

This time she did smile. "That sounds like a good idea."

Debra Erfert

Lee started unloading tacos from the bag. "Harold said that there were two men in the truck." He nodded toward the binder. "How does that guy fit in?"

"Well," Anna said, smoothing her hand across the binder's page, "Wade Gaines went to prison for three years, the maximum sentence Greg could get for the assault he committed. Wade is a repeat offender. And he got out last month. He has a brother, Jeremy, who has been in and out of prison almost as much as his brother. He works in construction, so they'd have the tools to cut the copper wire." Anna smoothed her notes with her bandaged hand.

"And?" Lee passed her a taco. "How does this information relate to your husband's crash?"

Anna rolled her shoulder, the one she landed on during her one-sided fight with Razor. It hurt. "I have suspicions that maybe someone in prison . . ." She looked up into Lee's eyes. "Don't laugh, but I'm thinking Greg had a hit put out on him."

Lee shrugged. "It wouldn't be unheard of, but that usually comes with a high price tag."

She sat up straight. "You believe my theory?"

"Why not?" He opened the wrapper of his taco. "You've done so much work on all his cases, you probably know them better than he did—and from more angles. So tell me your thoughts."

Renewed, Anna told him her theory about a relative doing the deed for the brother.

"Hmm, that doesn't sound so farfetched." Lee tapped her binder with his finger. "What do you plan on doing with this new information?" He took out his phone. It buzzed in his hand while he looked at it. "Excuse me," he said, standing up. "I need to take this. It's my attorney."

Anna watched Lee walk to the foyer after he said a single word, "Yeah." Either he had expected the call or he didn't like his lawyer very much, which she could totally understand. Anna grew up around her dad's friends. He rarely let her date anyone who wasn't going to law school or who hadn't already passed the bar. There

A Strange Twist of Fate

was a certain "I'm better than you" mentality that came along with that career choice, and most attorneys believed their own press. Meeting Greg changed that image. He seemed genuinely interested in her as a person and not just as a judge's daughter. Even her mother didn't scare him away.

Margo Wright. To most people, her mother could be defined as eccentric. But Anna knew she had major obsessive-compulsive issues that would get tangled in with her hearing voices that weren't there. Her mother was just as serious about her routines as Anna was about her own, and that worried Anna sick. Over the years, her mother's odd behavior seemed to have amplified. The prescriptions the doctors provided only worked when she took them.

"Anna, I need to leave." Lee walked back to the table and picked up his soda.

"I guess you won't be able to eat—again."

He shook his head. "It's OK. You just take that nap. Get some rest."

"Where're you going?"

Anna wondered why she asked that. It was getting too personal.

Lee stopped, his shoulders slumping a little. "I'm going to sign my divorce papers."

~*~

Lee's attorney couldn't have had worse timing. Even an hour later would've been better than having to skip out so soon on his lunch with Anna. The firm he'd hired to represent him had passed his case to Beverly Richardson, their youngest attorney, and he hoped it wasn't a mistake. Lee didn't really care who filed the divorce paperwork as long as it was done correctly and expediently. Six months was the statutory time limit, and, right on the date, his papers were waiting for him to sign. Still, Lee hadn't seen it coming. His preoccupation with the pretty widow knocked his deteriorating private life off the grid. Having Anna to take care of was distracting as well as enjoyable. Having to leave sooner than he wanted ate at him.

The Braxton & Braxton Law offices were strategically located next door to the Maricopa Superior Courthouse. The location guaranteed them constant business of one kind or another. Being so close to the courthouse also caused a shortage of parking spaces. Lee had to walk over from the parking garage. He didn't get inside before being stopped by an old friend—an ex-cop, to be more exact. David Curtis had decided to get a law degree instead of taking police reports. He currently was an assistant prosecutor with aspirations of being a judge.

"Detective Adams," Curtis said, his arms full of binders, not dissimilar to Anna's files. He balanced the binders in one arm and held out his right hand to Lee. "How're you doing?"

Lawyers were crawling all over the place. Some he liked. Others, not so much. Curtis had a reputation for knowing everybody's business.

Lee shook his hand. "Doing OK. Just here on personal business."

"I heard about the divorce. Sorry about that, man." Curtis shifted the binders again, holding them in both arms.

"How did you hear about it?" Lee hadn't seen him in a good two years.

"I saw Crystal Ward—"

"Carolyn's attorney."

"Yeah, she was filing some papers and spilled what they were."

"My divorce papers?"

"I'm afraid so."

"Just great." Lee blew out a heavy breath. The end of one part of his life was becoming public, whether he liked it or not. At least he had something else he could concentrate on. "Do you have a few minutes to talk?"

"Sure. What's up?"

Lee looked around to see who else could hear him before he asked, "You remember Greg Eddington?"

A Strange Twist of Fate

"Sure I do."

"I'm curious about what happened to his open cases after he died. Do you know?"

Curtis's friendly grin spread into a knowing smile. "You've met his wife."

"I"—Lee looked around again—"ran into her last night, and we got to talking."

"Uh-huh," Curtis said, still with that irritating smile.

"About those cases, do you know what happened to them?"

"I know more now than when Mrs. Eddington grilled me nine months ago. Most of the cases hadn't even come to trial then."

"But they have now?"

Curtis shook his head. "His cases were divided between three desks—including mine. Most, I believe, were pled out to avoid a trial. We just didn't have the manpower to take up Greg's slack."

"It's not like the man inconveniently scheduled his vacation, David. He was killed!" Lee's pulse throbbed in his head as he tried to quell his anger toward David's thoughtless statement.

"I understand that, but I think Mrs. Eddington believes that we're involved with some kind of conspiracy.

"A theory you never checked into?"

"Checked into what? A conspiracy?"

"How many of those cases ended with the defendants serving jail time?"

"I . . . I'm not sure. I know mine were all probation and community service deals."

"Crap"—Lee ran his hand over his mouth—"David, do me a favor. Find out about the other cases."

Curtis's brows dropped. "You're taking this seriously? Look, I know Greg's wife is hot, but she's obsessed with finding someone to blame. She might be as nuts as her mother."

Lee frowned. "What do you mean?"

Curtis lowered his voice. "No disrespect to Judge Wright—I think he's a great man—but Greg would talk about his mother-in-law being a card-carrying schizophrenic. She'd hear voices that no one else heard. One minute she'd be calm, relaxed, and in the next, she would explode in anger and be talking nonsense."

Lee remembered Anna being timid last night at the station, not like she was today. "Did Greg say anything like that about his wife—that his wife was crazy?"

"Well, no, but maybe his death gave her a psychotic break. I understand mental problems like that can run in families."

"A psychotic break?" Lee scrubbed his hand over his mouth again. "Stress can do that, huh?"

"I don't know." Curtis lofted the binders in his arms. "Listen, Lee, I'll do some checking and call you."

Lee nodded. "I'd appreciate any help."

Curtis knew Lee, yet he'd barely agreed to look into a few simple files. What help did he give Anna? From the sound of it, probably none. How hard could it be? The files must all be stored on computers—unless Curtis already knew the outcome and wasn't willing to share. Lee strode to his attorney's door, aggravated at his friend. Speculation, that was all Curtis had on Anna's behavior. As far as Lee was concerned, she was rational and a logical thinker. She certainly didn't hear voices—did she?

"Good afternoon, Detective Adams," the receptionist said to Lee as he entered.

Lee nodded at Connie but then looked down the hallway to Beverly's closed door. "I was summoned."

"Yes, sir. Ms. Richardson is waiting for you. You can go right in."

Lee's foul mood had followed him, keeping him from being polite. He just turned and strode to Beverly's door, knocked twice, and opened it without waiting for a response. His attorney looked up from the large executive chair that seemed to swallow her. She was pretty enough, and she always had her dark brown hair up in a do high on her head. He'd never seen her without lipstick or makeup, or without wearing a tight, low-cut jacket that matched the skinny skirt he could see through the glass table she used as a

A Strange Twist of Fate

desk. She was petite. The high heels she had on only brought the top of her head up to his chin when she stood.

"Lee!" Beverly got up and reached across the desk with her hand outstretched. "Today you'll be a free man again."

Her hand was cold to his touch. Was she nervous? "I'm hoping so."

"Have a seat." She motioned to the leather-and-chrome chair in front of her desk.

As he sat, she opened a thin, brown file folder. Lee thought his divorce papers would be thicker, more complicated. Five years of their marriage sifted down to just a few sheets.

"This is pretty uncomplicated," Beverly said, moving the folder over to his side of the tabletop. "These clauses state that Carolyn willingly signs off on any part of your retirement, and she wants you to sign off on her 401(k) and any other retirement investments she might hold in the future." She passed him a pen. "I believe you already moved what belongings you wanted to keep out of the residence—"

"Only what I could take at the time," Lee told her.

Beverly kept going. "This is the total in the shared savings account." She looked up at Lee. "It's been frozen per court order since you were served."

"I know."

"The account will be closed out, and the contents will be shared equally."

"How generous."

"You will be paid ten thousand dollars upon your signing over your half of the residence—"

"What?" Lee snapped.

Beverly pulled back the paper and looked at the clause again. "Your wife is buying out your part in the home. Since you're the one who moved out, we thought that would be adequate."

"Adequate?" Lee took a couple of quick, deep breaths to control his anger. "We bought that house at a great price, with a very low interest rate. *I* made the sizable down payment as well as

Debra Erfert

the mortgage payments. And now she thinks I'll be happy to get a tiny bit of my down payment back?"

Beverly gave him a calming smile. "But she will have full responsibility for the mortgage and taxes from now on."

"So? She earns more than I do."

"OK, your wife's attorney said to go up to twenty thousand dollars if you seemed put off by that clause. Also, Mrs. Adams keeps her car, and you keep the one you're driving—"

Lee cut her off. "Who are you working for anyway? Me or my wife?"

Beverly innocently batted her lashes.

Lee got up and paced across the large office. "What about my dog?"

Beverly flipped another page. "He'll remain in Mrs. Adams's custody."

"Like hell he will," Lee snapped. "Why is she holding onto *my* dog so tightly?"

He strode to the door and swung it open. "Connie," he called down the hallway. "Please come in here."

Connie's green eyes were popped open wide as she came into the office.

"Do you take notes?" Lee asked.

With her gaze bouncing between Lee and Beverly, she nodded.

"Then write this down and get it straight." Lee rapped his knuckles on the glass tabletop hard enough it pinged. His voice took on a hardened edge as he spoke to Beverly. "Our home is to be sold at market price by a Realtor I approve of. And I have to sign off on it. The proceeds will then be split down the middle. I don't care if Carolyn buys it, but she will pay the same price as a stranger. I want the contents sold by a reputable estate sales and auction house, and the proceeds will be split evenly. Again, Carolyn can buy what she wants, and the same goes for me, but it must be at the market price the auctioneer puts on it. Understand?"

Both Connie and Beverly nodded but were otherwise mute.

A Strange Twist of Fate

Lee stared directly into Beverly's eyes when he told her, "And if I don't have my dog back in my custody by midnight tonight, then Carolyn will have to sell her car and split the proceeds with me—and she cannot buy it." He looked up at Connie. "Get to transcribing. This ends tonight, or I find a new attorney."

Debra Erfert

Eight

Anna awoke with a start. The darkness pressed in around her. After eating not only her three tacos but also the three that Lee hadn't eaten, she'd soaked in a hot bath before lying down wearing pajama bottoms and one of Greg's old T-shirts. She'd slept on the couch all afternoon, straight into the night.

The house was dead silent.

Until tinkling broken glass shattered the silence.

Anna's heart raced.

Another scraping noise had her reaching for her cell phone and her gun from atop the cedar chest. As Anna punched in the code, unlocking her phone, she slid off the couch. The noise had come from down the hallway—from a bedroom or Greg's office. The outside lights weren't on. If someone had walked in her yard, the sensors would've caught the movement and turned on the lights. Unless the bulbs had been loosened again.

Anna crouched beside the couch, hiding as much as she could.

She heard a woman ask, "911, what is your emergency?"

In a whisper, Anna told her, "I think I have an intruder in my home."

"What is your address, ma'am?"

Anna told her as quietly as she could.

"Are you alone?"

"Yes."

Might she have imagined the noise? Dreamed it? When she saw a flashlight beam move in the foyer, her heart nearly burst from beating so hard.

"Who are you?" Anna yelled. Without a word, the light pointed at her face. She used the hand with her phone to shield her eyes. "I have a gun! Get out, or I swear I'll shoot you dead!"

A Strange Twist of Fate

Her threat didn't stop whoever carried the flashlight from getting closer. She heard shoes shuffle quickly on tile, moving toward her. Anna had no choice. Aiming at the light, she fired her gun. And she continued to shoot again and again and again as she screamed.

~*~

Lee paced his small living room, drinking a Diet Coke. He knew his ultimatum to Beverly couldn't possibly be done in a single night. He had been more angry than rational when he made his demands—not that he didn't mean them. But he would see each one of them carried through before he signed off on the divorce. He'd get Rusty back if he had to haul his wife's butt to court.

After he'd left the meeting, he'd driven five miles on the freeway before he noticed he was going back toward Anna's house and not his own apartment. His first impulse was to go to her. That was an interesting revelation. But he figured she was napping, so he drove home instead. Home. That was an odd description of his apartment. It had never seemed like a home to him, but only a temporary stop on his way to someplace else.

His phone buzzed against the countertop, sounding like a trapped bee. He grabbed it and looked at who was calling. He'd hoped it was Carolyn, telling him she was on her way over with Rusty, but he didn't expect to see the City of Scottsdale calling him.

"Detective Adams," Lee said.

"This is Scottsdale dispatch, Detective. You wanted to be notified if there was any activity on East Gainey Ranch."

"Yes, ma'am."

"I've just dispatched officers there for an intruder and shots fired. I've lost contact with the victim."

Lee didn't respond to the woman or even bother changing out of his blue jeans and old ASU sweatshirt before taking off out the door. His only thought was to get to Anna. He gripped the wheel, driving hard and fast, skidding around corners. His personal car didn't have emergency lights. Even so, he wasn't pulled over by the police in the twenty minutes it took to pull up behind the line of marked units on Anna's street.

Her front door was open, and the courtyard had officers standing around. A photographer snapped pictures of blood on the ground. Lee's heart pounded as he approached.

"Detective Adams?"

Lee recognized Officer Sanchez from last night's call. His partner, Newman, came out of the front door and headed toward them.

"Officer Sanchez," Lee said. "What happened? Where's Anna?"

Sanchez's brows rose. "Anna?"

Lee shook his head in frustration. "Mrs. Eddington. Is she hurt?"

Newman stopped next to them. He had a small spiral notebook open. "Mrs. Eddington took care of that intruder herself with a Walther PPK .380-caliber handgun."

Lee looked over at the blood droplets on the patio. "Is he in custody? The hospital? Dead?"

Sanchez said, "No. He ran away. We lost the blood trail in the grass after he ran around the house. We'll get a perimeter set up—bring in other units and start a coordinated search. We'll get him."

Newman told him, "The perp broke a window on the same side of the house where we found that patio chair. The main power was turned off at the circuit breaker box outside the garage. The sound of breaking glass woke Mrs. Eddington, and she confronted him when he came into the family room. The dispatcher listened to her warning him to get out before she shot him, and then she must've emptied her magazine in his direction. She left holes in the wall and a chair, but as you can see, she wounded the perp, too."

"And Mrs. Eddington?" Lee asked, staring at the front door.

Newman scratched his head. "She's . . . too calm. I remember after I unloaded my gun for the first time on duty, man—I had the shakes for the next couple of hours."

A Strange Twist of Fate

"Keep me informed on your search, would you?" Lee asked as he headed toward the door. Each blood drop on the concrete patio had its own numbered placard set next to it. The highest number he could see was eighteen. He got past the few officers he didn't know in the foyer by holding up his wallet badge. More blood dotted the tiled floor, and there were more numbered placards next to each one. He spotted Anna standing near her dining table with her arms wrapped around her chest. She had no ponytail—her blonde hair spilled messily down around her shoulders. But it was her pallid face and wide eyes that worried him. She looked like she might faint. When she finally noticed him come in, tears quickly formed and spilled down her colorless cheeks.

"Oh, Lee." Anna held out her arms to him.

He didn't know who made the first move, exactly, but he had his arms wrapped around her about the same time her knees gave out. Lee kept her from slumping to the floor. She shook, and he held her tighter while she cried with her face against his neck. Lee looked around at the others in the room. They all were staring at her outburst. She'd flipped emotions. He needed to get her out of the crowd so he could talk with her. Lee lifted her legs and carried her around the blood-splattered spots and down the hallway to the room he'd seen her go into earlier that morning—her bedroom.

"I—I shot him!" Anna's muffled words tore at his heart. "He—he wouldn't stop coming at me. He was going to kill me—I know it!"

Lee set her down on the end of her bed and sat next to her. She kept a firm grip with both hands, clutching his sweatshirt. "Anna, tell me what happened."

As Anna explained everything, he felt her shiver. A crocheted coverlet on the bed was within Lee's reach, and he pulled it up around her shoulders.

"I was so scared," she said with her face pressed against his shoulder.

Lee understood how she felt. Once he'd searched a business late at night on a possible burglary-in-progress call, not knowing if the suspect was still inside. His heart had pounded so hard he couldn't hear anything besides his fast-beating pulse—and he wore a bulletproof vest and had armed backup. Anna had been alone and was dressed only in pajamas.

"That woman with the camera took my gun. She said it was evidence, like *I* did something wrong." Anna pushed back to look up into his face. Her anger had finally emerged. He could see it in her eyes. "*I'm* the victim here! I didn't do anything wrong, and I don't understand how she can treat me like that!"

"No, you're right." Lee stood up. "She made a mistake. I'll go get it back. Take a little a moment to"—he was going to tell her to calm down, but he'd been married long enough to know those were fighting words to any woman—"relax until I get back. We need to talk."

Anna closed her eyes and nodded. Her head fell forward. It looked as if that short outburst took all her energy. She needed more sleep, but Lee knew she couldn't stay here until the scene had been cleared and that perp captured. Her life was in danger, of that he had no doubt. He went outside and found the crime-scene investigator by an unmarked patrol car looking at the back of her camera, scrolling through her digital pictures. He took out his badge as he approached.

"I need to talk with you," Lee said to the woman.

"Yes," she said without looking away from her camera. Lee could see the pictures of a broken window in a bedroom.

"You made a mistake when you took Mrs. Eddington's weapon into evidence."

She then gave Lee a momentary glance before resuming her work. "Tell her whining to her boyfriend won't do her any good."

"I am not Mrs. Eddington's boyfriend. I'm Phoenix Police Detective Lee Adams," he said.

"Yeah, like you sweep every crying woman off her feet and know just where her bedroom is to carry her into."

"I didn't say I wasn't her friend."

"What a good friend."

A Strange Twist of Fate

Lee couldn't miss the heavy sarcasm in the woman's voice. He glanced back at the house and saw Sanchez and Newman watching them. Even in the low light of the patio, he could see the frowns on their faces. They obviously knew the photographer. He briefly wondered why they weren't out knocking on the neighbors' doors asking about seeing a stranger. Lee didn't bother to hide his irritation any longer. The night was too dark where he stood to be able to read the nametag pinned to her suit jacket. "What is your name?"

After an audible sigh, she said, "CSI Madeline Kline."

Now he didn't know what to call her. She might've been hired solely for evidence collecting, which left her out of the officer category. He had never addressed anyone as CSI before, and that stuck in his throat. But Lee knew enough about collecting evidence in Arizona that he had standing to question her procedures—and definitely her judgment.

"Ms. Kline, you should've released the gun back to Mrs. Eddington after photographing it and logging in the serial number."

"It was used during the commission of a crime." She kept on clicking through her pictures.

"Mrs. Eddington is not the suspect; therefore, she committed no crime."

Kline shook her head. "She shot a man."

"Protecting herself," Lee snapped.

"That's not my call," she told him.

Lee took out his phone. "Then your supervisor will confirm it."

Kline laughed softly. "It's after ten. He turns off his phone. You can call him in the morning."

"I'll call Anna's father then."

"I'm so scared," Kline said under her breath.

Lee paid attention to the woman's face while he added, "I'm sure Judge Jackson Wright will have his phone turned on for his only daughter."

Kline looked first at the house and then into Lee's eyes. "Julianna Eddington is—"

Debra Erfert

"Julianna Wright, widow of the late Phoenix prosecutor Greg Eddington."

"Oh, crap . . ." She groaned as she set the camera down next to the evidence box.

Lee told her, "If you haven't done it already, document the gun and return it to her—with an apology for the unnecessary anxiety you've caused her."

"An apology?" Kline asked with her voice raised. "Why? I was just doing my job!"

"Poorly, if you made such an injurious mistake."

"Please tell me, who did I injure?"

Lee stepped closer, getting in the CSI's face. "Mrs. Eddington was attacked. She fought off that attacker with her gun. Without it, she might've been killed. The perp got away, and you seized her only means of protection if he comes back. She's scared out of her mind, thanks to you."

The woman's breathing increased loud enough Lee could hear it. He'd either frightened her or she was angry. With the way she jerked the plastic package open from around Anna's Walther, his guess was anger. It was too bad her attitude would probably keep her from offering that apology.

Lee took the gun from Kline. "The slide is locked open. She emptied it."

Kline opened the plastic evidence bag holding the magazine. "We found three rounds in two different walls, and one round in that chair next to the foyer." Kline gave the mag to Lee.

"Anna said the man had a flashlight in her eyes as he came at her—blinding her." Lee looked at the weapon. She ran out of bullets.

"That might explain this." Kline turned on a small flashlight, directing it toward a bag containing a Maglite with a broken lens and a flared exit hole in the side.

"She shot that?"

A Strange Twist of Fate

"I'd say it was a damned lucky shot," Kline said. "He couldn't have held on to the flashlight. He took the quickest exit out of the house—the front door."

Lee would make a point of resupplying Anna's ammunition in the morning. "He'd cased the place out last night."

"He did?" Kline asked. "How do you know this?"

"I brought Anna home, and she found the courtyard gate open. Also, the bulbs in the auto-sensor lights had been unscrewed."

Kline picked up her camera again. "It sounds to me like the perp is someone Ms. Eddington knows—someone neighbors might not have questioned being on her property."

"You have, what—five bullets accounted for?"

"Yes."

"So she might've hit him three times." Lee nodded.

"Maybe, depending if she had a full magazine and a round in the chamber. And if we found all the places in her house she hit."

"Did you ask Anna about that?" Lee asked.

"She wouldn't talk to me."

"Because you were treating her like a suspect instead of a victim."

Kline set her camera down again. "She shot a man," she said in a quiet voice. "And until an investigation is done, we can't be sure why he was shot." She looked up at Lee. "It could've been a domestic."

"With the lights out and him using that flashlight? And he broke in the house. The dispatcher heard her screaming at him to get out before she fired."

"They might've had a fight, and she locked him out."

"Anna doesn't have a boyfriend."

Kline scoffed. "Seriously? Not even you?"

"I told you—I'm her friend."

Kline let out a heavy breath. "I don't get it," she said, putting the evidence case on the back seat of the car. She set her camera next to the case. A single low beep sounded, indicating the car alarm had been set. She then took the gun and magazine from Lee's hands and headed for the courtyard gate. "Mrs. Eddington had been very guarded from the moment the police arrived, yet when she saw you, she threw herself into your arms."

She did? Lee remembered it differently. He'd been so relieved to see her unhurt that when he saw her crying, he raced to hold her.

Sanchez and Newman were now standing with two more officers. Each had small notebooks out, and they were listening to their radios.

As Lee neared, he asked, "Have you found the suspect?"

Newman shook his head.

"We haven't given up," Sanchez told him. "We have dispatch contacting the hospitals and urgent care facilities in Scottsdale and surrounding cities, putting them on alert."

"But they're usually pretty good at calling in suspected gunshot wounds," Kline said.

"We've talked with most of the neighbors," Sanchez said. "The sirens brought them outside. They didn't see anything helpful, although some thought a neighbor had shot off firecrackers."

"The gunshots. How about the local security patrol?" Lee asked.

"The guard was first on the scene." Sanchez flipped back a couple of pages in his notebook. "Oscar Jones, twenty-four, was on the next block over and heard the gunshots. The front door was standing open. He had to talk to Mrs. Eddington from there. She wouldn't let him inside without proof of his identity."

"Good girl," Lee whispered.

Kline said, "She bluffed him with an empty gun."

"Yes, she did," Newman said. "We got in only because she remembered us from last night and recognized our voices."

"That was fortunate." Lee looked at the front door. "I'll talk Anna into staying at a hotel or with her parents until you find the perp."

"Good idea," Kline said, agreeing. "Let's get this gun back to your . . . back to Mrs. Eddington, so I can go home."

~*~

A Strange Twist of Fate

"I don't know what you said to get her to apologize," Anna said, looking over her shoulder at Lee, "but whatever it was, it worked."

Lee stood behind her in the hallway at the edge of the foyer, watching as CSI Kline stepped around the blood drops and picked up the number placards on the patio as she headed for her car. Her job at the scene was over. Lee shrugged. He didn't bother telling Anna how he dropped her dad's name to get Kline to cooperate. "Where did you say that other magazine is?"

Anna pulled the coverlet tighter around her body. "It was on the cedar chest, but I couldn't find it in the dark, so I couldn't reload. I didn't want to turn on a light or even use my phone as a light without knowing for sure he was gone."

"I understand." Lee went to retrieve her extra mag. He found it on the floor just under the couch. No wonder she couldn't find it. That probably was a good thing. It had saved her from having to aim a loaded gun at a young security guard. When he got back to Anna, she was leaning against the wall, pressing her fingers to her forehead, rubbing them in a small circle.

"Are you OK?"

Anna dropped her hands. "I've got a headache."

Lee slipped his arm around her shoulder, coaxing her back down the hallway. "Do you have something to take for it?"

"I have some aspirin in the bathroom medicine cabinet." Anna looked back into the foyer. "Who's going to clean up all the blood?"

"The city cleanup crew will do it, but they're the last to come in after all the evidence has been collected."

Anna pulled the coverlet tighter around her chest. "How did you know?"

"They get called out for all sorts of dangerous spills, like gas, oil, and blood after bad traffic accidents."

She stopped before walking back inside her bedroom and stared up into Lee's eyes with her brows pinched together. "That's not what I meant."

"What, then?"

"You showed up here tonight just when I needed you—uh, I"—Anna stuttered, blinked rapidly, and then said—"when I needed a friend the most. How did you know what happened?"

Lee ran a hand over his head and then rubbed the back of his neck. He hadn't thought about how he'd explain showing up. He didn't want to lie to her, and he was too tired to figure out how to skirt around the truth. "I told dispatch to call me if you had any trouble." He shrugged. "I'm sorry."

Anna nodded her head a few times while staring at the collar of his sweatshirt. "I was expecting you to come back, you know, earlier this afternoon after you finished your . . ." She looked up into his eyes. "I'm glad you came."

"I am, too." Lee stared at her blonde hair. The ends were tucked under the coverlet, but the same shorter strands hung along her cheeks and near her brown eyes. The small bandage he'd placed over the cut last night was missing. "Anna, you know you're not safe here."

"Yeah, I got that idea earlier tonight."

"You need to find another place to stay—until the police find the guy who tried . . ." Lee couldn't finish his thought.

Anna turned to her room and slowly stepped inside. "I guess we don't really know what he had planned, do we?" She moved stiffly across the thick carpeting until she stood at the foot of her bed. "If he'd only wanted to kill me, then he could've used a gun and shot me from the foyer when he first saw me." She turned around and sat, her wet eyes staring up at him. "What did he want from me?"

"I don't know." Lee sat on the bed next to her. "Maybe he had a knife."

Anna gasped. "Like Razor had?"

Lee groaned. He hadn't thought about him. "Does he know where you live?"

"I've tried very hard not to let anyone know my address." Anna tossed off the coverlet and went to her dresser. "But that doesn't

A Strange Twist of Fate

mean he didn't find a way to get it." She picked up her Walther and empty magazine before walking to the side of the bed and kneeling down.

Lee got up and moved far enough to see her pull a slim plastic box from under the bed. When she removed the lid, Anna lifted out a cardboard box of .380-cal ammunition and set it on the mattress. He watched her while she tried to insert the first bullet into the end of the magazine, but her hand shook, and she didn't seem to have enough strength to press down the stiff spring. Lee knelt next to her and gently relieved her of the job of reloading. Seven bullets later, he slapped the mag into the gun.

"I want a round in the chamber," Anna whispered.

Lee nodded and aimed the end of the barrel at the mattress as he pulled the slide back and let it go with a snap. He then dropped the mag out and inserted another bullet, giving Anna eight shots—the same as she had with her intruder, it seemed.

"Anna, calling your mom now would be a good idea. I can help—"

"No," she said, cutting him off. Anna sat down on the floor, bringing her knees up to her chest. "I can't call her this late at night. She'd . . . she's . . ." Anna shook her head.

Lee remembered what his assistant prosecutor friend David Curtis told him about her mom's mental health problems. He took the coverlet off the bed again and wrapped it around her shoulders before sitting next to her, resting his back against the bed. The pout on her lips didn't surprise him.

"You can talk to me." Lee tugged on the end of the coverlet. "We're basically strangers. I won't judge you."

Anna looked up sharply at him. "Oh, Lee, we're not strangers."

He leaned closer. "OK, wrong word. We're newly acquainted friends."

The corner of her lips tipped upward in a cute grin. "Better."

"So tell me, why can't you call your parents tonight?"

Anna let out a heavy sigh. "My mother has a heavy-duty obsessive-compulsive disorder, among other problems." She

Debra Erfert

looked around the extremely neat room. "I guess I might, too." She groaned, dropping her face to the tops of her knees. "My dad thinks I'm as nuts as my mom."

"He told you that?" Lee asked, incredulous that any father could insult his daughter in such a way.

Sniffing, she said, "Not outright, but I can see how he disapproves of the way I do things. He'd probably have me committed if he saw my investigation binder."

Lee nearly laughed at that, but he held back. "Anna, having drive isn't the same as being compulsive." He cleared his throat. "If you don't feel, uh, comfortable with calling your folks tonight, then what about going to a hotel?"

Anna shook her head. "It'll cost too much."

Lee glanced around her room. Everything looked expensive, yet she worried about money? "Can you call a girlfriend?"

She shook her head again while her eyes drifted over to a photograph sitting on her dresser. It was a picture of Greg Eddington in a dark gray tux next to Anna, looking beautiful in her wedding dress. She looked gorgeous when she smiled, as if she felt joy.

"I married Greg a month before I turned nineteen. Basically, all of his friends' wives became my girlfriends. Since he died"—Anna's gaze fell to her knees—"I haven't felt like talking to them very much."

Lee lowered his eyes. He didn't know how well his next suggestion would go over. "This may be inappropriate, but . . . I have a nice couch—"

"I'm not sure . . ." She looked up at him. "If it wouldn't be too much trouble . . . I don't mind sleeping on a couch."

He brought his gaze up.

Her eyes held hope in them. "I promise I won't be any trouble."

"How's your headache?"

"OK, maybe a little bit of trouble."

Lee got up off the floor. "Your head still hurts, I take it?"

A Strange Twist of Fate

Anna nodded. "I'll throw a few things in an overnight bag if you'll get me a couple of aspirin."

"I can do that." Lee held out his hand, and she grasped it. Lifting her up gave him a sense of relief. Not just that she'd be safe, but that he'd be able to keep her that way—at least for the night.

"In there." Anna pointed at a door as she headed for her dresser.

The master bathroom was appropriately huge, with a glass-encased shower and a Jacuzzi tub. The dual above-the-counter bowl sinks were sitting on black granite. Each sink had its own mirror above it. Only one sink had an electric toothbrush next to it. Lee used his power of deduction and two fingers to pull on the corner of the mirror. It opened. The contents were very organized. The top shelf held several over-the-counter pain medications, plus an amber prescription bottle. It was Valium, a sleeping pill. He looked closer at the label. It had been filled over ten months ago. Evidently, she rarely needed it.

Lee scanned the other shelves as he reached for the bottle of aspirin. A small first-aid kit was propped up next to a package of antinausea medicine. Next to that was a bottle of vitamins. His stomach dropped when his eyes landed on a used pregnancy test stick. There were two pink lines in the results window. Lee's pulse increased when he realized that two lines meant positive.

Anna was pregnant! She must've had at least one boyfriend since her husband died.

Debra Erfert

Nine

Anna stood in her closet, staring at all of her pretty tops. None of them fit her any longer, so what was the use of torturing herself? Maybe because she wanted to look nice for Lee. She couldn't deny he was handsome, and she was attracted to him.

She grabbed a couple of Greg's T-shirts off the shelf and the new pair of jeans she knew still fit—barely. As she reached for her favorite blue Keds, she stopped. She hadn't noticed that hole in the toe. She knew the canvas was getting thin, but she didn't know it had broken through. Was it during her fall after her fight with Razor? Goosebumps coursed their way across her arms when she thought about that drug addict. His anger that morning might've led him to her house tonight, but how did it explain the light bulbs being loosened last night? Claudia hadn't left him yet, so that didn't make sense.

Anna grabbed a newer pair of Reeboks and a small duffel bag from the top shelf. From a cubbyhole, she took out the kit that had her travel-size bath accessories ready to go before heading back to her bed. She'd folded her underwear and socks before entering the closet.

Lee was sitting on the end of the bed staring at the bottle of Tylenol in his hands. He looked pale. Maybe he realized that he had asked a woman to spend the night at his apartment and now he regretted it. He'd barely signed his divorce papers today. Something like that had to be traumatizing. Her heart skipped a beat. She didn't have any other place to go. Her bank account was getting much too low to spend even a single night in a hotel without a cut-rate deal.

A Strange Twist of Fate

She pushed back the fear building up in her heart and the anxiety making her lightheaded. She could feel tears coming. "Lee?"

He looked up at her, and his eyes went wide as he jumped off the bed toward her. Quicker than she could ask what was wrong, Lee had taken hold of her elbow, guiding her to the bed with his arm around her back. She sat, holding her clothes to her chest, confused at what just happened.

"Are you OK?" they asked at the same time.

"Me?" they said together.

Lee held out his hands in front of Anna, stopping her from speaking again. "I thought you were going to faint. You were whiter than a sheet of paper."

"I was? Well, you looked like . . . like you were going to take back your invitation."

Lee took the duffel bag from her hand and set it on the bed. "No, no." He went to the dresser and came back with a small paper cup he'd taken from where she kept it in the bathroom. It was full of water. After he dropped two Tylenol in her palm, she drank them down with all the water.

"You don't need to bother changing. Just throw on your hoodie sweater, and you'll be set," Lee said.

"I'll need my shoes on."

Lee looked at her wriggling bare toes. "That would be a good idea," he said, taking the empty cup from her hand.

Anna reached for her socks, but Lee grabbed them first. He gave them to her, almost reverently. It was then she noticed he was staring at her. "Are you sure you wouldn't rather I find somewhere else to stay tonight?"

Lee smiled. "No, my couch is yours." He looked around the room. "Where's your sweater?"

Anna nodded toward her closet. "It's on a hook just inside the door."

While Lee went to get her sweater, she put on her socks. "I'll need to hire someone to fix that bedroom window, but it's too late tonight." When he came back carrying her hoodie, she asked, "Should I get something to board it up with until then?"

Lee laid her sweater down on the bed, then knelt down in front of her, taking one of her shoes and loosening the laces. "The police will have a detail here all night, so don't worry about someone getting in." He held the shoe near her toes as if waiting for her to put her foot inside. Suddenly, she felt like Cinderella.

When she didn't move, Lee lifted her foot and slid her shoe on before tying the laces, then repeated the process with the other shoe. He must've believed she was still shaken up. He could be right. She couldn't even load a simple bullet into a magazine.

"I haven't had anybody put my shoes on me since I was a kid." Anna leaned over her knees. "You did a good job. Thank you." She looked up in time to see Lee lifting her sweater, but she didn't miss the satisfying smile on his lips.

Lee held up the hoodie sweater. If she didn't stand up right away, what would he do then? Pull her up? Anna shook her head and complied. Before he went so far as to pack her bag, she quickly did that on her own. She grabbed her pillow, and on the way out, she stopped in the family room and loaded her investigation binder and laptop into a padded bag—which Lee quickly took from her. He carried her duffel, too. She caught him staring at her handbag, but she wouldn't even let him near it as she put her gun and extra mag inside.

On the ride over to his apartment in Phoenix, Anna said, "Lee, I think I could use a cheeseburger and fries."

The turn signal clicked, and he took the exit. Five minutes later, the inside of his car smelled heavenly, and Anna sipped on her chocolate milkshake and nibbled on the fries the rest of the way to his apartment building's parking lot. She carried the paper bag, her pillow, and her purse to his door while Lee carried everything else.

His apartment was on the first floor. The two-story building wasn't the newest, but she'd seen older and in worse neighborhoods. Lee had to set her computer bag down to insert his key in the lock. Anna reached for the bag.

A Strange Twist of Fate

"No, don't," Lee told her, brushing her hand aside. "I'll carry it. Lifting something heavy isn't good for you."

What did he mean by that? "I'm fine now."

He was just being weird about doing things for her, not that putting her shoes on her wasn't strange enough. He pushed the door open before picking up the bag again and waited for her to go inside first.

He'd left a light on in the small living room, making it easy to see the brown suede sectional she'd be sleeping on. It took up most of the space. Anna had considered buying one nearly like it since their family room was so large, but Greg didn't want something that intrusive. In Lee's apartment, it overwhelmed the room. She sat on a matching ottoman, still clutching her pillow to her chest and holding the bag of burgers.

"The couch and my bedroom set are the only pieces of furniture I own."

Anna glanced up at the big-screen television hanging on the wall and then lifted an eyebrow.

"That doesn't count," Lee said, setting her bags next to a doorway. There were only two. Anna could see into the bathroom from where she sat. In the other room, a bed nearly touched the edge of the door. The small kitchen had a breakfast bar, not dissimilar to hers, separating it from the living room. There weren't any barstools to sit on, but there was a small dinette table in the corner.

"Why not?"

Grinning, he said, "I consider a TV a necessity."

Anna shook her head and studied the big sectional again. She hadn't seen a show or movie in nearly a year. But lying on this, snuggled in a blanket, she'd even watch a football game. "This looks brand new."

"Six months old." Lee sat down on the edge of the couch, facing her. "I know this looks like a tight fit, but this was the one I wanted. And since I don't plan on living here too much longer, I didn't want to waste money buying a smaller couch I'd only use temporarily when I'd turn around and buy this bigger one once I moved, you know?"

"I guess." Anna motioned from the front door to the back of the apartment where the bedroom and bath were. "At least you left a path."

Lee laughed and took the paper bag from her hand. "Would you like something else to drink? Some milk?" He got up and rounded the breakfast bar. She heard the fridge door open. "I could heat it up—to help you sleep."

"Warm milk?" Anna had finished her icy milkshake a few minutes ago. For some reason, that sounded delicious. "Yes, I'd love some."

She pushed off her shoes and set her handbag on the ottoman. After she took off her sweater, she climbed onto the couch and scooted into the corner. She shoved her pillow behind her neck, put her sweater over her chest and shoulders like a blanket, and relaxed. The soft couch conformed to her body, making her drowsy almost immediately. But then she remembered Razor and how Lee thought he might've been her attacker. She wasn't sure, but one thing she needed to do was make her notes about tonight before she forgot the details of what had happened.

Tossing off her sweater, Anna got up and went to her computer bag. Just as she lifted it, Lee startled her so badly she nearly dropped the bag.

"Stop! What're you doing?" He set the mug and paper plates of burgers on the counter. "You shouldn't lift that—it's heavy!"

Too stunned at his outburst to resist, Anna let Lee take the bag from her. With his free hand, he gently guided her back to the couch. She stared at him, trying to see if she had angered him somehow, but his brow was scrunched like he was worried. His whole demeanor had been caring since he arrived at her house, but from the time she said she would stay with him, he acted . . . overprotective.

His behavior worried her—gnawed at her. "Lee, is—is there anything wrong? Have I done something . . ."

A Strange Twist of Fate

Lee put the case down on the floor. With a gentle hand, he tugged on her arm, coaxing her to sit down again. He moved to the ottoman, facing her—their knees touching. That worried look on his face intensified.

"Oh, Lee," Anna whispered. "What happened?"

He took her hands, grasping them tenderly. Her heart beat faster with every passing second.

"I wish you would've let the paramedics take you to the hospital this afternoon." He lifted her hand and ran his fingers alongside the bandages near her elbow.

"I'm not hurt, badly. You don't need to worry about me."

Lee nodded so subtly it was barely noticeable. "I am worried about you. Um . . ." He kept his eyes lowered to their hands. "You took a hard fall, and you should have a doctor check you out to make sure you and . . . and the baby are doing OK."

Anna gasped. "I look pregnant?"

Lee lifted his gaze only far enough to look at her baggy T-shirt. She pulled it away from her stomach, embarrassed by her figure.

"I saw your pregnancy test in the medicine cabinet."

"The test . . ." Anna gasped, remembering that test stick sitting on the shelf. "My baby . . ." Tears flooded her eyes, and she covered her face with her hands. Crying seemed like her only recourse to the sudden stabbing pain in her heart.

"It's OK—I understand," Lee said very softly, moving next to her on the couch. He wrapped his arm around her shoulder. "Your husband died, and you were lonely—these things happen." With a gentle hand, he swept her hair back from her face. "If you don't have the father in your life, then . . . then let me help."

Anna leaned heavily against Lee's chest, crying, relieved that somebody else finally knew about her baby. He just didn't know everything. After she pushed back some of the excruciating pain that never really seemed to go away, she lifted her head and tried to explain.

Debra Erfert

"I've never told anyone about—about my baby." Anna sniffed, her nose running. Lee got up and grabbed a couple of paper napkins from the counter.

"Not even your mom?"

Anna blew her nose on one of the napkins. "No, no! My mother could've never handled knowing about my pregnancy."

"You won't be able to hide it forever," Lee said quietly. "No matter how baggy you wear your shirts."

She dried her face with a clean napkin, sniffing back more tears. "You don't understand."

"I can try."

Anna got up, putting distance between her and Lee. Was his sympathy real? She had to take the chance that it was. She needed a good friend—someone she could count on no matter what, and he seemed sincere. The mug on the counter had milk in it. She touched the outside of it. He'd heated it up. She'd used warm milk on a few occasions to help her sleep when she didn't want to take her prescription. After a few sips, the tension in her shoulders began to ease. She set the mug down and turned to face Lee.

"I took that pregnancy test two weeks before Greg died."

Lee's head jerked back. With the way his brows creased together, she could see him trying to work things out in his head.

"But those tests are known for having false positives. I didn't want to tell Greg until after I was sure. I had an appointment with my obstetrician the same day Greg went up to Flagstaff on business. She confirmed that I was ten weeks along." Anna crossed her arms over her chest and hugged herself. "I never got to tell"—hot tears blurred her vision—"Greg died before . . ."

Lee had his arms wrapped around her before she could take in another breath. His embrace kept her from bawling again. With her face pressed against his neck, she said, "I had a miscarriage two weeks after his funeral."

"I'm so sorry, Anna," Lee whispered.

"That pregnancy test is the only evidence I have of our child."

"And you never told your mom?"

A Strange Twist of Fate

"I never told anybody. When I lost it, I almost died! The only thing that kept me . . . kept me sane after losing the baby was trying to track down who killed Greg—who drove that truck and pushed him off that road." Anna slid her arms around Lee's back, appreciating his warmth and his strength. "Having my investigation gave me something to concentrate on every day, and I needed that so desperately."

"And you didn't have to think about yourself," Lee said, moving his arms to her waist and squeezing her a little tighter.

"You do understand," Anna said with a sigh. Drooping, she whispered, "Oh, Lee, I'm so tired."

"It's late."

"It's not only that."

Lee smoothed his hand down her hair. "Then what?"

Anna rested her face on his shoulder. "Over the past eleven months, I've talked to hundreds of people, followed leads that I thought were strong, and few of them ended with arrests, they just had nothing to do with solving Greg's death. I feel like I've been running at fast-forward speed trying to catch my husband's killer, but the answer seems far enough out of my reach I can't solve it. I don't want to give up, but I . . . I'm tired."

"From what I saw of your research, your logic is solid, and although I don't agree that a civilian should be putting herself in dangerous situations"—Anna straightened, but Lee tightened his grip around her waist—"the information you've gathered is impressive."

"Really?"

Lee gave her a timid smile. "I think *you're* impressive."

Anna saw him look at her mouth, and her heart fluttered. Could he be thinking about kissing her? When he licked his lips, Anna tilted her face upward with excited anticipation, accepting—desiring—to receive her first kiss in nearly a year.

Three loud knocks came at the door, startling Lee into letting her go. He actually jumped back like Anna had turned scalding hot in his arms.

"Holy crap!" He looked at his watch. "I forgot!"

"Forgot what?" Anna watched him rush to the door and look out the peephole.

"It's Carolyn—my wife," he whispered.

A Strange Twist of Fate

Ten

"Your wife? I thought you were divorced?"

He shook his head. "I didn't sign the papers."

"So you're still married?" Maybe he withdrew the petition—changed his mind about the divorce. In an instant, Anna knew she didn't like that thought. A heated wave of jealousy flashed through her body. It made no sense. She barely knew Lee.

"I can't let her see me." Anna took off to the bathroom, snatching her purse off the ottoman on the way, to give him privacy. If he didn't sign his divorce papers earlier today, something unexpected must've happened. He never talked about his life. All Anna did was talk about hers. What an idiot she had been, opening up her heart to him when he was still tied to a wife. And Anna would never kiss another woman's husband—ever!

Being a curious person, she didn't close the door all the way. Surveillance, in this case, eavesdropping, had been a very useful tool to Anna. She heard . . . whining. A dog?

"Rusty!" Lee said, the happiness in his voice apparent. "It's good to see you, boy."

Anna peeked out the door and watched Lee kneel down level with a golden retriever that immediately began licking his face.

"He was too much trouble anyway," Carolyn said sharply. The woman wore a fashionable, well-fitted business jacket and matching pencil skirt. She held out a large manila envelope. "I did everything you asked. I hope you don't want anything else from me."

As Lee took the envelope, Carolyn looked around the room. When her gaze fell on the couch, Anna knew she saw her pillow stuffed in the corner. Carolyn lifted her chin and twisted a smile on her painted lips. "Oh, poor baby. Still sleeping on the couch—alone."

Lee didn't say anything, probably to protect Anna. But something about the woman's patronizing words irked her enough for her to give in to an impetuous thought. With a flick of her hand, she turned on the light and stepped out of the bathroom.

Carolyn's lips parted, and her eyes widened. She stared at Anna. Lee gave Anna a tired grin.

He took the leash from the woman's hand. "Good-bye, Carolyn." Lee closed the door with the woman still standing in the hallway.

"I hope I didn't embarrass you," Anna said, coming into the living room. "But she wasn't very nice." She dropped to the ottoman, and the dog came to her, poking his nose in her face, his tongue tasting her in greeting. "Hello, Rusty," Anna cooed as she petted his soft golden fur.

Lee tossed the envelope next to the mug of milk. "She didn't start out that way." He leaned his hands on the edges of the counter, his head hung low.

"What happened?" It was time he talked about his life, even if it was nearly midnight and she was about to collapse. When he didn't answer, Anna got up to stand beside him. With her hand on his back, she rested her face against his shoulder. "Don't tell me . . . you beat her on a regular basis?"

Lee scrunched his face up like he'd smelled something repugnant and shook his head.

"You . . . cheated on her?" Anna hoped not.

Lee let out a heavy sigh. "No."

"Did she have an affair?"

He lifted his shoulders. "I don't think so."

"Hmm . . ." Anna turned and leaned her hip against the breakfast bar. "Couldn't keep her happy in bed, then?"

He lifted an eyebrow and started to lean in toward her. "I could prove to you otherwise."

A Strange Twist of Fate

Anna stopped him cold with a hand to his chest. "I don't even kiss married men."

He gazed at the manila envelope again.

"Come on, Lee. You can talk to me. We're newly acquainted friends, and I won't judge you."

That brought out a cautious smile. "Do you want the rest of your milk?" he asked.

When Anna shook her head, he lifted the mug to his mouth and sipped a few swallows before he took it to the couch and sat down. The dog quickly got comfortable at his feet. With his gaze steady on the mug, he said, "I met Carolyn at a retirement luncheon for our chief. This was in Scottsdale. She was one of the waitstaff serving the private room. I flirted a little, and she flirted right back. Before I left, she slipped me her phone number on the restaurant's business card. I called her two days later." He grinned up at Anna. "You can't be too quick about things like first dates, or it looks like you're desperate."

Anna wasn't desperate, but she was lonely. She wondered how he saw her.

"We dated for three months. She even had Thanksgiving dinner at my sister's home. The whole family was there. Carolyn held my youngest niece like she was her own. I fell in love with her believing we had a lot in common—especially the love of family. I thought we wanted the same things when I proposed. We were married that March."

Anna stayed quiet, giving him time to think, maybe even time to grieve for the life he'd just said good-bye to. Lee took another swallow of milk, and then he drained the mug before he spoke again.

"That July she registered for her first semester at the university. Three years later, Carolyn graduated with a degree in business. A year after that, she got her Realtor's license and was working full time with a broker. We never argued about anything until I brought up the subject of having a baby. She flat out said no."

Lee finally looked up from the empty mug in his hands.

Debra Erfert

"It turned out she wanted to earn a lot of money and not have any children to get in her way of success. But what about me?" Lee asked, slapping his hand on the couch.

He jumped up, scaring Rusty into hopping away from his feet. "Would I have fallen for her if she had told me from the beginning that she had no intentions of having kids? Not a chance—no matter how attractive she was or how much she came on to me. We would've been no more than friends."

He set the mug on the counter with a light tap. He took several deep breaths before he said, "I started looking at life differently—at *her* differently. I wanted a family while she wanted a career. The love I had for her . . . changed. It faded. Resentment filled the gap where passion once had been."

"And then you filed for divorce," Anna said, touching his arm.

Lee turned his head enough to look into her eyes. "Carolyn filed."

"She . . ." It didn't take a detective to understand what happened. "She used you to finance—to jumpstart her career?"

Lee hung his head again. "It seems that way."

Anna gasped, and Lee looked at her. "You were cheated out of your own child. Oh, Lee, I'm so sorry!"

"You're sorry? What did you do wrong?"

"You were deceived by your wife and then by my old pregnancy test. Even unintentionally, I contributed to your pain, and I'm sorry."

"Anna . . ." Lee gathered her in his arms again. "You are special."

"I think my dad used that word to describe me on several occasions." Anna moved her arms around his back, hugging him. "But I'm sure he didn't mean it the same way as you."

~*~

Sunlight coming in from the bathroom window illuminated the living room enough for Anna to watch Lee soundly sleeping. He was on the other part of the couch, lying chest down, with his arm hanging over the edge, his hand resting on his dog. Rusty was still

A Strange Twist of Fate

asleep, too. Carolyn had chided Lee about sleeping on the couch. He later confessed that he usually did and offered Anna the bedroom, which felt wrong to her. She'd spent the last year sleeping on her own couch. This time she didn't technically sleep alone. They slept toe to toe, and she now had a perfect view of his handsome face.

He needed a shave, although Anna liked the thick coating of dark stubble; it balanced the weight of his short black hair. Greg's brown hair was nice, but he blended in with most everyone else in Arizona. Lee's dark blue eyes were beautiful, so different than Greg's brown eyes.

Anna was wrapped in the only blanket in the apartment. Lee had insisted. He went to sleep last night with a thick terrycloth bathrobe over him. He'd since kicked it off, and it was lying on the floor.

Lee still wasn't divorced. Midnight hadn't been the right time to read over a contract to find any hidden clauses put there by a devious woman. But today was Saturday, and Lee was off work and could get the job done right. He'd also promised to help Anna move her things over to her parents' house, not that she wanted to go there, even for the weekend.

She hadn't been completely honest with Lee about her mother's mental stability. But how did she tell someone she barely knew that her mother was a certifiable psycho, and if she didn't take all her meds on time, she might mistake her own daughter for one of the voices she heard in her head and smother her in her sleep?

There had been several close calls over the past year—one of them bad enough where Anna's dad had to have her mother sedated by the housekeeper. Of course, the woman working for them was really a registered nurse posing undercover as a housekeeper, or her mother would never have let her stay. It had been a reasonable alternative to committing her to the psych ward at the hospital. After all, how would it look if Judge Jackson Wright had an insane wife?

Debra Erfert

Anna knew her dad loved her mother without question, or he would've had her locked up decades ago. From doing research on the subject of mental illnesses a few years ago, she knew that kind of sickness ran in families, which was probably the reason her parents never had another baby. Anna's biggest fear was becoming like her mother.

Lee moved. He turned onto his side and sniffed. Was he waking up? Anna continued to watch him. Before going to sleep last night, Lee had changed into pajama bottoms and a tight-fitting dark blue T-shirt that hugged his muscled chest and biceps quite nicely. Anna had tried not to stare then, but he wouldn't notice her doing it now. From what she could see, the detective looked ripped. Oddly, it was hard to remember Greg's body without a picture to remind her.

Lee took in a deep breath. He was waking up, but he didn't seem to be in a rush. Greg had always been first to get out of bed in the mornings, usually for work. Even on the weekends he brought cases home to study. He had an end goal of running for district attorney. Anna thought back on the conversation they'd had the Valentine's Day before he died. One more year, that was all Greg needed before his dreams could come true, and then he promised Anna they would start a family. She hadn't known then that she was already pregnant.

"How long have you been awake?" Lee asked.

His voice startled Anna. His eyes didn't look open. How long had he been watching her—watching him?

"Not long." She sat up and stretched, feeling every injured muscle in her body complain. "Ow! Oh, I'm sore."

"A hot shower will fix you up, plus some aspirin." Lee sat up. Immediately, Rusty headed for the door, whining.

"You better take your dog on a walk or you'll be losing your deposit."

"I hear you." Lee ran his fingers through his messy hair and retrieved the leash looped around the front doorknob. Rusty

A Strange Twist of Fate

wriggled, making it difficult for him to hook the leash onto the collar.

"Are you going to put your shoes on, at least?" Anna asked, staring at his bare feet.

Lee grinned. "We'll only be a couple of minutes. I'll be fine."

Before Anna could try to find his shoes, he and his dog disappeared out the door—barefooted. To keep from worrying too much about Lee catching a cold or, worse yet, pneumonia, she stayed busy, putting the blanket neatly back on his bed, hanging his bathrobe up in his small closet, and washing the few dishes in the kitchen sink. By the time she had them dried and had found the right cupboard to put them away, Lee came back in with an excited dog.

"Good, you're not in the shower yet," Lee said, unleashing Rusty. As the dog came loping into the kitchen, Lee hurried into the bathroom and pushed the door closed.

"Good morning, boy." Anna stroked the retriever's soft face. "You came without any food, didn't you, and I bet you're just as hungry as I am."

The two uneaten burgers were in the fridge. The thought of eating hers now grossed her out. But for Rusty, the meat, broken into bits, mixed with some cold cereal Anna saw in the cupboard, would do until Lee went shopping. He had a couple of bowls she was sure he wouldn't mind sharing with his dog. One bowl she used for water, which Rusty drank as she peeled the burgers apart.

"Good idea," Lee told her. He'd stopped on the other side of the breakfast counter and watched Anna tear little pieces of beef patty into the other bowl. "But what are we going to eat for breakfast?"

Anna scoffed. "Not old hamburgers. I can cook something at my house."

"Sounds good."

After Anna poured a few Cheerios on top of the hamburger, she set the bowl on the floor. Rusty stuck his face into his breakfast as Anna scrubbed her hands free from the grease and ketchup that had coated the patties. "I want to shower here. The thought of going to my house and staying there longer than necessary worries me too much. At least until they arrest the person I shot last night."

Lee headed for the fridge. He took out the gallon of milk. "I'll call Sanchez this morning to see if they've got anything new."

"I need to write some notes in my binder before I forget them," Anna said as she wiped her hands on a paper towel.

"About?"

"We were thinking that maybe Razor might've broken in last night, except his girlfriend didn't leave him until earlier yesterday, so the time line is wrong for him to be the guy."

Lee puckered his lips and nodded, but his eyes weren't on her. "You're right about that, but you had a drug deal"—he smiled and brought his gaze down to her—"a sort of drug deal for information that went bad the night before, and if he was angry enough, Bivens could've reached your house before we got there."

"But that doesn't make any sense. Why would he retaliate against me when he didn't get in trouble? He ran away free. I'm the one who got arrested."

Lee leaned against the counter, setting the jug down next to him. "Yeah, but you dangled a hit of cocaine in front of his nose, and he could've been coming to get it from you. He didn't know it was powdered sugar, and he might've even thought you had more than that one baggie. When we arrived before he got inside, he ran off again and returned last night looking to get more than the coke from you."

"Oh, crap . . ." Anna leaned against the counter, facing Lee. "That was totally stupid of me."

"It's just a theory."

Anna hugged herself. "It's a good one." She let out a sigh. "I need a shower."

~*~

"Mother, what are you doing here?"

Anna stood at the edge of the foyer with her arms folded tightly across her stomach, panicking as she watched her mother

A Strange Twist of Fate

straighten the photographs lining the top of the antique sideboard. Lee stood behind Anna. He would be witnessing firsthand one of Margo Wright's obsessive sprees. Anna didn't need to get any closer to know that each frame would be spaced evenly apart and facing in exactly the same direction, depending on which way the light was coming through the windows. If there were reflections on the frames' glass, then she'd turn them enough to eliminate that glare. Anna didn't have any pictures hung on the walls out of deference to her mother's difficulty.

Without looking up or stopping her straightening, Margo said, "A city dispatcher called and said that someone broke into your house. I came to help you pack." She brushed her hands together as she rushed to the kitchen sink, squirted soap into her palm, and scrubbed her hands under a fast stream of water.

"Mother," Anna said as she walked farther into the family room, "I was going to call you this morning to tell you what happened—"

"Don't bother!" Margo shouted, slapping the water faucet off. Anna recoiled at her tone. Her mother tore off a single paper towel and dried her hands without looking at Anna. The trash can had a sensor. With a wave of her hand, the lid opened, and she dropped the used towel inside. In a softer voice, Margo said, "Dirty frames. When was the last time they were cleaned?"

"Um . . ." Anna glanced over her shoulder at Lee. He was still standing in the foyer near the hallway leading to the bedrooms. It didn't seem like the right time for him to meet her mother at the moment. She couldn't blame him. "I let Ella go."

"What? You fired your maid? Of course she fired her maid; she just said that." Margo tapped the cabinet door handle, and then the next one, and then the next one, alternating hands as she went through the kitchen. After she finished, she washed her hands again. "I'll send Vicky over after she gets through today." She tore off another paper towel and dried her hands.

Anna certainly didn't want to have a nurse come over and clean her house. "Mother, you don't have to—"

Debra Erfert

"Don't argue with me," Margo snapped. Anna stiffened and hugged herself tighter. She could tell by the outbursts and repetitive motions that her mother's problems were getting worse. Margo threw the paper towel away before heading into the family room.

"How did you get in?" Anna asked quietly.

"The security boy let me in—what the hell is that?" Margo pointed at the wall by the foyer. Anna stood still, knowing she'd seen the bullet holes. Lee was gone. He must've ducked into the closest doorway. Margo then spotted the hole in the chair. "He shot at you? Why didn't you tell me?"

Anna froze as her mother turned to her with her green eyes shining with unshed tears. "My baby," she cried, sweeping Anna into a viselike hug. "Are you hurt? Are you shot? My baby!"

"He didn't have the gun, Mother. I did," Anna said, holding her hands at her side. She knew her mother didn't like to be touched.

"You?" Margo let her go and moved back. "You have a gun?" Her eyes lost focus. "Of course she has a gun—how do I know where she got it?"

Anna looked over at the foyer again. Lee was standing at the corner, watching them. Before she could explain, her mother rushed over to the sideboard and began moving frames—again. Except this time, her hands jerked with each movement. Anna panicked. She shouldn't have said anything about her shooting a gun or her even having a gun. It had upset her mother. Why had she come over by herself? Did she take a taxi or walk? Anna took out her phone from her purse. Just as she dialed her dad, she heard his baritone voice coming from the foyer.

"Bring the warrant by the house this morning, and I'll sign it. Not a problem." When her dad walked into the living room, he slipped his phone into his pants pocket. The relief that Anna felt was physical, like a weight being lifted from her back. He would deal with her mother. Two steps behind her dad was Vicky. The older nurse was dressed in khakis and a plain white button-down

A Strange Twist of Fate

shirt, like every other time Anna had seen her. Today, she carried a small bag that didn't exactly look like a purse.

"Dad, would you take Mother—"

"*No!*" Margo screamed. Anna turned in time to see her mother sweeping her arm across the sideboard, flinging pictures off. Some crashed onto the tile floor; some slid hard and fast across the dining room table straight at Anna. Shocked, she turned away from the shattering glass and black frames as they hit her.

"Anna!" Lee ran into the room, his hurried steps crunching on glass. He wrapped his arms around her shoulders.

Lee wasn't the only one to help. Anna's dad rushed to her mother, and so did Vicky. The bag the nurse carried was dropped on the table, and while her dad held her mother's arms, Vicky took out a hypodermic from the bag. As if they'd practiced the maneuver, the nurse plunged the needle into her mother's arm while her dad talked with his face pressed against hers. He distracted her enough she never noticed the shot.

"She has a gun, Jackson," Margo said calmly, still in his arms.

Her dad looked sharply at Anna, his gray eyebrows pinched together. "I know. I know. Let's go home."

"I want my baby to come home," Margo said. Vicky took her arm, and after a nod from Jack, she began leading Margo through the mess on the floor. "But not with a gun."

After the nurse had led her mother out through the foyer, her dad slowly gazed around at the broken glass and torn pictures with tired blue eyes. He had been there when most of those photographs were taken. "Are you moving back in with us, Julianna?"

Anna stepped back from Lee, and he let her loose. "I was going to call you this morning, Dad. Last night wasn't . . . If it would be all right, just until the police catch the man who broke in."

Jack studied Lee for a moment before he turned his gaze on Anna and nodded. "Your room is just as it was before you were married. You're welcome to it. It would be better if you left your weapon locked up here." He walked through the glass scattered on the floor and left the house.

Debra Erfert

Anna looked at the destruction that happened in such a short time. She needed to clean up the mess, but Lee was staring at her very oddly. He might even be worried about Anna's mental health.

"I'm not like her!" she cried before rushing toward her bedroom. At least she wasn't yet. Anna went directly into her closet.

Lee followed her into the room. "Wait up."

Standing in front of the rack of too-small shirts, skirts, and slacks, the tears she felt like crying when her mother broke her framed memories spilled over her lashes.

"I'm sorry, I . . ." Lee ran his hand down the back of her arm. Even through her sweater, her skin went prickly with goose bumps from his touch. "I'm not usually so cautious when meeting new people, but . . ."

Anna turned toward him. His face was in shadow from the light coming in from the bedroom. She reached beside him and flipped on the switch. "Lee, you're trained not to walk into dangerous, unpredictable situations without backup. You acted exactly how you should have, how I would've told you to if I had known my mother was here. You really should've stayed in your car with Rusty."

A smile moved Lee's lips. "You're not mad?"

Anna noticed his teasing grin. "Very funny."

"Honestly, I don't think you're anything like your mother." He lifted her chin with a tender touch. "Anna, you have the most beautiful brown eyes I've ever seen. I noticed your mother has green eyes, and your father's are light blue." Lee ran his fingers along her temple and into her hair. "You look like a natural blonde. Are you?"

Anna mouthed, "Yes," yet the word didn't escape her lips.

"I thought so, but your mother is a brunette, and your father has gray hair. You stand at least eight inches taller than your mother, and you're even taller than your dad. Odd, don't you think?"

A Strange Twist of Fate

"I . . ." She caught his hand. His touch gave her shivers—the good kind. "I guess I inherited recessive genes. Right?"

Lee used his other hand and ran his fingers along her cheek. "You have more curves than her, and your face isn't even shaped like your mother's or father's." He gazed at her. "You have the most beautiful high cheekbones that neither of your parents have. Granted, your father's skin gets pink when he's upset, like yours, but your mother has an olive skin tone. It makes me wonder . . ."

"What?" Anna asked softly.

"Is there a chance that you're adopted?"

Debra Erfert

Eleven

"Adopted?" Anna blinked rapidly and said again, only softer, "Adopted?"

"Yes. It's not so farfetched. Lots of people are adopted."

"Oh . . ."

Without saying anything else, Anna stepped around Lee and went to her bed and sat down, looking confused.

Lee moved next to her, taking her hand. "I guess you never thought about that."

"I'm so much like"—Anna looked up quickly at Lee—"I mean, I like things neat and orderly. I always have. Just like my mother."

"That can be a learned trait," Lee told her. "Your mother had to have order, so you grew within those boundaries." He didn't like the worried look creasing her pretty brows. "Do you hear voices, like your mother apparently does?"

"I talk to myself." Anna shrugged.

Lee grinned. "I talk to myself too, especially when I'm working a tough case. It helps me think things through."

"Really?"

"Yeah, and I've walked in on my division commander when he was doing the same thing. The only difference is if you hear voices answer you back," Lee said. "Do you?"

Anna let out a soft sigh. "No."

Lee studied the scratches on the palm of her hand. "Your dad has gray hair, but it wasn't always that color." He looked up into her eyes. "Do you remember what it looked like before it turned?"

"Umm," Anna gazed up at Lee's black hair. "I'm not sure. It's been gray a very long time."

"Can you find out? Do you have some pictures?"

A Strange Twist of Fate

"Sure, we have family pictures. But they're at my folks' house." Anna got up and walked over to the chest of drawers to her framed wedding picture. "I'll find the oldest album and sneak it out of the house. We can have lunch and go through it together."

"Anna?"

She turned around, giving him her attention.

"What would happen if you just asked your parents if you were adopted?"

She didn't answer immediately. By how slowly she strolled across her room, he could tell she was giving his question serious thought. He also noticed her sexy figure as she moved. Baggy shirts only covered so much, but her tight blue jeans didn't conceal anything. She had curves in all the right places, more than what he saw in the pictures. She had been too thin back then. She obviously wasn't used to being on the shapely side if hiding inside her husband's T-shirt made her feel better.

When she turned around, she caught him looking at her body. Her face clouded over.

"Do I really look pregnant?"

"What?" Lee jumped up from the bed. "I never said that."

Anna pulled at her shirt again. "But you assumed I was since I'm not wearing my small clothes." Lee opened his mouth to remind her about the pregnancy test, but she didn't give him the chance. "It's been very difficult since Greg died, and I've gained some weight—"

"Whoa, Anna," Lee said, holding out his hands to get her to stop talking. "I can't keep my eyes off you—you're so beautiful!" He moved close enough to slide his arms around her waist and snuggled her up against his body. "I hope you understand that." When Lee lowered his lips to get that kiss he missed out on last night, Anna ducked her head.

"I don't kiss married men!" she said, laughing, and squirmed out of his arms.

Debra Erfert

"I've got to sign those papers," Lee moaned as Anna opened the top dresser drawer. "You're not going to leave your gun here, are you?"

"Not a chance." She took out a handful of underwear and several bras. "You worked too hard to get it back for me. I'm not going to leave it behind now. But I'm not going to let my mother see it," she said as she took her clothes to the bed.

"Do you want help packing?" Lee asked, reaching for the underwear.

Anna slapped at his outstretched hand, making him chuckle. "Cute. Oh! I forgot . . ."

"What?"

Anna took her phone out of her pocket and dropped onto her bed. "I need to get my window fixed."

"Who're you calling?"

"My insurance agent." Anna glanced up into Lee's eyes. "I don't want to pay for it."

"While you do that, how about I go clean up the glass?"

Anna lowered her phone. "Are you sure?"

"Yeah, I know how to clean." Lee's heart warmed at the beautiful smile she gave him.

"Then, that would be great. There's a broom in the pantry just off the kitchen."

"I'll try to save as many pictures as I can," he said, walking toward the hallway.

"Lee?"

He stopped at the door. "Yes?"

"Just so you know, I have most of those pictures on CD, and the rest I have saved on my computer's photo program."

Lee nodded, giving her the slightest grin, but he had his doubts about how many actually survived her mother's rampage. Most of the family room's floor had small bits of glass strewn about it. Fortunately, the tile would be easy to clean, easier than understanding what he'd witnessed.

A Strange Twist of Fate

Anna had told him her mother had an obsessive-compulsive problem. She'd displayed that when she seemed drawn to touching each picture frame as well as each kitchen cabinet handle even though she'd felt a need to wash her hands afterward. When she had answered out loud to someone who wasn't there, Lee knew instantly Anna's mother had much deeper problems.

The pantry was next to the fridge. The glass panels on the bifold door read "Pantry" and "Let's eat," making it easy to spot. Inside, the shelves were as organized as the bathroom's medicine cabinet had been. Anna insisted that she was not like her mother, but then again, she reluctantly admitted she was like her.

Lee found the broom and dustpan hanging near the doorway. He took the lid off the trash can at the end of the breakfast bar and brought the wastebasket into the family room.

He picked a photograph up off the floor. The glass that hadn't broken free during the fall hung on the edges of the frame like tiny guillotines that could draw blood at the slightest movement. Before the outburst, Anna had stood still, holding her arms around herself, looking like she had been afraid of her mother. For that matter, Lee had been frightened, especially when the frames had been used as weapons.

Lee dumped the glass in the trash and then looked at the picture. Multiple cuts throughout the middle of the paper made the photograph little more than garbage. He gazed at Anna's beautiful image. One of the slashes went across her face and through her husband's throat.

What if Lee was trying to convince himself that Anna was adopted because he knew he was falling for her? Could the thought of getting involved with a woman who could have a psychotic breakdown terrify him more than facing an armed robber—or being alone for the rest of his life?

He'd told Anna about Carolyn's deception and how he wouldn't have fallen in love with her if he knew she never wanted a family. But if Lee knew the future with another woman would be filled with voices only she heard, unpredictable sudden fits of violent anger, and uncontrollable repetitive actions, would he be opening himself up to a worse heartache? How could he do that to any possible children?

Anna acted terrified when her mother hugged her. He had to wonder what kind of a childhood she'd had. The thought of her having to deal with a mentally ill mother all those years saddened him. But what bothered Lee more was the idea of him selfishly needing assurance that Anna was mentally stable before he would let his heart completely fall in love with her—and he hated himself for that.

~*~

Anna's dad hadn't been kidding—her room was exactly the same as before she was married almost seven years ago. Of course, it was immaculately clean. There wasn't a speck of dust anywhere. Sadly, the clothes she brought with her didn't fill two drawers. She stepped in front of the full-length mirror hanging on the back of the closet door. When she'd married Greg, she had dozens of pretty shirts to take to her new home, none of which she could button up over her breasts or hips any longer.

But Lee told her she was beautiful. Maybe she was being too hard on herself. She wasn't a teenager anymore, and her body had been pregnant—at least for a while. A grown woman shouldn't be teenager thin. And Anna shouldn't continue wearing Greg's old shirts. Although she couldn't afford shopping in the same high-fashion department stores as before, looking homeless didn't make much sense.

Anna stepped closer to the mirror to study her face. She had always envied her mother's green eyes, and she had often wondered why hers were brown. The blonde hair was a plus, in her opinion. It got even lighter during the summer months without her having highlights put in. She turned her face to the side. Although their noses weren't too dissimilar, they weren't the same, either. Anna had more prominent cheekbones, especially when she smiled. Her mother's face had more angular planes, her jaw sharper. What if . . . what if Lee was right? Why did it take a virtual

A Strange Twist of Fate

stranger to make her question her heritage? That could also be the reason Anna's body was so different from her mother's, too.

Margo Wright was short but model thin—always had been. She looked beautiful on her dad's arm. Anna put her hands on her waist, cinching in the loose T-shirt. It probably was proportionate to her bust and hips. Since she had no clothes that fit, a trip to the department store was necessary, especially before she started applying for employment. Finding a job was another necessity. She had no other options after nearly a year of living off Greg's insurance benefits. But shopping could be postponed until after she found the photo album.

The door to her parent's bedroom was closed, but she could hear voices coming from inside the room. Although she didn't understand what was being said, she heard her dad's voice talking in a subdued tone. At least he was occupied, and chances were good her mother was still asleep from the shot Vicky had given her.

Sneaking downstairs went without event. In the den, Anna knew exactly where the albums were kept. The organization had never changed since—ever. The bookcases that lined two walls held every book they owned, including her dad's law books. She went to the bottom shelf, far left side. The second album from the left was the first book that she was in. She slid it inside an extra tote bag she'd brought with her from home, and she took the first album too, just for fun. It wouldn't do to get stopped at the front door and then have to explain the whys of her actions.

When Anna came to the den's doorway, she saw Vicky standing at the antique phone table next to the bottom of the staircase, writing on a small tube. Anna knew exactly what the nurse was doing. Every three months, Vicky would draw blood from Anna's mother to check on the medication levels in her system. Anna couldn't stand the thought that her mother was getting worse.

An idea popped into her head, a sure way to discover if she had been adopted without ever asking her dad and causing hard feelings. The answer was in the vial. The nurse always drew four.

Debra Erfert

After a few moments, Vicky put the vials inside her bag and then closed it before taking out her phone and walking up the stairs. Anna waited until the nurse had reached the top landing and then snuck over to the bag.

The snap closure was worn enough it hardly made a sound as Anna opened it. She only took one of the vials and then closed the bag again while listening for unwanted footsteps on the stairs. She made it to her car parked at the curb with the vial clutched in her fist, tote bag over one shoulder and her purse with the loaded gun dangling from her arm. No one saw her do it.

Lee had gone to the pet store to buy Rusty some essentials. But he had promised to come over after he was through and take her target practicing until she had to be back at her house to meet the window repairman at four. He'd left over an hour ago. How long could it take to buy dog food and a foam bed? Instead of standing around, Anna got inside her car and sent Lee a text from her phone.

Are you almost done?

His response took several minutes. He must've been driving.

Nearly to your house.

Anna pushed the ignition button, starting the car. It wasn't hot outside, but she wanted to have the air conditioning on to cool the interior, keeping the vial from spoiling. She needed a place to take the sample to have it typed. Anna already knew her own blood type was AB positive because she regularly donated. Since she stole her mother's sample, she'd need to get the cooperation of someone she could trust and who would do the work without needing paperwork from a doctor. Anna smiled. A friendly face popped into her mind. Larry Tug. She dated him a few times in high school, without her parents' knowledge. And, serendipitously enough, he owed Anna a favor.

Six months ago, Larry got arrested for leaving a restaurant without paying his bill. He'd had a few drinks, but he insisted that he had paid. He had called Anna, knowing her dad was a judge. Anna didn't talk to her dad about him, but she did pay his dinner tab, gave the waiter a double tip for the "misunderstanding," and

A Strange Twist of Fate

hooked him up with one of Greg's friends who took the case pro bono. Larry worked at Vista Labs, and they were open on Saturdays.

After Anna pulled up Larry's cell number on her phone, she sent him a text: *I need a favor.*

He responded within seconds. *Sure.*

I need to have my blood typed. Can you do it? It took a few seconds longer before he replied.

Off the books?

Yes.

Come over. I'm at work. Text me when you get here n I'll come out.

Anna felt a wave of relief wash through her, followed just as quickly by anxiety. She was really doing it—following an impulse that could change the course of her life, the way she thought about herself. *Thanks. See you soon.*

Anna stashed the vial in her purse just as Lee pulled up behind her. She wouldn't involve a police detective in something that could be considered illegal—at least unethical. No, stealing somebody's blood and having it tested had to be against the law.

Lee knocked on the driver's window. After she lowered the glass, he asked, "Are we taking my car?"

Anna didn't know how she felt about Rusty clawing his way in the back seat of her new Impala. The leather was pristine. "I think so." She grabbed her computer bag and the tote with the two albums while Lee opened her door. He quickly took her bags even though he knew she could safely carry them. She appreciated his thoughtfulness. Anna carefully got out. The vial containing the blood was rugged enough, but the lid might pop off in her purse if she wasn't cautious.

Lee opened the passenger door of his car for her. Rusty quickly poked his nose against her neck after she slid inside. "Hello, boy," Anna said, turning and stroking his face. The back was empty of anything but the dog and Anna's bags Lee had dropped down on the seat. She guessed his shopping items were in the trunk. Lee got behind the wheel and pulled out around Anna's car.

"I know a great shooting range off Black Canyon Boulevard. It has a pistol range, but it's a good forty-five minutes away. Do you want to get lunch first?"

"I'm not really hungry right now, but I do have another stop I need to make before we go shooting, if you don't mind."

"That's fine. Where?"

"Vista Labs, 600 West Montecito Avenue."

"A lab?" He took the corner onto East Dynamite Boulevard.

Anna didn't offer any more information. Instead, she changed the subject. "Did you buy Rusty a dog bed?" She knew she'd asked the right question when his handsome smile appeared. He loved his dog. She could tell that last night when Rusty first arrived.

"Two of them, plus four kinds of dog food, wet and dry," Lee said, glancing over the seat at Rusty. "I got him a watering tower, and a food dish that has a bone painted on the bottom of it."

Anna laughed. "Like he has something to look forward to if he eats all his food?"

"Yeah," Lee said, chuckling. "He now has a metal brush that I already tried out on him."

"Did he like being brushed?"

"Immensely." Lee reached over the seat and rubbed his dog's neck. Rusty sat with his head between their two shoulders, looking out the front window.

"Shouldn't he have a seat belt?"

"A harness, yes, but the store was out of his size. I'll have to order one online."

"May I ask you a question?"

"Yeah, sure."

"Where're you from?"

Lee gave her a longer look than what made her comfortable, considering he was driving. "Here, now, but I was born in Salt Lake City, Utah."

"And you moved to Arizona to become a cop?"

A Strange Twist of Fate

"Uh-huh. I didn't want to work out in the snow, like my dad did before he retired."

"Are your parents still in Utah?"

"Part time. They have a house down in Queen Creek where they spend the winter. They'll head back next month."

"Any brothers or sisters?"

Lee looked at her with his brows scrunched together. "Yeah, one of each." He took her hand. "Why so many questions?"

Anna squeezed his fingers. "I guess I'm just feeling a little isolated. I'm an only child. I don't even know if my mother has any siblings. She never talks about them, if she has."

"How about your father's parents?"

"They don't get along. I don't think they've spoken a dozen words in the past ten years. And I have no idea what their quarrel was about."

Lee grunted. "You are isolated."

Anna fingered the edge of her purse. Knowing that her mother wasn't really her mother would make her even more isolated. Maybe she shouldn't have taken the blood. As dysfunctional as it was, at least right now she had a family.

"Does it bother you much being back in your old bedroom?"

Anna clutched her arms over her stomach, hugging herself. The sounds of some of the late-night fits her mother had still echoed in her mind. She wasn't sure she'd ever be able to forget the screaming, the crying, and then the dead silence where all Anna could hear was her own heart thudding from fear. "I'm not sure how well I'll be able to sleep."

"After what I saw this morning, I can understand why," Lee said softly. "And you can't stay at a hotel?"

Anna let her gaze linger on his handsome face. "To be truthful, I'm going to need to find a job soon." He glanced at her with concern but stayed quiet, giving her time to tell him why.

"After Greg died, the mortgage was paid off by a special insurance policy, and so was my new car. And I've been living off his life insurance. It was a considerable amount, but with all the expenses—the maid, the landscaper, electric, gas, water, food . . ." Anna took in a deep breath and let it out in a heavy sigh. "I had to let go all the help my husband had hired because I was burning through the money too fast. I don't mind cleaning. I enjoy it. And I hired my elderly neighbor's grandson to cut the grass. He does an acceptable job, but the money isn't bottomless, so I need a job."

Lee took her hand again. "I understand. What were you doing before you married Greg?"

"Graduating high school."

His grin came out once more. "I forgot you were only eighteen. So how old are you now?"

"Twenty-five. And since we're spilling all of our darkest secrets, how old are you?"

"Thirty-three."

"Greg was thirty-five on his last birthday. You don't look your age."

Lee laughed. "Thank you, I think. Did you work while you were married?"

"You mean paid employment that I can put down on a résumé? No. I stayed at home for Greg. I was there when he had parties I needed to attend with him. I was making a home for future children . . ." Anna couldn't continue. That part of her life had ended.

Lee squeezed her hand. "So you didn't go to college."

Anna blew out a breath before answering. "No."

"How about going now?"

She sighed again. "I've been too busy to even think about it, really." Anna pulled out her phone.

Over the next fifteen minutes of their drive to the lab, Anna did a search on community colleges. It wasn't enough time to do the research justice. She'd try again later, after she crawled into bed, when she could use her laptop and find out about scholarships she might apply for.

After Lee parked, Anna shot off a text to Larry: *I'm here.*

A moment later, he answered: *Meet me at the alley door.*

A Strange Twist of Fate

"Stay here with Rusty," Anna told Lee as she quickly got out of the car. She shut the door before he could say anything. When she walked past the main entrance, she glanced over her shoulder to see if he noticed she didn't go inside. From the frown on his face, Anna was sure he was suspicious about what she had planned. She slipped around the corner of the building to find Larry standing outside a closed door. The alleyway was otherwise deserted.

"Hey, Anna." Larry had a packet in his hands. It had a syringe in it.

Anna took out the vial, but before she handed it over to her friend, she peeled off the label that had her mother's name on it.

Larry lifted a single eyebrow, but he didn't ask whose it was. "I don't need this much blood. If you can hang around, I'll give you back the rest of the vial in five minutes." He put the sample in his white jacket pocket. With a lowered voice, he said, "Uh, Anna, if you're looking for paternity with just a blood type, I have to tell you that this isn't the most reliable way of doing it. I'll get you a DNA kit that you can send in to a lab. The directions will be on the package. You'll need two samples, yours and whoever's this is. It can take a few months to get the results back, but that's the only way you will know for sure." Larry looked over her shoulder with pinched brows and then went back inside the lab without saying another word.

Anna could feel Lee staring at her. When she turned around, she saw him standing at the corner of the building with a deep frown. She gazed around the alley. Not the worst place to have an argument, if things went downhill. The way Lee stared at her gave her chills, like he could bore a hole through her head with his eyes. Still, she couldn't look away as he strode to her.

"What are you doing?" he asked.

"I can't tell you."

"Why not? Don't you trust me?"

"Of course I do, but"—Anna looked down at her hand resting on her purse—"I don't want to involve you in something illegal, so please don't ask me any more questions."

Debra Erfert

Lee glanced at the lab's door. "Is it real drugs this time?"

"No! Please go back to your car—"

"I'm not going until you tell me what you're doing."

"I'm only trying to protect you—and me." Anna felt herself blush. She turned away, angry that he could even think she would deal in real drugs. But what choice was she giving him?

Lee caught her arm. He wouldn't let her walk away. "Anna," he said with his voice soft and low near her face. "I'm your friend. Don't shut me out."

He stood so close. She felt every rapid rise of his chest against her arm he held. "I wanted some blood typed."

"Blood?" Lee's brows eased a little. "Whose?"

"My mother's," Anna whispered.

"Your . . ." His hand relaxed. "How did you get some of your mother's blood?" Lee dropped his hand and said, "And please don't say your father keeps a supply of it in his fridge."

"That's gross," Anna told him, but then she cracked a grin. "I stole it."

Lee's eyes widened. "How did you steal it?" He held out his hands in an effort to stop her from talking. "No, no, never mind. You do have the right to remain silent."

Anna's heart stopped. "You're going to arrest me?"

"I was kidding! It's a figure of speech. I'm sorry—I didn't mean to scare you." He wrapped his arms around her back, giving her a squeeze. "I promise I will never arrest you—I could never arrest you." He hesitated. "Anna, I'm fall—"

The door opened, and Larry came out, prompting Lee to let her go.

"Well?" Anna asked. Larry handed her a four-inch-square plastic-covered test. With noticeably shaking fingers, she took it. The chart wasn't hard to read. It was similar to her early pregnancy test. Each of the four blood types had a little window next to it, and only one was filled in with red. "She has type O blood."

"What type do you have?" Lee asked in a whisper.

A Strange Twist of Fate

"AB positive." Anna looked up at Larry. "Could I be related to someone. . ." She lifted the card.

Larry glanced at Lee before looking back at Anna. "No."

Debra Erfert

Twelve

Larry shuffled his feet and gave a curt nod at the test. "Anna, AB is one of the rarest types of blood, but I've never heard of a parent with type O having a child with AB blood, or the other way around, either." He handed her another kit and the vial. "Remember what I said about the DNA testing." He leaned in and gave her a kiss on her cheek before going back in through the door. It clicked closed, making the results indisputable.

"Are you OK?" Lee asked. He'd watched her face drain of color at the reality of the results. That wasn't good. She was in shock. If Lee would've known what she'd planned, then he might've been able to prepare her for a negative outcome. It was his idea in the first place to find out if she had been adopted. He'd planted that seed of doubt because he was apprehensive about becoming involved with a woman who might—*might*—someday have a mental illness. But there were no guarantees in life. He'd come so close to telling her he was falling for her before that door opened. If he told her now, it would look like he had waited to know if she would end up like her mother before committing his love. He'd missed his chance.

"She's not my mother?" Anna turned around, facing him. "Who am I, then?"

Lee put his arm around her back and started walking them toward the parking lot. "You're Anna Eddington, the same woman you were before you found out the results of that test." He stopped her before they reached his car. "Tell me, do you feel different?"

Lee didn't like the way she crossed her arms over her ribs like he'd seen her do so many times before. When tears started to puddle near her lashes, he knew her answer wouldn't be good.

A Strange Twist of Fate

"Yes." Anna closed her eyes as tears rolled down her cheeks. "I feel"—she gasped a breath—"alone."

Lee quickly wrapped her in his arms. She was trembling. He'd been so stupid, causing her more pain. She had lost her husband, and now, because of his selfish observations, she'd lost the only parents she'd ever known.

"I'm sorry. I'm sorry. I never should've said anything." He pressed his face to her hair. "Just forget that test."

"How can I forget that my parents have lied to me all my life?"

Lee kissed her head. "Let's talk this through—but not here."

It didn't seem like Anna had intentions of moving from his arms, not that he minded. Lee broke the embrace and moved her to the passenger door. After he had her inside, he rushed around and got into the driver's seat. He noticed she was still staring at the blood type result. He started the engine and backed out. Rusty stayed quiet in the back seat. Even he must've felt the depressed mood in the car.

After Lee shifted into drive, he said, "You don't really need to do that other test, do you?"

"I don't know. Larry seemed pretty definite about my blood type being rare." She turned the square cardboard test over. "It has a graph on the back. It shows the only types who can have an AB child are AB, A, or B. Not O under any circumstances. Oh, Lee," Anna wailed. "I'm adopted! Why didn't my parents tell me?"

Not telling a child about being adopted did seem unusual in this day and age. "Just because they didn't tell you doesn't mean they don't love you."

Anna sniffed, and Lee looked closer at her face. She still had tears rolling down her cheeks.

"It could also be that they had planned on telling you, but then your mother had her mental breakdown, and then maybe he couldn't discuss something that emotional without hurting her."

Anna wiped her face. "OK, that sounds good, in theory, for a kid. But I'm an adult. He's had ample opportunity to talk to me without her knowing, yet he never did. At least then I wouldn't have been worried sick that I was going to end up like . . . her."

"Yeah." Lee saw a fast-food restaurant down the street. That would be a good one to stop at. Eating in the car seemed like the best thing in her current state. "That's a good point."

Anna's phone rang. She dug it out of her purse and looked at the caller ID. "It's the City of Phoenix. Why on earth are they calling me?" She touched the green phone icon and said, "Hello? . . . I'm Julianna Eddington." She turned her wide eyes to Lee. "Where? What for?" Anna shook her head. "I don't understand. I need to do what?" The next moment, she groaned and said, "Yes, I'll come right over."

"What is it?" Lee asked.

"That was the police department's dispatcher. I was asked to go to meet an officer at the corner of West Clarendon Avenue and North 55th Drive to . . . oh, no!"

"Anna, what is it?"

Her voice softened to the point it scared Lee. "I'm being asked to identify a dead body. I think I know this address."

~*~

The dispatcher hadn't given Anna a name for the body she needed to identify or even why they called her to do it at a house instead of in the city morgue. There had to be something else going on. As Lee turned his car around, she looked up an address to confirm her suspicion. When she had started her investigation on the men Greg had put in prison, she'd visited and subtly questioned each of the women living at the houses. Some had been married to the imprisoned men, but most were only living with them, like Claudia had been. More than a dozen of those women had become her friends. Anna saw them every Friday at their self-defense class. A sick feeling began to churn in her stomach as she remembered Christina's hasty exit when her boyfriend Frank found her at the Salvation Army building. Anna scrolled to Christina's address. It was on Clarendon Avenue.

"Oh no . . ." Anna whispered.

A Strange Twist of Fate

"Tell me," Lee said.

They were within a mile of the meeting place. "You know the ladies I told you about yesterday, the ones Caesar is teaching self-defense to?"

"Yeah, sure." Lee glanced over at Anna as he drove.

"Christina Bush had to leave on Friday when her boyfriend showed up. Frank Morrison is a violent felon. She told him that she was going to her sister's house, not to the class. I thought she'd smoothed things over with him before she got into his car, but now . . ." Anna hugged herself. "We need to look out for Frank's car—an old orange Dodge Charger."

"I know that car," Lee told her. "He's about six feet tall, brown hair, blue eyes."

"That description fits half the men in the Phoenix metropolitan area."

"Cleft chin?"

"That's him."

"I've given that man a speeding citation, and I nearly had to Taser him. He took a swing at me—over a simple speeding ticket."

"How long ago was that?"

"Uh . . . four years ago."

"And you remember him?"

"I remember every creep who takes a swing at me."

"Over a ticket?"

"Yeah." Lee pulled up to a curb near a police car. The cruiser had its overhead lights rotating, and it was blocking off the intersection. Anna was now positive whose house they were going to. Her heartbeat accelerated in anxiety. An officer started walking toward them with a grim expression. They were in Lee's personal car and not his city unmarked, and as Lee got out, Anna watched him remove his wallet. The glint of the sun reflected off his gold badge as he opened his wallet. Anna got out and walked around the car to meet them.

"Detective," the officer said. "What can I do for you?"

Debra Erfert

Lee motioned toward Anna with a lift of his hand. "Mrs. Eddington was called by dispatch to come here to identify a dead body."

"Eddington?" The officer stared at Anna. "You Greg Eddington's widow?"

Anna read the officer's name tag. "I am, Officer Benjamin, and I'm supposed to meet with Detective Caine."

"Huh." He frowned, nodding. "Follow me."

Anna didn't need to follow the cop to know where to go. A coroner's wagon parked in front of the house reinforced the death. The closer she got to Christina's front door, the further her heart dropped to her feet. Three officers lingered outside the door and stared at her as she entered the empty carport.

"His car is gone," Lee said loud enough for only her to hear.

"I expected that," Anna whispered.

"Detective Caine," Lee greeted a plainclothes older gentleman who had stepped outside.

"Detective Adams." Caine's gaze turned to Anna. "Julianna Eddington?"

"Yes, Detective. How did you know to call me?"

Caine held out a sandwich-size plastic baggie with a piece of paper inside with writing on it. It was evidence. "We found this on the floor near the body."

The body. Anna felt sick. She recognized the slip of paper. It had written on it: *Call me if,* along with her cell number. Anna hadn't signed it; that's why they had asked her name. She looked up into the detective's hard eyes. "I wrote that and gave it to my friend—just in case things got too violent."

Caine nodded. "It got that way. Come inside, but don't touch anything."

Anna faltered until Lee put his arm around her back and squeezed. She needed his support—wanted it.

They walked into a horrible mess. The couch cushions were strewn across the floor. The two glass table lamps had been broken and were lying on their sides, with their shades crushed. Pictures

A Strange Twist of Fate

that once hung on the wall were now on the floor, broken. Holes the size of fists were beaten into the drywall. There were a couple of Jim Beam whiskey bottles on the coffee table, lying on their sides, mostly empty. Someone had been very angry and most likely very drunk. Anna hugged her arms over her stomach, trying to keep her nerves from overwhelming her.

They followed the detective down the hallway, and Anna knew she was moments away from having her heart broken.

Caine turned at a doorway, staying in the hall. "Remember, don't touch anything."

"I understand." Anna breathed through her mouth. The acrid, coppery-scented air inside the house smelled of spilled blood and lost bowels. The body lying on the floor next to the bed had a bloody sheet covering it, and a man stood next to it, writing on a clipboard. His white jacket suggested he was the coroner. "I'm here to identify . . ." Her voice warbled, but she nodded at the bloody sheet.

"Are you squeamish, Mrs. Eddington? You won't faint at seeing a dead body, will you? There's a shot in the face."

When Anna hesitated, Lee spoke up. "She's got a constitution of granite, Phil," he told the coroner. He was such a liar. Anna might just faint, or throw up, or both just at the thought of her friend lying there dead.

Phil took hold of the top edge of the sheet and started to pull. Anna closed her eyes and held her breath, steeling her nerves. When Lee grunted, she opened her eyes.

"I didn't expect that!" Anna said, letting out her breath.

"Frank Morrison," Anna and Lee said at the same time.

"Are you sure?" Detective Caine asked.

"His cleft chin," Lee and Anna said simultaneously.

"Can you lower the sheet past his hands, please?" Anna asked.

"Why?" Caine asked. "You've identified him. That's all we asked. We'll take it from here."

Anna stood upright, putting her fists on her hips. "I want to see if he's been in a fight."

Debra Erfert

Phil's gaze went to Detective Caine, who had stepped closer.

"His hands show abrasions, so yes." Caine squinted at her. "Do you have an idea who he might've fought with, other than the walls?"

Anna hated the idea that Christina could've shot her boyfriend, but there might've been extenuating circumstances. Claudia left Razor after she had been beaten. Not everybody in the same situation reacted in the same way.

"Send a unit to the Salvation Army on East Broadway Road and South 14th Street to see if there's an orange Dodge Charger or a 1990s silver Honda Civic parked in their lot," Anna told them.

"You have a theory?" Caine asked.

"I might." Anna looked around the bedroom, but she didn't see Christina's laptop computer. "Frank had a girlfriend. Christina Bush." As she walked to the hallway, she said, "He came to our self-defense class yesterday, very angry. Christina had to lie to him about where she was. I'm not sure how, but he tracked her down to that Salvation Army building. She went home in his Charger, leaving her Honda in the parking lot."

Still talking, Anna hunted for the laptop. "Frank was released from prison three months ago after serving time for battery with a deadly weapon." She found the silver MacBook on the living room floor, partially hidden by a couch cushion.

"I need to find Christina and talk with her . . ." Anna grabbed the computer.

"Don't touch that!" Caine shouted.

"My prints are already on it," Anna said, sitting on the floor and putting the laptop on her legs.

"Why would your prints be on it?" Caine asked, crouching in front of her. Lee took the same position next to him, watching her.

"Several months ago, I helped her install an app on her phone to help find it in case it was stolen." She looked up at Lee. "Mostly, she was afraid Frank would take it from her. Anyway"—Anna opened the laptop and began to type—"I'll be able to find where

A Strange Twist of Fate

Christina is on the map that pops up, or at least where her phone is."

"You know her username and password for that app?" Caine asked as he looked over the screen.

"I told you—I helped her set it up." A map of the city of Phoenix came on the screen, with a red pin stuck in a location. Anna knew that place. She'd had lunch at Christina's mother's house two times over the past year.

"I want to go and talk with Christina to see if she had anything to do with Frank's death," Anna said as she quickly shut off the program.

"Wait!" Caine made a grab for the computer, but it was too late; the program had already disappeared. The detective didn't appreciate it. "You're interfering with a police investigation."

"No, I'm not." Anna straightened. "I came and identified the body, just like you asked. I even gave you a tip on who I last saw him with yesterday and where her car might be. But I didn't say she was guilty. Remember, Frank is—was—a violent felon, and his friends were, too. You don't know he wasn't offed by one of them."

Caine looked at Lee with a hard glare. Lee shrugged. "Her husband was an attorney. Her father's a judge. She's bound to pick up—everything!"

"I think I'm done here," Anna said, getting up off the floor. "Gentlemen."

Neither man tried to stop her as she crossed to the front door, although she knew they had a right to. She made it outside before they called her bluff. Without looking back, Anna strode to Lee's car. The windows had been rolled down a few inches to give Rusty flow-through air, but Lee had locked the doors. She waited with her hand on the door handle and listened to one set of footsteps coming up behind her. The alarm beeped once, and the locks popped up. Anna got inside. Lee took his seat behind the wheel and started the car.

"Where to?"

131

"Will you take this intel to Caine?"
"Not right away."
Anna nodded. "Good enough."

A Strange Twist of Fate

Thirteen

Lee pulled to a slow stop where Anna had told him. She didn't explain where they were, and he wouldn't press her for that information—not yet anyway. He'd given her the time that she seemed to have needed while he drove. She'd also done some research on her phone during their short trip.

He looked at the cars parked in the carports and side yards. Then he checked to see where Anna was looking. She wasn't so sneaky. Her eyes were trained on the pink stucco house two places down. From his point of view, the trunk of a silver Honda was visible between two cars. She found Christina. Now either he could call dispatch for backup or go with Anna and back her up as she talked with her friend.

"What did you want to do?" Anna asked.

Lee jumped, startled. Her dark eyes were intently on him. "Whose house is this?"

"Emily Bush's, Christina's mother."

"Any brothers?"

"Yeah, I thought about that. She has one brother and two sisters. They don't live here, but if she came home after having a deadly fight with Frank, then they might be here to support her. You should stay—"

"No! That's not going to happen." Lee got out, leaving the windows down again for his dog, and headed for the house. Fast-paced steps assured him Anna had followed. Not wanting to be seen as he approached, he stayed low and used the two other cars in the driveway as shields. When he looked to see how well Anna was doing at being stealthy, he saw her standing on the sidewalk grinning at him.

Debra Erfert

Anna walked past Lee, saying, "Christina is my friend. If you want an introduction, stay close to me," and continued to head toward the narrow front path leading to the house's entrance. Lee dropped his pretense of being covert and fell in step behind her. When he told the coroner that she was fearless, he'd hoped to bolster her courage. He'd severely underestimated her mettle.

The front door opened before they got to it. Lee flinched, his hand reaching for his duty weapon holstered in the back of his waistband.

"Hello, Emily," Anna said to the woman behind the steel security screen door. "I need to talk to Christina, please."

Lee could see that the woman's eyes were red-rimmed, but he didn't smell alcohol coming from inside the home, only cooking beef. When she looked at him, Anna made the introduction.

"This is my boyfriend, Lee Adams."

Her boyfriend? Lee immediately put his arm around her waist. No sense in losing an opportunity to hold her.

"Are you alone?" Emily asked.

"Yes," Anna told her.

A click came from the knob before she opened the screen door. She must've had a deadbolt thrown. Anna went through first and hung near the door while Lee came inside. Emily threw the deadbolt again, locking them in.

"Christina's in the kitchen," Emily said with a warbled voice. She led the way.

Lee waited for Anna to go first, but before she moved, she quietly unlocked the deadbolt. He didn't expect that. She then took his hand and led him through the empty living room and into a kitchen, where several women and two men were sitting around a dining table. Only one woman had a black eye and a puffy lip. When that woman saw Anna, she burst into sobs.

"Oh, Christina . . ." Anna rushed around the table with her arms out. Lee stood near the cupboard while the two women held each other, crying. He studied the others in the group. The mother had tears on her face again. An older man might be the dad or an uncle;

A Strange Twist of Fate

he looked about the right age. There was a younger man sitting next to Christina, near her age. He was probably her brother. Everyone seemed angry—either with Frank, or they might know he was a cop. He couldn't even fool Harold.

"I tr-tried to call you, to get out . . ." Christina choked to a stop.

Anna gripped her shoulders, staring into her eyes. "I'm here now. Let me help you." She brushed Christina's dark brown hair away from her wet face with a gentle hand. "Start from the beginning, OK?"

The young man got up and gave his chair to Anna. She moved it even closer to Christina before she sat down. Emily took the chair on her daughter's other side.

"How did you know something happened?" the older man asked.

Anna gave him her attention. "The detective found my number on the floor next to Frank, and he called me, not knowing who I was. He asked me to come identify the body." Anne stared at Christina. "I thought Frank had killed you."

"I was afraid he was going to," Christina whispered. "He was angry that I had lied to him about going to Dee's house yesterday. I didn't think he'd check with her."

"I'm so sorry, Christina," Dee whined softly.

"It's not your fault," Emily told her, placing her arm around her shoulder. "We all knew Frank was bad news."

"Mom—I told you, I'm sorry!" Christina covered her face with her trembling hands.

"Did you and Frank fight all night?" Anna asked, stroking Christina's hair.

She cupped her bruised cheek. "Basically. He accused me of cheating on him. The more I denied it, the angrier he got. It didn't matter what I said anymore, and I knew it. I told him I wanted to leave, and he started hitting me. When he said he'd rather see me dead than let me go, I ran to the bathroom and locked the door."

"Whose gun was it?" Anna asked.

Debra Erfert

"Frank's. I was surprised to see it." Christina looked up at Lee. "He's not supposed to carry a gun. He's a felon."

"Are you a cop?" the younger man asked sharply. He stood behind Anna's chair. With the way his shoulders pushed back, Lee sensed a fight coming.

"Leave him alone, Scott," Emily told him. "He's Anna's boyfriend."

"Anna, you got a boyfriend?" Christina asked softly.

"Uh-huh, and he's a very nice guy. Tell me, how did you get a hold of Frank's gun?"

"Me?" Christina's eyes went up to Scott. "I called my brother this morning from the bathroom. He came over . . ."

With her voice low, Anna asked a straightforward question. "Christina, did you shoot Frank?"

"No, I didn't," she said, staring at Anna.

"Who did?" Anna asked.

Christina glanced up at her brother before she looked down at her hands. Scott took off toward the living room. Lee stood in his way. He only had time to put up his hands before Scott slammed him against the cabinets, knocking him to the floor and running toward the front door.

"Lee!" Anna ran to him as he recovered enough to get up off the floor.

Lee shrugged her off. "Stay here!" He took out his gun. When he rounded the corner into the living room, he aimed his weapon at a man pinning Scott facedown on the carpet. Scott's arm was twisted up high behind his back in a hold that Lee recognized from the police academy.

"Caesar!" Anna rushed into the living room. "You made it!"

Lee lowered his gun and looked at Anna. "Caesar? Your self-defense instructor?"

Christina ran in next. "Please don't hurt him. Scott was only protecting me!" She hung on Anna's arm. "Please help us. He only wanted to get me out of that house, but Frank was so drunk, he—"

A Strange Twist of Fate

"Shut up!" Anna shouted with her hands clenched into fists. "You have the right to remain silent!" Christina choked back her next words and stayed quiet.

Lee stared at Anna. She had amusingly arrested everyone in the room, including him. Lee nodded at the ex-marine still pressing one knee between Scott's shoulder blades, evidently Frank's killer. "Nice to meet you, Caesar. I'm Lee, Anna's boyfriend."

Caesar smiled up at him. "So did you sign those divorce papers yet?"

~*~

Anna was a logistics genius. Lee watched her make arrangements for Scott's attorney with someone that she'd known for several years, and then they all met at the police station for his official booking and quick bail release. Christina's brother never actually spent any time in jail. Self-defense, that was what Scott would plead, and with the violent record Frank had, chances were solid, in Lee's opinion, that the jury would agree with him.

It was too late to go to the shooting range, they'd missed lunch, and Lee was so hungry he could eat Rusty's leather dog chew. But over the past few hours, Anna had held his hand at least a dozen times. He almost did feel like her boyfriend. Now he needed an hour or so to read through those divorce papers and sign them, and then maybe he could consider another relationship.

Lee opened the back door of his car, and Rusty jumped inside. He'd had a good walk along the greenbelt near the police department. Anna sat inside, quietly typing on her phone. She must have her whole investigation on that thing. Her binder might be a backup.

After he turned over the engine, Lee asked, "Where to now?"

Anna let out a soft sigh and leaned her head back. "I'm hungry." She looked in the back seat. "How about we get some groceries and go back to your place? I'll cook. You read your divorce papers."

Lee laughed and shifted into gear.

Debra Erfert

"And then after dinner, we can look through my family albums and discover the answer to my dad's hair color."

"Does that make a difference now?"

"It might, if he had an affair and my mother adopted me from that liaison."

"That would be an interesting twist." Lee took hold of her hand, and she squeezed his fingers. "Are you feeling any better about—you know—the test results?"

"Honestly, Lee, I haven't had two minutes to think about it."

"That's because you've been too busy taking care of a whole family." He gently squeezed her hand. "Have I told you how much you impress me?"

Anna gave him an impish grin. "I think you might've mentioned it before."

He kissed the back of her hand.

"I told you, I don't kiss married men."

"You didn't kiss me." And to prove it, Lee kissed her hand again, this time a little slower. Anna sighed softly. He took that as a good sign.

"Guess what I missed?" Anna said after he stopped distracting her.

"I can't imagine."

"I was supposed to meet with the window repairman an hour ago. He called while you were walking Rusty to reschedule for Monday."

"That's right. I'd completely forgotten about that."

Anna smiled widely. "He said he wouldn't charge me for this missed call, so that's good news."

"Yeah . . . You said you needed to look for a job before long?"

She dropped her head against the headrest. "I think so. Going to college will take too long. Or I could do both at the same time, I suppose."

"Have you thought about applying for the Phoenix Police Department?"

She straightened. "What?"

A Strange Twist of Fate

"Come on. With your mad investigating skills and logical thinking, you'd be an asset to the department."

"What would I have to do?"

"Well, there's a written test and a physical agility test, and if you pass those, then there's an oral board, where I know you'd wow them. And in Arizona, you don't need a college degree to apply. After you're hired, you'll go through the police academy."

Anna looked down at her body. "Physical agility? I'm so out of shape, I don't think I could compete with the men who apply."

"We could go jogging together, and I could help you with the sit-ups and push-ups." Lee grinned. "I'll find out what the requirements are so we can have something to work toward." Lee gazed at her face. The satisfied smile on her lips gave him a deep burning feeling in his chest.

"I'd like that," Anna told him.

Lee drove to his neighborhood grocery store. Shopping with Anna felt . . . natural. They didn't disagree about any food selections. He even let her talk him into buying more dinnerware, flatware, matching placemats, and cloth napkins. Since he had nothing to actually cook in, he also bought a set of pots and pans, too. Although she didn't like the quality of the items, she said they'd do—for now. Lee noticed Anna didn't flinch at the huge bill he paid at the checkout. His detective's pay wouldn't go as far as a lawyer's. He wondered if she could live within a budget. Interesting how he let his thoughts wander that far ahead.

When they were settled back in his apartment, Anna in the kitchen and Lee sitting on the couch reading the divorce papers with a pen in his hand, she brought up possibly applying to the police department again.

"Lee?"

He looked up. Anna was chopping carrots with one of the new butcher knives he bought. He'd purchased two. He didn't even know he needed two different sizes. "Yes?"

"How much does a rookie cop get paid?"

Debra Erfert

"Ten years ago when I was hired, I started at a little over fifty thousand a year." He got up when her hands stilled, yet her eyes were on the knife. "What is it, Anna?"

She looked up at him. "That's before taxes."

"And retirement." Lee leaned on the breakfast bar and watched her face.

"That would leave, maybe . . . fifteen hundred dollars in a paycheck?"

"Yeah, that sounds about right."

Anna continued cutting the carrots. "I guess I'll need to sell the house. It's too big for me anyway."

"But it's paid off."

"I know, but the expenses associated with living there are just too much." Anna scooped the carrots into a dish. "I need one with a smaller lawn that I can take care of myself. And who needs a music room and a den? The homeowners' association's fee is five hundred dollars every month."

"Ouch!" Lee took one of the carrot bites and tossed it in his mouth.

"That won't be within my budget from now on. How's your reading coming along?" Anna added some water to the dish and then butter and honey before putting it in the microwave.

"I'm nearly finished. It seems like they made all the changes I'd asked for. I have to sell my house."

"Your house?" Anna's shoulders drooped. "Oh, I guess you'll lose it in the divorce."

"Pretty much. It looks like the attorneys have settled on a Realtor. I just want to make sure it sells for market price."

"Who's the contracted broker?"

"Uh . . ." Lee went back to the couch and found the right page that had the clause containing the house sale. "Rockbury Real Estate."

"My friend Lisa is a Realtor with Home Town Brokers. Let me make a call."

"Are they reputable?"

A Strange Twist of Fate

"Absolutely." Anna wiped her hands on a paper towel. "I'll probably get her to sell my house."

"Do you think the Realtor at Rockbury might make a special deal with Carolyn and screw me over somehow?"

"Your wife is going to buy it?"

"Soon-to-be ex-wife, and yes, that's her plan."

"Huh." Anna picked up her phone and headed for the couch. "Didn't you want to keep it?"

That thought had crossed his mind, but he couldn't be sure it wasn't out of spite or if he really wanted the home he'd lived in for the past five years. "Carolyn found the house. I agreed with her on the purchase, so, no. But I don't want her to steal it from me, either. She tried to get me to sign my interest over to her for half of what I paid on the down payment."

"That was a lousy thing to try." Anna tapped on her phone and then sat back. A moment later, a smile graced her pretty lips as she spoke. "Hello, Lisa, this is Anna . . . yes, I'm doing much better; thank you so much for asking. Listen, I'm going to be putting my house on the market, and I was wondering if you'd be interested in coming over and giving me an appraisal and then listing it for me." Anna smiled over at Lee. "Wonderful, thanks! . . . Oh, not until next week. I'm having some repairs done. I'll call you when they're finished.

"Listen"—Anna leaned forward and moved Lee's divorce papers to where she could read them—"while I have you on the phone, I heard of a house on East Captain Dreyfus Avenue that might be on the market. Could you find out if it's a multiple listing? . . . Yes, that's the one . . . It is? Good! Do you know what the list price is?" Anna tapped the paper with her finger several times. "Two ninety-five?" she repeated with her gaze on Lee.

He mouthed, "That's what we paid for it when we bought it."

Anna shook her head. "Is there an offer on it yet? . . . One? At full price? . . . I'd like to make an offer." She smiled again. "Three hundred fifty thousand . . . Uh-huh. With the contingency of my house selling . . . That's right . . . OK, we'll talk later. Bye!"

Debra Erfert

"You can't be serious," Lee said in shock.

Anna leaned back again. "Of course not."

"Then . . . What?"

Anna got up and went back into the kitchen.

"Anna, tell me what just happened," Lee said as he followed her.

She twisted the stove's, knob and a flame burst under the grilling pan. "I just got you twenty-five thousand more dollars"—Anna looked over at him with a sly grin—"well, a little more than that when Carolyn comes back with a higher offer."

Lee stared at Anna calmly putting two steaks on the hot grill like she hadn't done anything underhanded or sneaky. She'd done both, but the only sign she gave that she might've done something duplicitous was the subtle grin on her lips.

"I've got to sign those papers," Lee said softly.

"Please do. I'm not comfortable dating a married man."

Lee stepped closer. "Are we dating?"

Anna set the stove's timer, and while the steaks sizzled, she turned to Lee. "Am I cooking you dinner in your apartment?"

He gazed around the kitchen. A salad filled a bowl, veggies were cooked, and the most delicious meat was grilling not three feet away from him. "It certainly looks that way."

"I don't know about you, but to me, this feels like a date," Anna said with an alluring smile.

"How can I argue with that kind of logic?" Lee stepped close enough he stood nearly flush against her body. "Usually at the end of a real date—"

Anna stopped his advance with a firm hand to his chest. "Not until you sign those papers!"

"Fine . . ." Lee leaned in and pressed his lips to her forehead, giving her a kiss.

"You have six minutes before the steaks are done," she whispered.

Lee moved his lips down to her cheek. "OK." He then kissed his way down to her soft neck. The sigh he heard gave him hope.

A Strange Twist of Fate

"Lee Adams . . ." Anna pushed against his chest.

"OK, OK," he said, chuckling. "I get it. Sign the papers first, then a real kiss."

"But after dinner, so you don't rush. These steaks will be ready before you know it." Anna turned away from him and took the salad bowl to the small dinette table where she'd set the placemats, plates, silverware, and glasses.

Lee hurried to the bathroom and washed his hands and took a couple of minutes to run a razor over his face, something he'd neglected to do that morning. He'd looked scruffy all day.

Rusty sat on the floor next to Anna's chair throughout dinner. Lee witnessed her feeding him three times. The dog had always been his dog, but now Lee was afraid his Rusty's heart belonged to Anna, bribed away with lean steak.

After they had the dishes washed and put away, Lee did something he hadn't done since moving into his apartment—he lounged on the couch with his feet up on the ottoman, holding a beautiful woman in his arms while watching a football game on his big-screen TV. Rusty had crawled up next to Anna.

Lee wasn't paying particular attention to the game. Neither was Anna. She'd taken out the rubber band from her hair and had fallen asleep on his chest, and he was reading through the rest of his divorce papers. It looked the same, with the exceptions of the additions he'd requested. The savings account would be released and divided evenly upon being filed in court. Lee would sign off on Carolyn's 401(k), and any other retirement investment she might hold in the future . . . The clause ended there.

"What the—" Lee said out loud, waking Anna. He might've said it a little too loud with the way she jerked away from under his arm and quickly stood. Rusty jumped from the couch, startled by her sudden movement.

Anna stared at him as if he'd turned into a killer, but that look didn't last more than a few seconds before her hand plastered onto her chest. "Lee! You scared me!"

Debra Erfert

"I'm sorry." Lee sat up straight. "I found something." He slapped his stapled copies down on the ottoman.

Anna sat down and slid her arm around his back. "What happened?"

Lee turned it back one page and pointed to the retirement clause. Anna took a moment and read it. "It sounds reasonable that you don't attach her retirement account, as long as she . . ." She took her arm from around his back and picked up the packet, looking at it closer. "Where is the clause stating Carolyn signs off on your retirement?"

"It's not there."

A Strange Twist of Fate

Fourteen

Anna stared up at Lee. "That hardly seems fair. Why should she be entitled to half of your retirement if you don't get any of hers? After all, you paid for her education."

Lee thumped his knee with his hand. "It was there in the last draft."

"What? What . . . do you mean your attorney took out that clause?"

"Or Carolyn's did to screw me." Lee jumped up and scooted around the ottoman. He needed to pace. He walked to the front door and then turned around. "All I know is, it isn't there now."

"Who's representing you?"

Lee stopped pacing. Anna had an odd look in her eyes. "Braxton & Braxton, but a junior associate got my case—"

"Beverly Richardson?"

"You know her?"

"I know practically every attorney in and around Arizona, thanks to Greg and my dad, and the many parties we attended over the years, and I wouldn't trust Beeve the Cleave to file my nails." Anna glanced at her watch. "Would you mind if I get you a new divorce attorney? I'll make sure you get your retainer back from Braxton."

Lee saw firsthand how swiftly Anna gave hope to Christina's brother Scott when he was booked into jail. And right now Lee felt like he was condemned to a life sentence. "Beeve the Cleave?"

Anna picked up her phone from the ottoman. "Don't tell me you never noticed her abundant cleavage and the way she doesn't quite button her top up properly."

Lee started to smile but cleared his throat instead. "Make the arrangements."

Debra Erfert

"Good. I'll call Homer Peabody." Anna sat back, tapping on her phone. Within moments she said, "Hello, Homer?" She smiled. "Yes, this is Anna. How are you? . . . I'm doing fine, thank you . . . No, really. I promise! . . . I'm sorry for calling you so late, but I have a good friend who has found himself in a little trouble. Do you have room on your calendar for an easy divorce case?"

"Easy?" Lee asked.

Anna waved at him. "Can he speak to you now?" She waved at Lee again but motioned for him to come back to the couch. "Thanks, he's right here."

Lee relented and took the phone she held out, pacing while talking. Mr. Peabody's voice sounded as old as Lee's grandfather's, but the questions the man asked gave him confidence in his ability to get the job done expediently. He'd only grunted when Lee told him about Beverly. By the end of their thirty-minute conversation, Lee had his instructions. He was to bring the divorce papers by his office Monday morning and sign a contract with Peabody Law Office. Although Peabody's current specialty was contract law, he would personally see Lee's case through inside a week. He would also threaten Braxton & Braxton with a breach-of-contract lawsuit. He expected a quick settlement of his retainer returned, plus enough to cover Peabody's payment and maybe a little more.

When Lee went to return Anna's phone to her, she had fallen asleep. Rusty had curled up below her. She looked so peaceful, lying on the couch with her sweater over her shoulders. But he knew she'd be cold before the night was over. Lee set her phone on the ottoman and went to his bedroom to get the blanket. Before he left his room, he found his bathrobe hanging in the closet and took his pillow back to the couch.

After he spread the blanket out over Anna, he turned off the TV and the light and lay down on the other side of the couch, this time with his head near hers.

"Lee?" Anna whispered.

A Strange Twist of Fate

He felt a tug near his shoulder, and he reached up and took her hand. "I thought you were sleeping."

"I was."

"Did you want me to take you home?"

"And where is that, exactly?"

"At your folk's house?"

"According to that blood test, I don't know where my mother lives."

Lee kissed Anna's hand. "Your parents are your folks. They raised you, even if they didn't tell you that you were adopted."

"I'd rather sleep here with you."

He noticed she didn't agree with what he'd said about her parents. "My couch is yours for as long as you want it. May I ask you a question?"

"Sure . . ." She sounded sleepy.

"If Carolyn doesn't come back with a higher offer, what do you plan on doing?"

"Hmmm . . . Is your house nice?"

"It's beautiful, and the neighborhood is wonderful."

"Any homeowners' association fees?"

"None."

Her voice became softer. She must only be inches from his face, but it was too dark to see her. She sounded like she was about to fall asleep. "Would you mind if I bought it, then?"

Would Lee mind having Anna living in his house? He could easily visualize her sleeping in his bedroom. Carolyn hadn't cooked many meals in their kitchen, but he could almost taste the ones Anna might prepare. She had already proved she was a great cook.

"If I had a choice of who I'd like to see in my house," Lee whispered, "I'd rather it be you." Anna didn't respond. Her hand felt limp. She'd fallen asleep.

~*~

Like the morning before, Anna woke up first. This time, she didn't hide the fact that she was watching Lee while he slept. Once again, he was on his chest with his arm hanging over the side of the couch, his hand on Rusty. In the brief time that she'd glanced through his divorce papers, she'd seen the clause where he would retain custody of the family dog. That was how important Rusty had been to Lee.

Evidently, Anna was important to Lee as well. Yesterday, just before Larry had come out of the door with the results of the blood test, Lee had been a few syllables away from telling her his feelings for her. She wasn't stupid. Unless he was about to faint, he was going to tell her he was falling for her. And he looked terrifically healthy to her. What she couldn't understand is why he hadn't said anything since then. She'd given him plenty of openings. She'd held his hand, and he'd touched her often enough for her to know he wanted more. Could that be the problem? Was he only interested in someone he could bed? It would be interesting to see how long he would hang around if that were the case. Anna already had romantic feelings toward him. If she were being honest with herself, she probably was in love with him.

"Good morning," Lee said, startling her out of thoughts.

How anyone could look so good first thing in the morning was beyond her. "You're awake." Anna sat up and stretched while Rusty lopped to the front door and scratched at the bottom.

"I know—I'll lose my security deposit." Lee got up, but before he moved away, he leaned over and kissed Anna's cheek. Then he and his dog were out the door in seconds, leaving her alone.

After a bathroom trip, Anna picked up the tote bag containing the two albums, carried it over to the breakfast bar, and took out the album with the earliest pictures. She wanted to see her parents before she was born.

The very first page was from their wedding day. No surprise there. She'd seen it before. What Anna didn't remember was how utterly happy and carefree her mother had looked. Her mother—who now seemed more like a stranger. How long had Margo Wright carried the secret of Anna's birth before she had her mental breakdown? Had Anna's adoption contributed to it? At some point

A Strange Twist of Fate

in Anna's life, Margo must've known she would want to find her birth mother. Anna thought all adopted children go through that stage. Some had happy reunions—she'd seen them on TV. Logically, there were women who gave up their babies so that they weren't reminded of traumatic events, like rape, and seeing the child they gave up years later might not be a good idea. Had Anna's mother been a victim? Did Anna really want to know? Would she ruin her birth mother's life by finding her now? She had so many questions, but only one starting place.

The door opened. Rusty came bounding inside, pulling Lee in with him. The joyous smile on Lee's face filled Anna with happiness, a sensation she hadn't felt since before Greg died. Anna gazed down at the photo album again. Did she have any right to intrude uninvited into her birth mother's life, possibly making her miserable by even the attempted contact?

"You look worried. What's wrong?" Lee asked as he unhooked Rusty's leash and looped it around the doorknob.

"I was just thinking." Anna flipped the page. "I know I'm adopted. I'm wondering about the ethics of finding my birth mother."

"You're looking at your family album?" Lee walked up behind her, sliding his arm around her waist. His jaw rested against her cheek. "Well . . . your dad has dark red hair. You don't even have red highlights."

Anna leaned her hands on the edge of the counter. "Yes. Red and brown does not make blonde. I thought about searching out my birth mother, but what if I find out she is in prison for murder or something equally as horrible?" She flipped to the next page. "Or that she's happily married with more children. What if I show up telling her I'm the baby she gave away, but she'd never told her husband about ever having one before she'd married him? I might ruin her marriage, ruin her life!"

"Yeah, I can see the ethics behind your problem. But you can't do anything without your dad's cooperation." Lee kissed her cheek, went into the kitchen, and then took out Rusty's bag of food from under the counter.

"Why not?"

Lee scooped out a heaping cup of kibbles into Rusty's dish. "Think about it as an investigator would. Where would you start?"

Anna flipped to another page. "I'd . . . look at my birth certificate. It would have my place of birth—which hospital, and the exact date, just in case they'd lied to me about it."

"Where do you keep your birth certificate? Do you want to go get it this morning?"

Anna lost her smile. "I don't have it. My dad does."

"You didn't take it with you when you married Greg?"

Anna shrugged. "I didn't question my dad when he took care of my legal paperwork for my marriage license. I rarely question anything he does. He's a judge. He knew what he was doing." She looked down at the album again. But he hadn't been a judge back when he was first married. No, he was an attorney, like Greg had been.

"Haven't you needed to use your birth certificate since then—like to get a mortgage?"

"I got my driver's license and passport when I was seventeen. I don't remember needing to prove my birth to the bank. It just never came up before."

"So you'll need to send for a copy from the state if you don't want to ask your dad about it."

"Maybe . . ." Anna studied the picture before her. Something was odd. She flipped to another page, specifically looking at the house and not the people. She didn't recognize it. "They lived someplace else before moving to the house I grew up in. If I could find out where it was, maybe a neighbor would know something."

The pictures were held down by little black triangles glued to each corner. With a little tug, she lifted it off the page. She turned it over, looking for any writing. Nobody left a note of any kind, but there was a printing date: September 28, 1990.

A Strange Twist of Fate

After turning several more pages, she took out another photograph in the same way, taking care not to tear it. Anna studied each picture with new eyes, looking at the house for any clues on where it could be located. A picture taken outside, on the back patio, showed a landscape of cacti and desert brush with a mountain in the distance. So they had lived on the outskirts of a low desert town. The big backyard had green grass, like their house did now. Most expensive homes had swimming pools in the backyards, but Anna had known for a long time that her mother had a fear of water. There wasn't anything but bliss on her mother's face as she sat on the ledge of the low block wall. Anna's heart skipped a beat at the way her mother's shirt hung over her stomach.

"Oh, Lee . . ." Anna turned to the next page. That was where the album ended.

"What is it?"

Anna shoved that album aside and grabbed the other one from the bag. "Mother was pregnant."

"What?" Lee put down the box of cold cereal in his hand and rushed around the breakfast bar to stand beside Anna.

She tapped the picture that showed her mother on the wall and said, "Look," while she opened the next album.

"She does look pregnant, doesn't she?"

"You think?" She poked the picture again. "I never noticed it before. She's not very big, but I'd say she's at least six or seven months along there, and I know that it wasn't with me."

"So she either had a miscarriage or the baby died. There's nothing sinister about that."

"Look here," Anna said, moving the album with her baby pictures in it closer to Lee. He did what she asked. The photograph was one that she'd viewed several times and never thought twice about. "That's Mother standing by my stroller, wearing the same dress, except she doesn't look pregnant anymore."

"Right," Lee answered slowly.

He didn't get it. Anna's heart beat faster. She lifted the picture out from under the little triangle tabs and handed it to Lee. "Look at the trees!" He held it closer, studying the picture. He took too long to answer. "That tree is deciduous, and the leaves are turning yellow."

"Uh-huh. Right."

"Now look at this other picture." Anna lifted the photograph of her mother looking pregnant out from under the tabs. She handed it to him so he could see it better. The apartment's lights weren't that great, and the only natural light that came into the living room was from the bathroom window. As Lee held up the two photographs next to each other, Anna noticed the dates stamped on the backs. She grabbed his wrists to move them higher for a better look.

She gasped and turned his hands around for him to see the backs. Anna's stomach twisted in disbelief.

Lee looked at one and then at the other, then turned the photographs around to see the pictures again. "What in the world?"

Anna swallowed the thickness in her throat so that she could talk. "Those pictures were taken within a month of each other. Look at the dates stamped on the back."

He was quiet for a moment before he said, "At least they were developed within a month of each other, but that doesn't mean they were taken that close together. Maybe they just forgot to have the first one developed after they finished the roll."

Anna pushed away from the counter. "Oh, come on! The trees in the yard are still dropping leaves—they aren't another year taller. And knowing my mother, she wouldn't wear the same dress two years in a row."

Lee set the photographs down on the counter. "OK . . . OK, so she had a miscarriage and then they adopt . . ." He stopped midsentence, with his dark brows pinched together. He was staring at the picture with Anna's stroller.

"Why would they even have considered adopting if she was pregnant?" Anna paced across the room. "And if she did have a miscarriage, how could they have qualified for an adoption inside a month?"

A Strange Twist of Fate

"When were your parents married?"

"In January 1992, and my birthday is October 5, 1992. A time lapse of ten months works for a natural birth. How long does an adoption take?"

Lee stacked the pictures together. "Is there a way for you to get that vial of blood back into your parent's house without anybody seeing you? Put it back where you found it?" He closed the albums. "The albums too?"

"What? Why?"

Lee picked up the tote bag and stuffed the first binder in it. "Because you couldn't have been legally adopted."

Debra Erfert

Fifteen

"His car is gone." Anna stood on her toes, peeking into the garage. "He usually plays golf on Sunday mornings."

"Does your mother go with him?"

She dropped down and turned to face Lee. "She hasn't in the past. I don't know why today would be any different. Give me my bag." Anna reached for the tote Lee carried. "You stay in your car with Rusty."

"Where's the vial?"

Anna tapped her purse hanging over her shoulder. "I never did the DNA test."

"How are you going to get a sample of your dad's DNA?" Lee asked, giving her the bag.

"I'll think of something."

"Are you coming back out after you replace these things?"

Shaking her head, Anna said, "I need a shower and a change of clothes." She looked up at Lee. "Maybe you should go and come back for me later. It won't look right if you're sitting in your car. A neighbor might call the police."

Lee glanced up at the front door. "OK. Text me if you want me to come back sooner than, say, thirty minutes."

"I will." Anna headed for the front door as she took her keys out of her purse. She'd always had a key to her parents' house and never thought about returning it after she'd married Greg. As she quietly inserted it into the doorknob, Lee drove off. A moment of panic made Anna hesitate before opening the door. She would've rather gone with Lee. But she knew how important it was to get the albums back on the shelf before her dad noticed they were gone.

Getting inside wasn't hard. Nobody heard her come in. Her running shoes made little noise as she tiptoed over to the staircase.

A Strange Twist of Fate

Vicky's bag wasn't there. Anna didn't expect it to be, either. But she had a plan. Larry had used very little of the blood, so she placed the vial against the floorboard underneath the antique phone table. It would look like Vicky had accidentally dropped it there.

Replacing the photo albums came next. Since the den was empty, Anna took care in making sure she had them in order and perfectly lined up next to the other dozen albums on the shelf. Even with her mother's illness, they had pictures taken, usually around holidays, birthdays, and special events. If Anna hadn't been in a hurry to distance herself from them, she'd have liked to go through the rest just for memory's sake. Not all of her childhood was a nightmare. There were times where she could actually have said she was content—but not many.

With that unpleasant task done, Anna went upstairs to her room. She found her shower kit, clean underwear, jeans, and a T-shirt and took them to her en suite bathroom. The towels hanging near the walk-in shower had a fresh lavender scent to them, like they had recently been washed. They most likely had been.

The shower felt wonderful, and since she had an extra few minutes, Anna let the hot water run down her neck after she had rinsed the conditioner out of her hair. Her thoughts went to Lee. She loved his kind and caring manner. He had a gentleness that spoke to her heart. He'd told her she could sleep on his couch for as long as she wanted. Being at his place would be less stressful than spending time with her parents, especially after finding out about her mother's pregnancy.

The glass shower door suddenly opened.

"Mother!" Anna pushed the faucet knob, shutting off the water before taking the towel from the top of the glass.

"Julianna," Margo said quietly, almost sleepily. "Why are you here? Did you have an argument with Greg?"

Anna froze. She didn't know how to answer. Memory regression was a new symptom. Lying might be the best course. "My water heater is broken." Anna smiled. "I hope you don't mind."

Debra Erfert

"It's good. It's good." Margo watched Anna dry off. The bruises and cuts couldn't be hidden, but her mother didn't mention them or how her body had changed from rail thin before she turned around and slowly wandered out of the bathroom.

That wasn't something Anna had missed—unexpected intrusions. Dealing with her mother had become difficult after Anna reached high school. Locking her door had never been an option when it would send her mother into a panic so bad that only an injection could stop the hysterical rant, similar to what had happened yesterday.

While combing out her wet hair, Anna heard the garage open. Her dad was home. Nervous butterflies sprouted dragon wings in her chest. She'd have to face him before she could leave the house, and she would need to explain why she wasn't staying with them any longer. Telling him she was going to stay with a friend—a male friend—wouldn't be wise.

Anna draped the used towel over the shower surround before going to her room. Her mother had fallen asleep on the bed. It took a bit longer for Anna to get dressed and gather her remaining stuff together, but her need to be quiet overrode her desire to get away quickly. After she had her clothes in her overnight bag and was about to leave the bedroom, Anna turned and gazed at her mother. She hadn't moved at all. Lying so still on Anna's quilt, Margo looked peaceful and innocent. Mostly, she seemed normal, like other mothers might be.

Then it occurred to Anna—that the woman sleeping so calmly wasn't her natural mother, and according to Lee, she couldn't have even adopted her legally. That was speculation on his part. Who knew what an attorney could get done twenty-five years ago in a short amount of time. Maybe Anna wasn't officially adopted until she was a year old, yet had been in their custody since her birth. For as long as Anna could remember, Margo Wright had taken care of her—when she was able to. But what Anna didn't question was the love that her mother had shown her over the years despite the illness she suffered. She truly loved Anna, and Anna loved her. She

A Strange Twist of Fate

was the only mother she'd ever known. Anna longed to hug her. They had a miscarriage in common, yet she couldn't tell her, couldn't share in the pain or console each other.

After Anna set her bag down, she quietly walked back over to the bed. A lock of her mother's brown hair had fallen across her cheek. Anna carefully moved it off her face before leaning down and lightly kissing her forehead. "I love you, Mother," she whispered, as tears of emotion wetted her eyes. Anna made it out the bedroom door and down the stairs without actually crying, something that her dad would detect in an instant.

"Julianna!"

Her dad's voice had a hard edge to it. He was in the den. Those butterflies in her chest took flight again as she dropped her bag by the front door before stepping inside the den.

"Good morning, Dad." Anna pulled her sweater around her body, crossing her arms over her stomach, intimidated by the stern look he gave her. He sat behind his large oak desk with a file folder open in front of him, exactly like the way she'd seen him hundreds of times in the past. Jack Wright was a solidly built man, with shoulders wide enough they offset his barrel chest. Anna knew from the old pictures that he'd had thick red hair, but now his gray hair had greatly thinned. His face was touched with pink—the complexion of a redhead. That wasn't something she had ever noticed before. His blue eyes stared unflinchingly at her.

"I see that you're all right."

"Yes." Anna had to quash the impulse to look over at the albums.

And then her dad lifted his gray eyebrows—his classic look showing that he was waiting for an explanation. Well, she wasn't going to give it to him this time.

"Dad, thank you for letting me come back here, but I'm going to stay with a friend until it's clear for me to go home."

He nodded, sitting back in his big executive chair. "The friend you slept with last night?"

Debra Erfert

Anna felt heat rush up into her face at the insinuation. "I didn't—"

"You worried your mother sick when you didn't come home. How could you do that to her?"

"I didn't do anything to Mother—at least not intentionally." Now he blamed her for her mother's condition. *Was* she to blame? Was that why her mother was so doped up she fell asleep in Anna's room?

"Who were you with last night?" Jack sat forward. "Was it that cop who was at your house yesterday?"

"How do you know—"

"Grow up, Julianna. Adams has testified in my court—of course I'd know him. He's not good enough for you."

Anna dropped her hands and clenched them into fists. Over the year since Greg's death, she'd grown, not only in being independent, but she'd also routinely dealt with dangerous people. Why should she be frightened to stand up to her dad?

"You can't tell me who I can date or who I can fall in love with. I'm a grown woman, not an ignorant teenager."

"Don't talk to me like I'm one of your snitches, young lady."

"My what?" Anna took a half step away from him as he stood up. He strode to the window overlooking the side yard and stared outside.

"I let you have this past year, hoping that you'd stop believing that Greg was murdered. I thought if you went through the motions, asked your questions, it would be therapeutic for you, and you'd see for yourself that your husband's death was an accident." Jack turned to face Anna. "But dealing with drug addicts to get information is going too far. You put yourself in real danger, and I can't let that go on."

Anna gasped, holding her hand to her throat. "You knew?"

"You said you weren't ignorant, Julianna. Of course I knew about your little investigation. I'm a highly respected judge in our city. I've had calls about you poking your nose in where it doesn't belong. How do you think you've stayed out of jail this long?"

A Strange Twist of Fate

The only way he could've known about her trying to get information out of Razor was either Lee had told him about it, which he'd never do, or that creep of an officer, Zim-something, who had arrested her had called him after Lee proved she was innocent.

Jack walked back to his desk and opened the top drawer. When he lifted a vial of her mother's blood, Anna couldn't breathe.

"Why did you take this?" Jack asked.

Anna had to swallow the cotton of emotion balled in her throat before she could answer. "What makes you think I touched it?"

He turned the vial around to where a tiny piece of label could be seen. She'd forgotten about peeling off the label—most of it anyway. "Don't lie to me, Julianna!"

Anna had never been able to lie to her dad before. She straightened her back and lifted her chin. "Why didn't you tell me I was adopted?"

Her dad's neck streaked scarlet red.

Anna motioned toward the vial. "Mother has blood type O. I'm AB. It's impossible for her to be my mother." And then her temper seethed. "You must've known how scared I was about having a mental breakdown, yet you kept my adoption a secret, even after I became an adult. That was wrong!"

It took a few moments before Anna realized that her dad hadn't answered her accusation. But he didn't deny it, either. "I want my birth certificate."

"You don't need it," Jack told her.

"I will at some point in my life. Where is it?" Anna asked, going over to the bookcase. There must be a fire safe that she had missed seeing shelved among the books and artifacts he'd collected over the years. She looked up at him. "Why are you refusing to give it to me?"

"I don't know where it is." The color on his neck intensified.

"Are *you* lying to me?" Anna asked softly, not believing what she heard. Judge Jack Wright was one of the most organized men she'd ever known. For him to suddenly not know where a piece of paper was filed—something was up. When the muscles in his jaw jumped, she knew she'd caught him in a lie.

"Don't expect me to keep you out of jail next time you ask the wrong person a question."

A Strange Twist of Fate

Sixteen

Anna choked back a reply. There wasn't any other way to take that except as a threat, especially after what he'd told her. He must've known about Greg's files she'd kept. But would he actually go after her with charges? Now she was frightened of him. The tears she'd kept at bay after saying good-bye to her mother spilled freely from her eyes. Her throat had closed tightly enough that speaking became impossible. Anna ran from the den, crying. She picked up her bag and ran out the front door. She continued running until she made it far enough down the street and saw Lee's dark sedan driving toward her. He pulled over.

"Anna!" Lee rushed around the car and caught her. "What happened?"

"Oh, Lee!" Her words were muffled against his neck, but that was all she could say as he held her. He got her in his car, which was a wise move. She thought she could hear the faint sound of a siren.

Lee didn't ask any more questions as he turned the car around. She couldn't have answered them anyway. He drove while she controlled her emotions with Rusty whining from the back seat. They ended up stopping at a neighborhood park. As soon as he took the car out of gear, he turned in his seat.

"Honey, I can't stand seeing you so upset. Please, talk to me—tell me what happened."

Anna told him about what her dad had said and his threat about jail. But she wouldn't tell him about how her dad didn't think Lee was good enough for her. It was a despicable thing for him to have said. Lee didn't respond right away—he slowly ran his hand over her still-wet hair, much like he would do with his dog. Surprisingly, it calmed her.

Debra Erfert

"So he didn't give you your birth certificate," Lee said in a low voice.

Anna shook her head.

"Then we'll get it another way. Write in for a duplicate."

Anna sniffed. "I guess there's no other way, is there?"

"Maybe. Maybe not. If your parents filled it out at your birth and not your birth mother . . . I just don't know enough about this subject to give you any definite answers. I think you need to talk to an attorney."

"Good suggestion." Anna took his hand. "Would you let me go with you to see Homer Peabody?"

Lee leaned over and kissed Anna's cheek. "It's settled. We'll go together." He looked at the bag near her feet. "What're your plans now?"

"I couldn't stay there any longer, not after . . . I don't feel comfortable . . ." Anna dipped her head. How could she explain? Her feelings about her mother were jumbled. "You offered me your couch?"

He smiled. "For as long as you want it."

Anna let out a held breath. "Thanks." She glanced at Rusty. "Could we go by my house and measure that broken window? If you could nail up plywood until the glass guy can get there, I'd feel better."

"Anything you want." Lee put the car in gear and took off.

The ride over to her house went quickly. Anna didn't live far from her parents—her dad had made sure of that when he made the generous down payment as a wedding gift. At the time, Anna hadn't seen it as his being controlling, only loving. But now it seemed like he'd manipulated her into staying close. After she sold it, she would give him the money back.

When Lee turned down her cul-de-sac, the short street had a couple of fire engines, a rescue unit, and several police cars parked in front of her neighbor's house. Two paramedics were rolling a gurney up the walkway to the neighbor's front door.

A Strange Twist of Fate

"I hope Mrs. McCarthy is OK," Anna said as Lee pulled into her driveway.

"Mrs. McCarthy?"

"She's nearly eighty years old. I'd hate to think she fell and broke her hip or something." Anna opened her car door. "I don't know why the police would be here for that. I'm going to check on her, and see if her grandson needs help."

Lee followed her across the street. "Is he the kid who cuts your grass?"

"He's not exactly a kid. He's twenty-one." Anna walked across the street, with Lee staying next to her.

A uniformed police officer stopped them before they could enter the house. Lee, wearing jeans and a light gray button-down shirt, took out his wallet. The cop didn't look at Lee's off-duty badge but stared at Anna as he pinched the small microphone attached to his shirt and said something she didn't understand.

Lee froze. It seemed *he* understood what the officer said.

"What is it?" Anna asked in a whisper.

"I don't know." Lee finally slipped his wallet into his back pocket, then put his arm around her waist. "But he just called his sergeant."

Anna panicked. He called his supervisor after just looking at her. Did her dad have anything to do with it? "I think we should leave."

The sergeant came to the door. The officer nodded at Anna, and the sergeant's brows tightened when he saw her.

"Sergeant Melville," Lee said.

"Officer Adams," Melville said, briefly glancing at him.

"I'm a detective now with the Phoenix department," Lee told him.

Melville nodded, then returned his eyes to Anna. "Who are you?"

"This is Julianna Eddington." Lee held her closer. "She lives across the street. What happened here?"

Debra Erfert

"Is Mrs. McCarthy . . ." Anna couldn't finish her thought. If the police had been called, it was more than a broken hip.

Melville looked down at Lee's arm around her waist. "I read that you had a break-in a couple of nights ago."

"I did. Where is Mrs. McCarthy?" Anna asked louder.

"She's in the bedroom. The paramedics are with her. She's holding up."

Anna leaned against Lee. "Thank goodness."

"I think you should see this, Mrs. Eddington," Melville said. "Detective, you need to come with her. Follow me."

Lee kept his arm around Anna as they walked into the living room. The house smelled disgustingly pungent. Anna's heart started racing. Something grave had happened. When the sergeant led them into the kitchen, she saw the blood on the tile outside the door leading to the maid's quarters. Mrs. McCarthy only had a part-time housekeeper who came in twice a week, and not a live-in helper. Did the man she shot hide out here? Lee's arm tightened around her.

"This way. Watch where you step," Melville said as he entered the room.

"Oh, Lee," Anna whispered. She hesitated to follow the sergeant.

"Do you want to stay out here? I'll go in alone."

Anna couldn't let him go someplace that frightened her. It wouldn't be right. She straightened, deciding to follow the sergeant, even though her head told her to leave. "No. I'll go."

Lee released her and went in first, shielding her from the room as a whole. She kept her gaze on where he stepped. The repugnant odor grew stronger, and the blood wasn't confined to the tile floor—there were smears of it on the white wall, punctuated with handprints. She looked at Lee in an effort to keep from getting nauseated. He was staring across the room, next to the unmade queen-size bed positioned under the window. The blinds were closed, but an overhead light illuminated the room enough she

A Strange Twist of Fate

could see a small desk next to the bed, and the wall above it was papered with pictures of a woman with blonde hair.

Pictures of Anna.

There had to be a hundred photographs of various sizes, overlapping one another, some in color, others in washed-out black and white. Anna moved closer to the desk, where she saw her wedding picture—the one that had been in the newspaper. Her hand moved to her throat. She recognized most of them as ones that were taken at public events—they must've been downloaded off the Internet. But there were others of her shopping, coming out of the Salvation Army building, and taking bread to her contacts—and of her naked, drying off with a towel.

Anna screamed, feeling violated. She pressed her fist to her lips to keep from screaming again.

It was then that she heard Lee breathing hard. His mouth was pushed down in an angry frown, matching the dark storm of emotions in his eyes.

"Who lives in here?" Lee snapped at the sergeant.

"The homeowner's grandson, Travis Marley. Mrs. McCarthy told us she was out of town visiting his mother in Idaho for four days. When she came home this morning, she wanted to ask him if he'd go to church with her today. Evidently, Travis had been in trouble before. He had been released from Adobe Mountain six months prior.

Anna looked at Lee.

"Arizona juvenile correction facility," he said.

"Travis was stalking me. Where is he now?" Anna asked, afraid of what her answer would be, considering all the blood on the floor and wall. She'd shot an intruder. Was Travis the intruder?

"His grandmother found him in the bathroom—dead. In here," Melville said as he headed away from them.

Anna gasped, the realization hitting her like a stray bullet. "I shot Travis!"

"We'll compare the blood from your home with his," Melville stopped at the bathroom doorway. "But it would have to be a tremendous coincidence for there to be two nonrelated shooting incidents on the same cul-de-sac, and considering those pictures."

Lee slid his arm around Anna's waist and started to move after the sergeant. "I can't," Anna said, looking up at Lee. The frown on his lips didn't waver as he nodded. After another glance at the pictures, he walked around the bed and stopped next to the sergeant in the doorway of the bathroom. Anna stared at his face and tried not to imagine what he saw. Her insides tightened like an overwound rubber band.

Another man entered the bedroom. He had a badge attached to his belt and a camera in his hands. He obviously was a crime-scene investigator. Anna panicked—her pulse accelerating at the thought of the disgusting pictures being photographed for a report that anyone could see. She couldn't think—her heart raced too fast—but she could react. Anna grabbed the camera as he aimed it at the pictures and tried to pull it from the investigator's hands. "You can't do this!"

The man yanked it away and seized one of her wrists. "Back off—now!"

Anna reached for the camera with her free hand, but he was prepared and held it up out of her reach.

"Let her go!" Lee ran to her side. Moments later, he had her in his arms.

"Oh, Lee!" she cried.

Lee let her go and started ripping the nude pictures of her off the wall.

"Cut it out," the photographer told him, grabbing Lee's arm. Lee shoved him away.

"Stand down, Brackman," Melville said, rushing over to them. He placed himself between the two men. "How would you feel seeing those kinds of pictures pinned up of your girlfriend?"

Brackman stared at Lee as he continued to pluck the last few pictures off the wall. "He's destroying evidence, Serge."

A Strange Twist of Fate

Melville shrugged. "He's only taking the ones that he doesn't want memorialized in your report. It ultimately won't change the outcome."

Lee took Anna's arm. "Let's go."

He didn't wait for her to agree before he started walking them toward the kitchen and guided her through the house. She didn't argue. Staying would mean having to explain to Mrs. McCarthy that she had killed her grandson.

Lee didn't let her go until after they were outside by his car and he needed his free hand to get his dog out of the back seat. Anna took all of her bags inside her house, since, evidently, it was safe for her to move back home.

Anna dropped her things next to the couch and went to stand by the window overlooking the backyard. She shivered as gooseflesh coursed over her skin. Travis had taken pictures of her through her bedroom window—her privacy had been completely invaded. He'd followed her to the grocery store, and she had never noticed. That would change. Anna would pay closer attention to who was around her.

"I guess I need to find someone else to mow my—" Anna choked, and a sob preceded tears. Lee was right there, wrapping her in his arms, letting her cry on his shoulder. "I . . . I didn't mean to . . ." She took in a shaky breath. "I didn't mean to kill Travis. I'm so sorry!"

"I know, honey. I know," Lee said quietly.

It took a while before Anna could stop crying. How long was long enough when you ended someone's life? When her energy had depleted, she leaned heavily against Lee.

"Am I going to be charged for this?" Anna asked.

"Honestly?" Lee let up on his tight embrace enough to look into her eyes. "I don't know."

Anna's heart jumped in fright.

"But what I can tell you," Lee said as he moved her to the couch and coaxed her to sit beside him, "is that all the evidence shows he was stalking you, and he broke into your home, and you shot to protect yourself. And they found a knife by his body. You are innocent of any crime."

"A knife!" She leaned against his chest. "But just the same, I should talk to Homer Peabody about this, too."

"I'd say that's a safe thing to do," Lee said as he swept some of her hair off her face. "I take it you're not moving in with me."

"Lee, I wasn't really moving in with you."

"A man can dream, can't he?"

Anna let out a heavy sigh. "You know, I thought it might've been Razor who broke in."

"Yeah, he was a good suspect."

"I wonder where he is."

"Do you really care?"

"He beat up Claudia. I'd like to see him in jail for that."

"There's still a warrant out for his arrest for pulling a knife on you. That won't go away. I promise you, we'll get him. I go back to work in the morning. I'll take backup with me, and we'll break down his door to see if he's hiding from us there."

Anna reached for Rusty's head and gave it a good scratch. He'd stayed by Anna's legs since she sat down. "I bet that's where he is. Or at his cousin's house in Tempe."

"You have an address?"

"Yes."

"Of course you do," Lee whispered with his lips brushing above her eyebrow. He then kissed her cheek before moving his mouth down her neck. "You're amazing."

Gooseflesh raced across Anna's skin, coursing out from where his lips touched. "Lee," she whispered.

"You're not kissing me," he said softly as he pulled at the neckline of her T-shirt and kissed the curve of her throat.

"What did you do with those pictures?" Anna asked.

He lifted his head. "Uh . . ."

"You still have them?"

A Strange Twist of Fate

Lee let go of her T-shirt and sat back. "I do." He reached into his back pocket and retrieved the dozen photos. "Would you like to burn them or shred them?"

Anna held out her hand. "I think I might do both."

Debra Erfert

Seventeen

Anna stretched her arms up over her head, completely rested after sleeping through the night in her bed for the first time since Greg died. Lee and Rusty had slept in the guest room that had the broken window. She imagined Lee lying on his stomach, his arm hanging over the bed, with his hand on his dog. Lee craved the physical contact, but so did she.

Anna got up to check if he'd left for his apartment to change for work. When she saw the bedroom empty, she continued into the living room. It was empty, too. Actually, she was glad he was gone. She had a few hours before they were to meet at Homer's office, and she had made up her mind last night that she would buy some new clothes. Truthfully, when Anna had looked over the pictures Lee took off Travis's wall, before she had shredded them, she had to admit that she didn't look fat, only curvy. All she had to do was find the right clothes to fit her body type.

Anna had a good reason to buy some properly fitting outfits. She wanted to apply to the police department, and while she didn't have an actual work résumé, the PD human resources department could certainly tell her how to go about starting the application process. Making a decent impression was a good idea. Anna showered after making sure the doors were locked and all the blinds were tightly turned down. Instead of wearing her hair in her usual ponytail, she used a blow-dryer and a round brush to style it. She felt prettier just with that small effort.

~*~

Lee had taken his dog to work with him. He didn't feel comfortable leaving him in an apartment for the next ten hours, and his sergeant didn't have a problem with him bringing his dog—as long as it wasn't a permanent situation.

A Strange Twist of Fate

Lee ran a hand down the back of his head. He needed a haircut. Tonight, he wanted to take Anna out for a romantic dinner. Hopefully, he could get away from work a little early to get that haircut and change into something more casual.

Two light taps came at his closed door.

"Come in," Lee said loudly.

David Curtis, his ex-cop friend who was now an assistant prosecutor, stepped inside his office, carrying a messenger bag. Rusty lopped over to him with his head low and tail wagging.

"Hey, puppy," David said, rubbing the dog's head.

"David." Lee came from around his desk with Rusty's leash and quickly clipped it to his collar. "What's up?"

David closed the door. "You wanted me to check into the cases Greg left open." He moved to Lee's desk and took a laptop out of his bag. "At the time Mrs. Eddington questioned me about them, I frankly figured she was being hysterical. After you talked to me about the same thing, I got curious."

He pulled up a chair, sat down, and opened his computer while Lee stood behind him, watching as his friend logged on.

"I knew the dispositions of the cases that landed on my desk—I told you that." David brought up a spreadsheet. "But I honestly had no idea what happened to the others. I wasn't worried until I got through looking at the first dozen Kenneth Baker was assigned, and then"—David tapped his finger on the screen—"look at that."

Lee studied the spreadsheet. "They all received probation."

David sat back. "Yes, just like what Mrs. Eddington suspected. But look closer."

Lee leaned in, scrutinizing the other columns. David had done considerable work putting all the important information together. Next to each perp's name was the arrest date, the bail amount, if the perp had been released, and who put up the bail if the perp was released. There was a column for the public defender's name and one for the judge.

"Is this a mistake?" Lee tapped the screen. "You have Judge JoAnn Clarkson on every one."

Debra Erfert

David took some file folders out of his briefcase and gave them to Lee. "Check them yourself."

Lee took the files and sat behind his desk. The cover sheet gave all the important information upon closing out each case. It didn't take him very long to go through all twenty-two cases. A single judge had given each perp a walk.

"Are you going to tell Mrs. Eddington about this?" David asked.

"I'm sure she'll be interested in who might've benefited by Greg being killed, as evidently everyone here did." Lee looked over the list again. "Can I borrow these for a while? I'd like to study them. I'll need to cross-check them with vehicle registration."

"Looking for that infamous dark pickup truck." David stood and closed his laptop before putting it back into his messenger bag. "Sure, but I'll need them back. I took them out of Main Filing."

Three taps came at the door a moment before it opened and Officer Martinez leaned inside, grinning. "Lee, a hottie says she's here looking for her detective boyfriend." His brows rose. "That can't possibly be you since I happen to know you're married."

Lee sighed louder than he had intended. "We're divorcing, Lito."

His grin slackened. "Yeah, I heard. Sorry, man." He nodded toward the report room. "You better get out here before Esperanza moves in on your new woman."

Lee put the short stack of manila files into his desk drawer, then followed Lito and David out of his office. The only people in the report room, though, were Officer Esperanza and his new trainee.

"Anna?" Lee called, looking around.

"If you're looking for the blonde," Esperanza said, sitting behind a computer, "she went into the ladies' restroom to, uh, powder her nose."

Lee nodded and then went to wait outside the restroom door. They had made a date to meet at Homer's office, not at his, although he was happy she came. Frankly, he thought she'd tagged

A Strange Twist of Fate

him her boyfriend just to get him inside Christina Bush's house to find out who killed Frank Morrison. Since she still continued to call him that, he got the feeling she wasn't kidding. Lee liked that idea. More than liked it, actually.

A couple of minutes later, a woman came out. She was blonde, but it wasn't Anna, so he didn't pay her attention. He was tempted to look inside. If Esperanza had hurt her feelings, then he'd pound the wolfish cop until he regretted it.

"Is Detective Adams still in his office?" the blonde asked Esperanza.

Lee stood upright when he heard Anna's voice. The blonde had been her? But she didn't have blue jeans on, or her husband's baggy T-shirt, or a ponytail. The blue, knee-length skirt and the jacket she wore fit her perfectly, hugging her waist and her every shapely curve. Her pretty blonde hair flowed in waves around her shoulders.

"He's right there," Esperanza said, smiling and nodding toward Lee.

Anna turned around. Lee's heart flipped. She was more beautiful than in the photographs her mother had destroyed or the pictures pinned to the dead man's wall. Anna had artfully used makeup to enhance her natural features, and the diamond earrings she wore sparkled against her skin. When she smiled, Lee felt as if his fast-beating heart would burst out of his ribs.

"Hi," Anna said, walking over to him. "I'm sorry for interrupting your work, but I came by HR to start my application process, so I thought we could ride over to Homer's together."

"She's applying for patrol?" Esperanza said, smiling. "I'll probably be her field training officer."

Lee's first thought was to pound him again, but for a different reason. Esperanza obviously couldn't hurt her feelings, not with the gorgeous way she looked, but he most assuredly would hit on her. Esperanza had gone through two wives in four years, and as far as Lee knew, he was currently dating several women at the same time.

Debra Erfert

"Are you ready to head out?" Anna asked, ignoring the officer's statement.

"I need to get Rusty." Lee quickly went back into his office and found Rusty had made himself comfortable enough on the couch to fall asleep. Lee took the end of the leash. "Come on, boy. Let's go see Anna."

Rusty jumped down and rushed to the door, tugging him along straight to Anna. He had to wonder if the dog had caught her scent. Lee had when she walked past him, then again when she stepped near him. The perfume she wore was so intoxicating that if the four other guys hadn't been watching, he would've kissed her neck, taking in a deeper breath of that heady scent.

"Hey, Rusty. You're such a good boy," Anna cooed, leaning down and scratching under his chin. He, in returned, licked her across her mouth, making her giggle. Yeah, his *dog* got to kiss her.

"Do you want to get lunch after we meet with Mr. Peabody?" Lee asked Anna while rubbing Rusty's shoulder. He took in another inconspicuous breath of Anna's perfume while he was close enough. When she smiled, his pulse sped up again.

"That sounds great." Anna straightened. "I was in such a hurry this morning that I missed breakfast." She pressed her hand on her stomach. "I'm hungry."

"This way." Lee held out his hand to Anna. "My car is parked out back."

"OK." After she tugged on the hem of her jacket, she fell in step with Lee out into the parking lot.

Lee looked around. They were alone when they stopped next to his car. He took full advantage of their isolation and pulled Anna against his body, dropping his face to her neck. "You smell delicious," he murmured against her skin.

"I thought you'd like it," Anna whispered. "Shouldn't we be going?"

After he quickly kissed her neck once, he released his grip on her. "You're probably right." Lee smiled. "The faster I get my divorce settled, the quicker I get to give you a real kiss."

A Strange Twist of Fate

Anna got in the car and smoothed her hand over her skirt. "I never actually said I would kiss you."

Lee had already swung the door closed just as he heard what she'd said. He stood staring at her through the window. Did she mean it, after all the times he'd kissed her face and her neck? He could tell she enjoyed every sensation he'd given her. At least he thought she had. He'd felt her press against his body. Could he have been mistaken? When she lifted her face to him, the grin suggested she'd only joked, and when she winked at him, he knew for sure. He shook his head. She was teasing.

A deep sense of love filled his quick-beating heart. How could he fall for a woman so fast, especially one who wouldn't let him truly kiss her? In reality, he wanted to do more than just kiss her, but he knew that wouldn't happen before he had a ring on her finger.

His heart thudded. He *was* actually thinking that far ahead.

Anna opened the door. "Is something wrong?"

Lee shook his head. "No, no. I was just . . . thinking," he said with a grin.

~*~

The meeting with Homer Peabody had put Anna in a foul mood. It had gone all right for Lee. Anna was sure that his divorce papers would be drawn up and signed before the Wednesday deadline he'd promised that morning, but when Anna had told him about the break-in and subsequent killing of her neighbor, he brought in his younger associate to act as her criminal defense attorney. Homer would be there for her if Travis's family decided to sue her for wrongful death. She couldn't afford even a settlement without insurance. And paying Homer as well as his associate would probably drain her savings account and take what money she'd get from the sale of her home. She'd find out after the inquest if she would have any criminal charges pressed against her.

When she got around to telling Homer that she had been adopted and that her dad refused to hand over her birth certificate, and for that matter, that he wouldn't actually admit that she had been adopted, he'd suggested hiring a private investigator—another drain on her shrinking recourses. He had two he trusted, and he would set his best man, who happened to be a woman, to task immediately. Anna had stolen her mother's blood to get her type, and now a stranger would be digging into their past, finding out everything, good or bad. Anna's mood fluxed between hopeful and very foul.

Lee had gone back to work after lunch, taking Rusty with him. For a few moments, Anna had seriously thought about asking if she could keep the dog with her, for companionship. But she knew how much he loved Rusty, and she thought better of it.

After Anna had changed into jeans and a pretty shirt—that fit—she found the perfect place down the block from Mary Beth Gaines's house to do surveillance. Slumping low in the seat so that she wouldn't be seen, Anna watched the house with the gray Toyota Corolla parked at the curb. Mary Beth, widowed for nearly ten years, had two sons in their thirties, Wade and Jeremy, both with lengthy criminal histories. They, most likely, were the "white dudes" Harold saw ripping off the alley's copper grounding cords. Now she just had to wait long enough to see if Jeremy drove a late-model, dark blue Ford F-150 with a black metal cage over the cab and bed. Harold gave her that information. If the information was good, she owed Harold, big time.

The dark truck hadn't been in the driveway when she first pulled up, but that didn't discourage Anna. She might have to come back several times before finding them. She was a patient woman—most of the time. But not today. In need of a distraction while she waited, she took her phone out of her purse and sent Lee a text. They'd had lunch at a very nice restaurant—a very date type of lunch. When he had walked her to her car, she had very nearly kissed him before getting into the driver's seat. The impulse had flustered and angered her at the same time. It wasn't fair that his scheming soon-to-be ex-wife would try to get a hold of his retirement. In doing so, she kept him from his divorce, and in turn, she kept Anna from a real kiss. Anna wanted lip-on-lip contact

A Strange Twist of Fate

from Lee. She kept Wednesday in mind as the target date while she sent her text.

So what are you doing Wednesday?

Lee responded immediately. *Signing papers in Homers office.*

Want to come over to my house for dinner?

What r u cooking?

Anna frowned. Her impatient mood didn't improve as she'd hoped. *Does it matter?*

Just wanted to know if I can bring anything.

That did make Anna feel better, and she smiled. *You allergic to shrimp?*

Love it.

Scampi?

Is that made with onions and garlic?

Steak it is.

lol! Lee texted back.

A car's engine pulled her attention to the road behind her, and she slumped a little farther down as a deep-blue Ford pickup drove by her with two dark-haired men inside. Anna's heart raced when she saw the black metal cage over the cab and bed that held an extendable wooden ladder on the driver's side. The bed was covered with a tan tarp, but it was bulging high with something. Every detail Harold had described just backed into Mary Beth Gaines's driveway.

Anna had only one problem with the truck—it was in rough shape, and she didn't get a good look at the passenger side as it drove by to see if there was any white from Greg's Cherokee transferred onto the blue paint. And when they backed into the driveway, she couldn't see it from the sidewalk, nor did she get a picture of the truck's license plate. OK, that was four problems—five if she wanted to get a picture of the contents under the tarp. If Harold was right, then it was full of stolen copper grounding cords, and he would be a hero.

Excitement percolated inside Anna as she slung her purse strap over her head, settling it on her shoulder. She wanted her gun close, but she needed her hands free to use her phone's camera to send a picture to Lee.

Anna took several pictures while she waited beside her car as the two men got out of the truck. They went to the tailgate and talked as she took two more pictures. They were too far away for her to hear what they were saying. They laughed and went through the carport door, disappearing inside the house.

Now was her chance. Anna sprinted across the street, staying low the closer she got, like Lee had done at Christina's mom's house. When she got to the end of the driveway, she took another picture of the front of the truck before she moved to the passenger's side facing away from the house. Once there, she took several pictures as she moved toward the tailgate, not stopping to review them. Anna had to make it quick, but she did take the time to look at the body damage the truck had along the front quarter panel, door, and back quarter panel. She didn't see white color transfer in the obvious damage it had, but any logically thinking bad guy would've buffed that off. They'd had a year.

Anna's heart nearly stopped. Greg died a year ago—today. She'd forgotten about the anniversary. She'd forgotten about her husband. The anticipation she'd felt a moment ago turned to explicit sadness. What were the chances that she'd found his killer a year to the date he'd died? Anna stayed low, making her way to the tailgate. The high mound under the tarp kept her hidden from anybody looking out from inside the house.

The ends of the tarp were tucked inside the edges of the truck's bed. Anna didn't see any tie-downs. Using one hand, she grabbed a fold and yanked up. The tarp loosened, and she was able to pull up a section over the wound copper cable. Harold was right! She yanked again and exposed more.

Anna stepped back far enough to get the whole back of the truck in one picture, including the license plate and copper cable. She sent it to Lee in a text as she rushed back along the side of the truck, staying as low as she could. When she neared the sidewalk, she heard the house door in the carport open, and Jeremy Gaines

A Strange Twist of Fate

looked between Anna and the back of his truck. She'd left the tarp up and the copper exposed. His angry gaze sent her running across the street to her car.

"What the hell—*stop!*" Gaines yelled, stepping out into the carport.

"Not a chance," Anna said, jumping into her car. With a touch of a button on the dash, she started the car. Her phone rang at the same time—her Bluetooth switched it to her car's radio. After she shifted into gear, she touched the Connect button.

"Anna, where are you?" Lee asked.

Anna floored the accelerator, and the Impala's engine roared. "I'm leaving Mary Beth Gaines's house in Avondale." Both brothers jumped in their truck as she passed the driveway. They were coming after her.

"Why didn't you tell me you were going to do a stakeout? I would've come with you."

"I may be in trouble." Anna saw the truck skid as it came out of the driveway.

"What is it?"

"I think the Gaines brothers saw me taking pictures of their truck, and they're chasing me." Anna took the corner onto South Avondale Boulevard, with the brothers only a car's length behind her.

"Where are you, exactly?" She could hear Lee's voice warble, like he was running.

"About a block away from West Buckeye Road, coming back to Phoenix."

"I'm headed your way."

Anna glanced in the review mirror. They'd caught up with her. She screamed as the truck slammed into her back bumper. A moment later, bullets pierced her back window and windshield at the same time, missing her by inches and leaving the safety glass shattered around the holes.

"Anna!" Lee shouted. "What happened?"

Debra Erfert

She swerved onto West Buckeye Road without slowing down and stood on the gas. "They shot at me!"

"Are you hit?"

"No." Anna wove around the cars in front of her, using the left turning lane. "Lee, help me!"

"I'm on my way, and I'm having backup called. They'll get to you before I can, honey. Just keep heading toward me—keep talking to me."

Anna glanced in the rearview mirror. Jeremy kept his truck hanging off her back bumper. "I can't lose them!"

"Help is coming," Lee told her.

Panic set in when she sped toward an intersection. The light was red, but stopping was out of the question. And she didn't want to get off Buckeye Road, either. That would be the only way for Lee to find her, for him to send her help. As she neared the intersection, the green turn arrow came on. Anna snaked through the cars, blaring her horn. She made it without hitting anyone.

The middle turning lane was empty, and Anna took advantage of that, speeding her way east toward Phoenix and hoping a cop would see her. Another impact from behind sent her into the fast lane. Jeremy pulled up next to her. Anna looked up and saw Wade reach his arm out his window, aiming a gun at her. She flinched away, knowing what would happen next. Loud bangs sounded. Holes popped in the driver's window. She screamed in pain as bullets struck her. She turned the steering wheel hard left, slamming her Impala into the truck, pushing it away from her. They bounced away from each other. The brothers careened into oncoming traffic. Her car slid off the road, landing in a shallow drainage ditch, making the airbags explode.

"Lee . . ." Anna's phone had fallen from her hand during the crash, and the dashboard had been shot, taking out her car's Bluetooth connection. She needed to get away before the brothers came back. She still had her purse over her body, with her gun hidden inside. Her left arm was useless—her ears were ringing, and

A Strange Twist of Fate

she was dizzy. Using her right hand, she opened her door and crawled out. She heard tires squealing, and she panicked.

Debra Erfert

Eighteen

Lee had been waiting for backup to serve the search warrant and break down Bivens's door when Anna had sent the picture. The officers had arrived at the same time she told him she was in trouble. Lee had one officer call the emergency into dispatch while they headed her way with lights and sirens, and he followed them. The information Anna had sent him was relayed over the police radio. Every officer would be on the lookout for that dark blue truck.

His heart sank as he'd listened to Anna being pursued. He heard gunshots a heartbeat before the line went dead. Lee had to concentrate on his driving to keep from panicking, listening to the emergency traffic coming over the radio. Civilians were calling 911 about a car chase and shooting, then a crash.

Dispatch confirmed that Tolleson police officers had arrived on the scene. The ten minutes it took him to get there seemed like an eternity. The road was backed up. He and his officers drove on the shoulder the last two miles. When Lee pulled to a stop behind a Tolleson police car, he saw Anna's crashed Impala sitting at an angle in a shallow ditch. The driver's door was open, and he ran over to it. Bullet holes punctured the door and windows. The seat had blood on it. Her phone was on the floor by the brake pedal. Lee grabbed it and turned around, looking for her.

A Tolleson police officer stood near his cruiser. Lee and his backup rushed over to him. "Where is Mrs. Eddington?"

Officer Kidrich shook his head. "The car was empty when we got here."

A Strange Twist of Fate

"Empty?" Lee looked at her phone. She'd never leave it willingly. "Anna!" he yelled. "Anna!" The dread he'd held at bay surfaced. The men who'd shot her must've taken her.

He heard a faint sneeze.

"Anna?" Lee couldn't tell where it came from or if it had been a woman who sneezed—or if he had heard it at all. The traffic had been blocked off, so it was quiet enough he could hear—barking. He had an idea. Lee rushed to his car and opened the back door. He said, "Rusty, go find Anna. Go find Anna! Go!"

Rusty darted from the back seat and ran straight to her car. Lee followed, watching as the dog whined and sniffed around the bloody front seat and then the ground.

"Get Anna," Lee told him again.

Rusty didn't lift his nose from the ground as he headed through the ditch, then into the citrus grove. Lee, along with the two Phoenix officers and the two Tolleson officers, chased after his dog, running through the trees until Rusty came to a stop.

Lee dropped to his knees next to his dog. They found Anna, lying on her side. The back of her shirt was saturated with blood. Blood soaked her hair against her head. "Get paramedics here!" he shouted at the Tolleson officer.

"I've got them on the way," Kidrich said. "Watch it—she's holding a gun!"

The officer was right—she had her Walther in her right fist. She was half lying on it, but she'd had it out, ready to protect herself. Lee gently took it and handed it to Kidrich, who dropped the mag and ejected the round in the chamber.

"Lee . . ." Anna groaned.

He leaned in closer to her face. Her eyes were half-open. "I'm here, honey. I'm here."

"Kiss . . . me." Her words were barely audible.

Lee looked at her trembling lips. She must be in shock. He took off his jacket and covered her shoulders. He couldn't understand why she would want him to kiss her now—here.

She groaned again. "Hurry . . . a real kiss."

Debra Erfert

Why was she in a hurry? A horrible thought occurred to him, and he got angry with her. "You are not dying. Do you hear me?" Lee kissed her cheek and told her, "You will not die. You have to be OK—for me. Please, please, live for me. I need you!"

Lee lifted his head to see what reaction his declaration had on Anna, but her eyes were closed, her face slack and pale. "Anna? Anna!" He looked up at the officers. "Where are those paramedics?" he shouted at them, like it would stop her from bleeding to death.

"They're here, Lee," one of his Phoenix officers said, kneeling down next to him. "You'll need to give them room."

Lee didn't move away from Anna until two firefighter paramedics knelt beside her. He'd seen them work before, rescuing trapped motorists or working on sick people. But he never would've imagined seeing someone he loved having her clothes cut away and IVs inserted into both of her arms. She'd been shot in the leg, too.

"She has AB positive blood," Lee told them as he picked up her discarded purse from the ground. "Make sure the doctors know that."

One of the paramedics looked up at him. "We will, Detective."

"Where're you taking her?"

"To John C. Lincoln. They handle level-one traumas."

Her wounds were covered, and she had a heavy blanket put over her body and an oxygen mask over her nose and mouth before she was rolled into the back of the rescue unit. All Lee could do was stand, watch, and worry.

"Detective Adams, the suspects' truck was spotted on the 85 going south toward Gila Bend," Kidrich said, giving him Anna's Walther and magazine. "Three DPS units are in pursuit."

~*~

The truck had been stopped by the time Lee reached the DPS line. A highway patrol officer stood behind his opened driver's door taking command of the scene. Lee instantly recognized Lieutenant Hargrove. It seemed the Ford had run out of gas, but

A Strange Twist of Fate

neither man would listen to orders to get out with their hands up. Considering there were highway patrol cars parked on both sides of them, plus a helicopter flying overhead, the men must've known they couldn't hold out forever. Still, they were armed, and Lee knew every officer planned on going home alive.

"So what now?" Lee asked the lieutenant.

Lieutenant Hargrove glanced at Lee while twisting open a bottle of water. "We could wait them out." He took a long drink and then said, "But I prefer to gas them out, especially after they shot a judge's daughter. I have SWAT on the way."

Two minutes later, a heavily armored truck lumbered to a stop beside the lieutenant's car. The back opened up, and six men outfitted with ballistic shielding jumped down, carrying automatic rifles with gas-grenade launchers secured above the sights.

"LT," Jones said, nodding at Hargrove. "Any movement?"

"They're still in the truck. I'll try one more time to reason with them, and then it's your turn." Hargrove picked up the mic from the seat of his cruiser and leaned his arm on top of the open door. "Attention in the truck. Throw out your weapons, and put your hands out the window. This is your last chance."

Hargrove waited a few moments and then shrugged. "I guess we do this the hard way," he said, turning to the black-clad men.

"Do you mind if I try?" Lee asked, holding out his hand.

Hargrove sighed. "If it will make you feel better." He gave Lee the mic to the car's loudspeaker.

He'd had an idea, thanks to the personal information Anna told him about the brothers. Knowing both men lived at home gave Lee an edge. He cleared his throat and said, "I just wanted to let you know—I called your mother."

Hargrove snorted a laugh.

"Mary Beth is on her way here now. Do you really want her to see her sons get tear gassed? And if that happens, what next? Are you going to shoot it out with your mother watching?" Lee paused for a few moments to let them think. He lifted the mic to his mouth again, but he didn't get to speak before he saw a gun tossed from the passenger window and hands being held out both sides of the truck.

"You gotta be kidding," Hargrove said softly, then louder, "Go! Go!"

With guns and rifles raised, the SWAT officers approached the truck. In seconds, the two men were on the ground being handcuffed.

"You a hostage negotiator now?" Hargrove asked Lee.

Lee shook his head. "No, still a detective. It was just a hunch. I need to question Jeremy Gaines in connection with Assistant Prosecutor Gregory Eddington's possible murder."

Hargrove seethed, "It was him?" He swung his head at the truck again. "A dark pickup truck. Mrs. Eddington was right—all this time?"

"And now she may be dying." Lee's chest hurt. Was she dead already? He should've kissed her, like she asked.

"We'll take those two to DPS headquarters on West Encanto Boulevard. Meet us there. I'll get you your interview, and I'll be in there with you."

Lee didn't drive straight to their headquarters. He had to stop by the hospital. Inside the emergency room, he found the nurses' station, where he caught the attention of a young woman in paisley scrubs.

"I'm Detective Lee Adams, and I'm looking for Julianna Eddington. She was brought in a half hour ago."

The nurse's gaze went up to a large clear acrylic board suspended over the counter that had a grid drawn on it with names written down several columns. Lee saw *Eddington* printed next to *Sg3 Luke*.

"She's been taken into surgery, Detective."

Lee breathed deeply. "She's still alive."

"Yes, sir."

He nodded. "Dr. Luke is her surgeon?"

"He is."

Lee kept nodding. "And after she comes out of surgery?"

A Strange Twist of Fate

"She'll be taken into ICU."

"OK," Lee nodded again, taking in another deep breath. "If I'm not here yet and she asks for Lee Adams, tell her I'll be back very soon."

The nurse smiled. "I'll remember, Detective Adams."

Anna had put her life on the line trying to get information on her husband's killer, and Lee planned on following it up. By now, Jeremy Gaines should be sitting in an interrogation room. Lee took out Anna's phone. He'd need to do some reading before that interview.

The smartphone probably had a security code he'd need to figure out before he could get into it. Lee touched the button on the bottom, and the screen lit up with a picture of Greg Eddington. He pressed the button again to get the number pad. Now all Lee needed to do was crack her security code. Would she use her address? He inputted *3546*. The phone shook. He tapped in the current year. It shook again. Two tries down. What if she used letters instead of numbers? Anna had Greg's picture as the first thing she saw when she used her phone. Lee smiled and inputted *GREG*, and the first page of app icons appeared.

Lee leaned against the wall and started scrolling through a note application. Each name was alphabetized. Gaines was just below Eddington. Out of curiosity, Lee opened the Eddington file. The information held there was a copy of Greg Eddington's DPS final report stating their findings—the March 10 crash was an apparent accident, with the driver of a dark-colored pickup truck leaving the scene of the crash. No suspects.

"March tenth?" Lee took in a fast breath. That was today's date. Anna hadn't told him it had been a year since her husband died. His heart sank. Something that important and she didn't want to share it with him. Truthfully, he had been crowding her with his time, even insisting that he stay with her last night, not letting her be alone or even asking if she wanted his company. He'd used the excuse of being worried about her safety with the broken window. And although she accepted his lunch invitation readily enough and acted like she enjoyed being with him, he couldn't understand why she would keep something so important quiet. Unless . . . she felt she needed to keep up a wall around her heart that Lee wasn't allowed to breach.

Lee took off to the DPS Headquarters, determined to find the answers to Anna's husband's case, and then he'd check on her condition before giving her some time and space while she recuperated.

Lee showed the clerk at the front desk his badge. She buzzed him through a secure door. The clerk also gave him directions to the interrogation rooms, where he found Lieutenant Hargrove sitting at a desk behind a computer, typing.

"It's about time you showed up, Detective," Hargrove said without looking up at him or stopping his typing. "How's Mrs. Eddington doing?"

Lee sank onto the plastic chair next to Hargrove, exhaling loudly. "She's alive."

Hargrove dropped his hands to the edge of the desk and slowly nodded. "That's everything with shooting victims."

Looking around at the closed doors, Lee asked, "Have you mirandized Jeremy Gaines yet?"

The lieutenant shook his head. "I didn't, but he asked for a lawyer already."

"Did you call one for him?"

"No. Don't plan on it until you've had time with him." Hargrove smiled. "I figure you can talk *at* him all you want, as long as you don't ask him any questions."

Lee shook his head as he took out his wallet, where he kept a copy of the Miranda Rights. "I need to ask questions. First, could you print out Jeremy Gaines's criminal arrest history? It might be useful. Where is he?"

Hargrove hit a few keys on the computer, and a moment later, Lee heard the sound of a printer. "Follow me," he said, standing up.

A Strange Twist of Fate

Before coming to the DPS Headquarters, Lee had read through what few notes Anna had on Jeremy and Wade Gaines. It wasn't much—not as much as Lee thought there would be anyway. Besides the personal information such as addresses and birth dates, she had uploaded Jeremy's last arrest report and the outcome of the case. He'd finished serving three months in city jail for disorderly conduct six months before Eddington had died.

Lee secured his gun in the same locker where Hargrove stored his. It was standard procedure not to take weapons in during an interview. The moment he stepped inside the room behind the lieutenant, he got angry, being near the man who shot his girlfriend. The man was two years younger than Lee, according to the report uploaded on Anna's phone, yet his skin was darkly tanned and weathered, making him look older by several years. She had told him that Jeremy Gaines worked in construction. The well-developed muscles in his shoulders and arms testified to his heavy lifting for a living.

Gaines hadn't bothered looking up. He'd kept his gaze steady on the table in front of him. He sat slumped in the plastic chair bolted to the floor, his wrists handcuffed to loops of metal protruding from both the sides of the chair.

Lee quietly read him his rights. Those familiar words got his attention, and his eyes glared up, first at Lee, then at Lieutenant Hargrove, as his jaw worked out.

"Do you understand your rights as I have read them?" Lee asked the man.

Gaines didn't say anything, but the muscles in his jaw popped again.

Lee nodded while he put the little card back into his wallet. "Well, you do have the right to remain silent." As he replaced his wallet in his back pocket, he said, "But you being silent isn't going to take back those bullets you put into Mrs. Eddington, the daughter of a superior court judge—"

"That wasn't me," Gaines said quickly.

Debra Erfert

Lee looked into the eyes of a man who'd basically laid the crime on the back of his brother—except in Arizona, all parties involved in a felony where a death occurred were just as guilty as the one who did the shooting—not that Anna was going to die, he had to remind himself. But Gaines might not know that law—yet.

"We have the gun," Lee told him. "We'll have fingerprints."

Gaines leaned his head back and grinned. "Then you'll see."

Lee looked at Hargrove. "Were there any gloves in the truck?"

"Yeah, leather work gloves," the lieutenant said, crossing his arms over his chest.

"Hmmm . . ." Lee walked over to the wall and leaned his back against it. "So we wouldn't know for sure who fired the shots that sent Mrs. Eddington into the ditch."

"But I was driving," Gaines said quickly, sitting up straight. "I couldn't have shot her."

"He might have something," Hargrove said, nodding.

"Like I said." Gaines relaxed in his chair again.

Lee thought he'd go to the reason Anna was in surgery—her husband's death. "From the sound of it, you're not very loyal to your brother. I'm surprised you'd go so far as to drive your truck into Greg Eddington's Cherokee last year."

Gaines's face didn't seem to register what Lee had said. He tried to say it in a different way. "We have your truck, Mr. Gaines, and we'll be looking for any trace of paint transfer from when you pushed Assistant Prosecutor Gregory Eddington off Interstate 17, sending him crashing down into the Bloody Basin canyon. His body was unrecognizable."

Gaines pulled at his restraints. "You think I had something to do with Eddington's crash?"

"He's quick," Hargrove said to Lee. The sarcasm was obvious.

Gaines shook his head, looking between Lee and the lieutenant. "I didn't have anything to do with that."

"It had to be you—your brother was still in prison. Can't argue with the judicial system." He pushed up from the wall and rushed over to the table. "Out of revenge, you got rid of the man

A Strange Twist of Fate

responsible for sending your brother to prison, and now you drove the truck so your brother could shoot his wife, the judge's daughter. You committed attempted murder. And if she dies? That's murder!"

"No way, man! I'm not going down for that. That was Wade, not me!"

Lee slapped his hands down on the table. "But you pushed Greg Eddington off that interstate, killing him! Admit it!"

"It wasn't me." Jeremy rattled his handcuffs.

"Wade couldn't have driven that truck. His butt was sitting in prison, doing the time Eddington had given him. And you were willing to speed alongside Mrs. Eddington in order for Wade to shoot her, just to keep your stolen copper safe—it's not a far leap from that to vehicular homicide."

Knocking at the door preceded its opening, and an officer leaned in with papers in her hand. "LT, you were waiting for this?"

"Thanks." Hargrove took the pages and started reading.

Lee straightened. "The death sentence will be on the table if Mrs. Eddington dies, Gaines. Either way, you'll never breathe free air again."

"Adams, take a look at this," Hargrove said.

He looked away from Jeremy's blushed face to the lieutenant handing Lee the report. After quickly reading the top page, he frowned. "You were arrested March fifth for aggravated assault with a deadly weapon five days before Greg Eddington's car went down the canyon. Your mother bailed you out three days before the crash." Lee slammed the report down on the table in front of him. "You didn't do it for your brother—you murdered the prosecutor for yourself. We have the truck you were driving and the remains of Eddington's Jeep. Right now our forensics team is hard at work finding paint transfer, if not on your truck then on Eddington's car."

Jeremy swallowed hard, and his shoulders slumped. "I want a lawyer."

Debra Erfert

"At this point, Gaines, you don't have anyone to help you, so why not just tell us the truth?"

The man kept his eyes on the report lying on the table, his jaw flexing. "I don't have to tell you anything. Where's my lawyer?"

It didn't sound like they'd get an easy confession. No matter. They had the physical evidence now to keep both of the brothers permanently off the street. Anna got shot getting that evidence—she might even have given her life to catch them.

A Strange Twist of Fate

Nineteen

"She's still unconscious," Clarisse said softly.

Lee had a friendly association with the nurse from when he'd been in patrol and she worked in the Phoenix ER; otherwise, he didn't stand a chance of seeing Anna. He looked through the window into the small room where she lay quietly on a bed, hooked up to a monitor. She had IV tubes running into her right arm from two bags hanging from near the head of her bed—one clear and one red. The plastic tube running across her cheeks and under her nose had to be oxygen.

"Why isn't she awake yet?" Lee asked.

"She'd lost a lot of blood. The doctor is hopeful that this will be the last bag she'll need to bring her pressure up." Clarisse gazed into Lee's face. "She also received a concussion from the bullet striking her head—"

"She got shot in the head?" Lee felt worse, remembering the blood saturating her hair. He'd thought she'd been cut by flying glass, not shot by a gun.

"Not exactly. It grazed her here." Clarisse pointed to her own head, above and behind her ear. "It didn't penetrate, but the force was hard enough to give her that concussion."

"And that's why she's unconscious?"

"That and she went through two hours of surgery to remove three bullets—two from the back of her shoulder and one from her thigh. We don't really know the reason why she hasn't come to."

Lee groaned, leaning against the glass.

Debra Erfert

"She'll be OK, Detective Adams," Clarisse said. "Why don't you go in and talk to her—help her wake up—until her father gets here."

"Her dad called?"

"Yes, not too long before you arrived. He should be here in an hour or so."

Soft beeping from the heart monitor floated through the air as Lee followed Clarisse into the room. Each beep reminded him Anna had survived. She had bruises under her eyes he hadn't noticed before that must've happened when the airbag had deployed and smacked her in the face. He looked closer. Her nose didn't look broken. The bandage around her head made Lee cringe. He would be forever grateful the bullet hadn't penetrated her skull. A sling held her left arm tightly to her chest. He hung back while the nurse took her temperature and checked her IV needle.

"She's all yours," Clarisse said as she walked out.

The side of her wrist had the IV's needle inserted under the skin and taped down. Lee gently picked up her right hand. Her skin felt cool to his touch. He kissed her cold fingers and said, "Anna, the doctor wants you to wake up now"—he leaned down next to her pale face and gently stroked her forehead—"and so do I, honey. I need to see your beautiful brown eyes—to know you're OK. We have things to discuss—so many more things to discuss."

The coolness of her skin worried Lee. She always hugged her sweater tightly around her chest. He thought it was more of an emotional response, but what if she was cold? When she'd slept on his couch, she would wrap up in his blanket, while he could barely stand having his bathrobe over him. Lee looked around the room and found an extra blanket on a shelf. He unfolded it and gently spread it over Anna, taking care not to disturb the wires for the heart monitor coming out from the top of her gown or the IV line in her wrist. He tucked it up around her chin before reaching under the blanket to take her hand again.

"Anna, we need to talk about my camping out in your guest room for a while." Lee kept staring at her face to see if he could

A Strange Twist of Fate

detect any changes. "I want to be close to you—to take care of you. If you have a problem with that, then wake up and tell me, and I'll give you the room you need, but please, don't sleep any longer."

Lee rested his cheek on her shoulder and closed his eyes. "Honey, I . . . I'd never been so afraid. When I heard you screaming through the phone, all I could think about was getting to you. When I reached your car"—he took in a shaky breath—"your phone was on the floor, and you were gone. I thought those men had taken you and that I'd never see you again. I've never experienced panic before like I did then. I was afraid—"

"Detective Adams!"

Lee jerked his head up to see Anna's father standing in the doorway. As he got up, letting loose of her hand, he wiped an escaped tear from his cheek with his thumb. "Judge Wright."

"In the hallway."

That wasn't a request but a demand. Technically, Lee wasn't supposed to be in her room at all. The nurse had bent the rules even discussing Anna's condition with him, let alone giving him permission to spend time with her. She obviously hadn't been able to give him a heads-up about Anna's dad coming in earlier than she anticipated.

Reluctantly, Lee left Anna's room. He expected her dad to be waiting outside the door, but he was walking out of the unit. They ended up in a consultation room. He must've wanted privacy.

"Are you involved with my daughter being shot?" he asked briskly.

"No, sir!" Lee said, straightening his back. "I was the one who found her."

The judge kept a hard stare on Lee. "What happened?"

Lee knew from Anna that her dad sat quietly by for the past year while she did her investigation, but he might not know how detailed it was or how much information she had gathered, and he probably had no idea about her binder or the information she had in her phone. He would keep those secret. But Lee did tell him Anna's theory about a relative being angry enough to kill for an imprisoned family member, along with Harold's detailed information about that dark blue pickup—the same kind Anna had been searching for—that led her to an ex-con named Jeremy Gaines and his recently released brother, Wade.

Wright's forehead held a sea of deep wrinkles. "Gaines—I know that name."

"You might. Jeremy was released on bail for a felony three days before Greg was killed."

The judge's brows lowered. "Julianna's theory is plausible?"

"Not only plausible, but Anna thought it probable enough to stake out their mother's house, where she believed they were living." Lee took out his phone and brought up the incriminating picture text. "She sent this to me, but they spotted her before she could drive away, and they chased her."

"They're in custody?"

"Yes."

"So Julianna solved Greg's death?"

"I believe so. We still have forensics to gather." Lee let out a sigh. "After your son-in-law died, his new defense attorney got him a plea bargain and probation, along with every other defendant that Greg was going to prosecute."

Wright rubbed his forehead with his fingers. "You said that all of Greg's cases received probation. How do you know this?"

"I, uh, asked a friend of mine who works in the prosecutor's office. He researched it. Judge JoAnn Clarkson cut them all the same deal, it seems."

"Clarkson?" Wright lifted his head higher, his face flushed pink. "I turned over my docket to her after the accident when I took time off for Julianna." He shook his head. "Clarkson released all those defendants—the ones who would've been in my court—and that one man who should've been in prison killed Greg and sent my daughter to the hospital with bullets in her body?"

"Yes, sir."

Wright reached for the doorknob. "I'll deal with her when I get back to work. You do your job and tighten the rope around

A Strange Twist of Fate

Gaines's neck." Lee started to follow the judge back into the ICU, but before they went inside, Wright stopped him. "You can't come."

Lee's heart thumped. "Why not?"

"You're not family."

Lee was tempted to tell the older man, "You're not either," but he held back. "I'm her boyfriend."

Wright shook his head, his mouth in a hard, flat line.

"Shouldn't Anna be the one to decide if she wants me with her?"

Wright looked at the door for a moment before he nodded. "That sounds fair—when she's conscious."

Lee remembered he had Anna's phone in his car, but he wasn't going to give up his source of her information. "She lost her phone in the crash—my cell number is on her speed dial. She probably hasn't memorized it yet." He took out his wallet and gave the older man his business card. "Please tell her I'll come as soon as she calls."

The judge took the card without ever looking away from Lee's face. Lee watched him turn and go inside the unit, and a sense of loss dropped heavily onto his chest. As much as Lee wanted to hold Anna, he had no legal right to intrude. He would just have to wait for her to call.

~*~

Lee sat behind his desk, trying to concentrate on a new case he'd been given that morning, but all he could think about was how quiet his phone was. Anna still hadn't called him all day. She must've regained consciousness by now, or . . . she took a turn for the worse. Would the judge call him if that happened? Lee wasn't so sure he would. It was nearly five. It might be a good time to go to the hospital for a visit or at least talk to Anna's nurses.

Several knocks at his door brought him out of his depressing thoughts. "Come in."

The door opened, and in strode a young woman carrying a messenger bag made from jeans fabric over her shoulder. She

Debra Erfert

smiled at Rusty for a moment before turning toward Lee. The woman's long, light brown hair had a bright purple streak hanging down one side of her face. Her dark blue eyes peered out from behind rectangular-shaped glasses with light blue frames. The pink-and-blue tie-dyed T-shirt she wore was knotted up around her stomach, showing off a jeweled belly-button piercing. Her acid-washed blue jeans were strategically ripped at the knees, and Lee promised himself he'd never, *ever*, let any daughter of his leave the house looking like that.

"Detective Adams?" the woman asked Lee. "I'm Candice Shane, and I need to speak with you in private."

"I'm headed out." Lee stood up and reached for his suit jacket hanging on the back of his chair. "Can this wait until tomorrow?"

"Homer Peabody sent me to find Julianna Eddington's birth mother."

Lee shrugged on his jacket. "You're a private investigator?"

"I am," Candice said, taking her phone out of her bag and sitting on the couch. Rusty bounded over to her with his ears perked up. She gave his head a good rub before continuing. "That's why I'm here talking to you since I couldn't get through to Mrs. Eddington."

"She's in the hospital."

"Yes, I know, Detective. The crash was in the newspaper this morning." Candice smiled at him. "Good job in finding her husband's killer, by the way." She held up her phone. "I've done some checking, and I can't find Mrs. Eddington's birth certificate in the Arizona vital records."

"You can search for records—not just the person whose certificate is being replaced?"

Candice put her phone down on her exposed knee. "I have a friend in that department who looked it up for me. I can't get a replacement copy sent to me. Mrs. Eddington would need to do that, but I can have it pulled up and see the names of her parents, where she was born, and junk like that. Only her name doesn't

A Strange Twist of Fate

appear on or around October 5, 1992, under the name of Julianna Wright."

Lee let out a heavy breath and sat back down. "I guess I'm not surprised."

"Oh? Why not?"

"What did Homer brief you on where Anna's case is concerned?"

"He told me to find her birth mother."

"Can you?"

"I can find anyone I set my mind to," Candice said, lifting her chin, a small silver ball piercing beneath her lip catching the light.

"I hope so. Anna's not getting her adopted dad's cooperation."

"Adopted dad? Are you sure he isn't her biological father?"

"No, actually. We only know for certain that her mother isn't her mother."

"Do you have any other clues that might make this any easier?"

Lee reached into the inside pocket of his jacket. "We went through her family album Sunday morning, and we found several suspicious pictures. See what you make of them." He passed them to Candice and watched her face as she studied the three pictures Lee hadn't let Anna put them back into the album. He'd known they could be important.

"That's awesome," Candice murmured, looking at the backs of the pictures. "The drugstore ID number is stamped on the back." She then scrutinized the two with Margo Wright wearing the same dress.

"You did say that Mrs. Eddington is adopted, right?"

"Yes."

"And the baby in the stroller is?"

"Anna."

"But the mother had been pregnant in the very same month?"

"It looks that way."

"Did the baby survive?"

"Not that we know."

Debra Erfert

Candice was quiet for a few moments before she said, "After Homer gave me this assignment, I researched the rules for adoption in Arizona. If you get pregnant while waiting for a baby, the agency will put you into an inactive status for the duration of the pregnancy. You can rejoin an agency once you feel you're ready again. That's usually when the baby is about a year old, or so. That changes if there is a miscarriage. You can become active again after you are healed from the loss." Candice looked at the pictures again. "I doubt an adoption counselor would agree that two or three weeks is enough healing time. If they decided to go forward with an adoption, it would take longer than what it appears happened with Mrs. Eddington."

Candice gazed at Lee. "Rules are rules, even if you're a judge. Now if the baby would've been adopted before she found out she was pregnant, that would be different. The state certainly wouldn't take a baby back."

"Yeah, but Anna would've been in the picture with Margo pregnant."

"So are you thinking the Wrights purchased their baby?"

Lee blew out a fast breath. "This is how I see it. Judge Wright loved his wife so much that when she had a miscarriage, he did whatever necessary to replace the baby she lost, no matter the cost. And no one questioned her having a newborn, considering her pregnancy."

"OK, that's why I couldn't find a birth certificate under Julianna Wright. That would be her alias, given to her by the Wrights." Candice tapped the pictures. "I'd like to know how she got her Social Security card, driver's license, or marriage license." In the next instant, she answered her own question. "They probably had a fake birth certificate to show, and because Jackson Wright is a judge, his word was never questioned."

Candice tapped one of the pictures. "I recognize the mountain in the background."

"No way." Lee gazed at Candice's smiling face. She had plastic braces on her teeth.

A Strange Twist of Fate

"Way. It's Mount Lemon, just north of Tucson." Candice squinted at Lee. "How long have you lived in Arizona?"

"I've never lived in Tucson."

"This, plus the store ID on the pictures, gives us a definite search area." Candice reached into her bag again. After a moment, she came out with a small photograph. Lee took a closer look. "Where did you get a picture of Anna?"

"From the Internet." Candice held it out. "Haven't you done a search on your girlfriend?"

Lee recognized the picture as one from Anna's stalker's collection. "That's not something I routinely do when I date."

"I thought I should have pictures of her adoptive parents, too." Candice took out an older picture of Jack Wright with red hair, holding his arm around Margo. They both were smiling.

"How did you get that one? That's not on the Internet."

Candice smiled, the plastic of the retainer-type braces shining. "I told you, I can find anything."

"Then find Anna's real mother."

"Let me do a little more research."

"Are you sure you're up to this? You seem very young to be working as a private investigator."

"I have my degree." Candice shrugged. "It also might have something to do with my being Homer's grandniece," she added with a wide smile. She stood up and adjusted the messenger bag hanging over her body. "Do you want to be in on the search for Mrs. Eddington's mother?"

"Yes, I would." Lee took out his phone again to check to see if he'd missed Anna's call. He hadn't. Still nothing from the hospital or from her dad. "And now is a good time to get on that."

"Listen, Detective, I know you're anxious, but how about we start early tomorrow morning. I'm sure we can get this wrapped up by tomorrow night. Right now, I'm hungry." Candice grinned and said, "And I owe someone dinner."

"Sure. OK. I can pick you up at Homer's office at eight."

"That sounds like a plan."

Debra Erfert

Lee liked her positive attitude, but he seriously doubted she could uncover a twenty-five-year-old secret in a single day.

A Strange Twist of Fate

Twenty

"Let's try to walk to the chair, Mrs. Eddington," Bunny said, encouraging Anna to stand and trying to give her an aluminum cane to walk with. She'd only been out of the ICU for a few hours, and they were already coaxing her to get out of bed.

"I really don't want to," Anna told the nurse as she took hold of her good arm, the one that wasn't in a sling.

"Are you in pain? On a scale of one to ten—"

"I know the stupid scale!" Anna said sharply. "Of course I'm in pain. I was shot today—I *should* be in pain."

"That happened yesterday, Mrs. Eddington," Bunny told her, still with her hand wrapped around Anna's right arm. "Remember? We've had this discussion twice now."

The last thing Anna remembered was seeing a gun pointed at her—everything after that had been wiped away by the bullet striking her head, or her doctor surmised as much. She couldn't even remember what day it was. She pulled out of the nurse's grip. "Leave me alone!"

Bunny straightened. "I'll have to report this to the doctor."

With her hand clutching the elbow of her shot-up shoulder, Anna asked, "Has Detective Adams checked in on me yet?"

Bunny moved to the IV stand and tapped the nearly empty saline bag. "I haven't seen or heard of a Detective Adams, so it would be safe to say no."

Anna didn't like her nurse. She didn't like not being able to remember what happened after she got shot. But what she liked least of all was Lee not coming to be with her once since she woke up. How could he not care enough to see how she was doing or even if she had survived being chased by the Gaines brothers? Her frustration led to anger—which only exasperated the titanic headache she'd had since waking up. Taking the hard-core pain medication wasn't an option. She learned a couple of years ago that any narcotic would make her throw up, leaving her feeling even worse. She would have to make it through the recovery using ibuprofen, ice packs, and self-restraint or her temper would make enemies of all those helping her.

"May I have my purse? I need my phone," Anna said. She'd call Lee if he wouldn't come on his own. She really couldn't understand what had kept him away. And then a horrible thought entered her aching head. What if he'd had an accident? Who would've called her to say he'd been hurt? Or killed?

"We don't have it," Bunny told her as she cut off the IV line. "I think your father took your personal items home with him yesterday."

Anna reached for the room's phone. "I need to call the Phoenix police department."

"What for?" her dad asked.

Anna looked up to see him coming into her room. He'd left earlier that morning after she'd been transferred up from the ICU to a room on the third floor, and it surprised her to see him again so soon. Unless it was Saturday and she'd lost a whole week, then he should be at work. "What are you doing here?"

His thick gray brows lifted upward. "I came to take you home."

"Home?" Anna dropped her hand to her lap. "What are you talking about?"

"Has Doctor Luke been in to see you this afternoon?"

Anna looked at Bunny, who shook her head. "I don't think so."

Jack headed for the chair that Bunny had wanted her to sit in a few minutes before and sat down. "He'll be in shortly to release you."

Bunny leaned over Anna and stripped up the tape holding down the needle in her wrist. "Dr. Luke did give me an order to

A Strange Twist of Fate

discontinue your IV, so I suppose he could want to send you home now, although it seems much too soon."

"But I was just shot today—I shouldn't be going home yet." Anna worried more that Lee wouldn't be able to find her once she left the hospital than she did about her own health. But then he knew where her parents lived, so why was she so concerned? Possibly because she'd have to go back to her mother's problems.

"That happened yesterday, Julianna," Jack said. Sitting forward in the chair, he stared at the nurse. "Is my daughter still having memory problems?"

"Yes, sir." Bunny slipped the needle out of Anna's skin and applied a bandage over the hole.

"Dad, have you seen Lee—Detective Adams? Has he come to see me?"

Bunny took the IV bag and left the room.

He sat back in the chair, and his gaze drifted to the window. "No, I haven't seen him. I'm sure he'll be around."

Anna lay on her right side, the only way that was comfortable. "I don't understand why he hasn't been by, at least for a few minutes. I thought . . ." What did she think? That he loved her? That they had a future together? He never actually told her as much. Maybe she fell into the desperate category after all—desperate for Lee.

~*~

Lee walked up to the ICU nurses' station while staring at Anna's window across the room. The light was off, but he could see movement inside. He couldn't tell if her dad was there or not. Clarisse wasn't on duty to sneak him in.

"May I help you?"

Lee smiled at the nurse sitting behind the desk, who was writing in an electronic chart. Her name tag read *Helen*. "I came to visit Julianna Eddington. Do you know if her father is with her?"

Helen's forehead wrinkled. "Let me check." She started typing on a computer keyboard.

Debra Erfert

"She came down from surgery. I was in here with her yesterday—Julianna Eddington," Lee reminded the nurse of Anna's name.

After a few moments, Helen gave Lee a warm smile. "Mrs. Eddington was transferred up to the third floor this morning."

"The third floor?" Lee nodded. "That's good, right?"

"Yes, sir. That's very good."

"I'll just go and see her up there." Lee tapped the desk with his knuckles before he turned to leave. If Anna had been transferred, she must be much better. They certainly wouldn't move her if she were still unconscious. He walked quickly to the hallway elevators and pushed the Up button. But then Lee thought about her not calling him to let him know she had been transferred. She must've had the opportunity to do so—yet she hadn't called. Could it be because her dad never gave her his card? Lee dismissed that idea. He knew how resourceful Anna was. She would've called the police department to get a hold of him that way.

The elevator doors opened, and Lee stepped inside. He pressed the button for the third floor and waited for the doors to close. Now he needed to speak to Anna, to hear from her if she needed space. It was the not knowing that bothered Lee more than her not calling.

The nurses' station was empty when he got to it. There were tall rolling carts with a few covered trays parked in the hallway. Dinnertime—everyone was busy. Since Lee didn't know which room Anna was in, he stopped the first woman he saw in scrubs as she came out of a room.

"Excuse me, please. I'm looking for my girlfriend. She was transferred up from ICU this morning. Her name is Julianna Eddington. Could you find out what room she's in for me?"

"Sure." The nurse walked behind the long desk and looked at a paper before saying, "Mrs. Eddington was released this afternoon."

"Released?" Lee took a step back. "She wasn't even here for two days. Who took her?" As soon as he asked the question, he knew the answer.

A Strange Twist of Fate

"Judge Wright had an ambulance waiting for her and assured the doctor she would have a private nurse."

"Her dad." Lee turned and strode down the hallway. He'd been manipulated into leaving, and now Anna was locked away in a million-dollar fortress where her dad could keep him away from her for as long as he liked. Lee had to figure out a way to get in to see her, but first, he needed to solve another mystery, one that could change her life for the better or leave her shattered—either way, Lee planned on being there for her. If she wanted him.

Debra Erfert

Twenty-One

Homer Peabody's office parking lot had several cars in it when Lee and Rusty pulled in and parked next to a shiny red BMW convertible with its black ragtop down. They all were high-end models, the kind that his soon-to-be ex-wife drove, unlike his seven-year-old Buick. He hadn't noticed how beat-up his car looked until then. Lee got out.

Since nobody was around, he took a few moments before going into the building to admire the pretty Beemer. Lee seriously thought about replacing his car, too, after his divorce was finalized. Something new and shiny, something Anna might like to drive. She would look good sitting on brown leather seats next to him, with her blonde hair flying in the breeze.

"Nice ride, huh?"

Lee looked up to find an attractive businesswoman strolling from the main door of Homer's office and headed for the Beemer. She was dressed in dark gray slacks and a short matching jacket cinched in at her waist. The frilly pink shirt she wore had a high collar. Tendrils of curly hair framed her smiling face, and she was staring at Lee. There was something familiar about her. Then he noticed a blue cloth messenger bag over her shoulder.

"Candice?"

She lifted out her arms, hands palm up. "What do you think?" She then turned around on her heel to show him her back and looked over her shoulder. "Tell me the truth—did you recognize me?"

Lee stared closer at her light brown hair. It was twisted up on the back of her head, and it was one solid color, no streak of purple.

A Strange Twist of Fate

She didn't even wear glasses, and her eyes looked green, not blue. "I swear, I had no idea until I saw your bag."

Candice swung around to face him. "I knew it." She jerked a thumb toward the office. "Uncle Homer needs to see you before we go. I'll watch Rusty for you."

Lee hesitated while Candice opened his car's back door, and she easily caught Rusty's leash as he hopped down. "I'll make this fast," he told her.

He hoped Homer had good news for him. Inside, the receptionist took a brief look at him and got up. "Follow me, Detective Adams. Mr. Peabody is waiting for you."

The frown on the woman's face discouraged Lee. If her boss wasn't happy, then the news couldn't be good. Lee knew Wednesday had been a quick deadline. He'd hoped for the best, but dealing with lawyers, he should've known nothing ever happened quickly. The longer things were delayed, the more each attorney made in billable hours.

Homer's door was standing open, and the receptionist announced Lee before turning back down the hallway.

"Come in," Homer said while sitting behind his desk. With a wave of his weathered hand, he motioned to the chair in front of his desk. "Take a seat, young man."

Lee sat, feeling his hope sink as the older man slid a red folder across the polished wood, with *Adams vs. Adams* labeled on the front.

"I'm sorry that I couldn't do better, but I thought you'd be more interested in time expediency than a higher cash result." Homer got up and made his way to a window, every movement slow, deliberate, and stared outside. "I want you to initial each clause after you read it."

Lee opened the folder and dutifully did as instructed. In just a few moments, he knew it had changed. "I'm getting my down payment back?"

Without turning to look at him, Homer said, "You paid it."

209

Debra Erfert

"I know . . ." But Arizona was a community property state, so Lee paid close attention to what else might've been changed to compensate his soon-to-be ex-wife for the money she'd be losing. The further he read, the more he realized that nothing else seemed different, except that he would keep his full retirement. He scribbled his initials in the little box at the end of each clause, next to Carolyn's. On the last page, she had her full signature, and that was when Lee's heart began to thud in earnest. He took a deep, calming breath and signed his name, knowing he had finally severed his marriage to a woman who had never loved him. All he wanted to do was find Anna and kiss her until his lips hurt.

"What do you think of my grandniece?" Homer asked, still staring out the window.

That particular view had captivated the old man's interest for several minutes already. Curious, Lee got up and stepped next to him to find that from this vantage point, he could see Candice sitting in her car, with Rusty in the passenger seat next to her. It amazed him how different her appearance was from last night. Yesterday, she looked like a high school kid. Today, she truly was a stunning grown woman. She sat behind the wheel of her expensive sports car, and it looked like she was texting, but Lee could be mistaken. "She's . . . surprising."

Homer chuckled. "Candy keeps surprising me, too. She's twenty-seven years old, and I didn't think she'd ever finish her formal schooling. I sat through all her graduations, praying each one would be the last."

Lee's gaze went from Candice kissing Rusty's face to Homer's shining eyes. "How many degrees does she have?" The wrinkles in the old man's face deepened as he smiled.

"Ask *her* about it." Homer turned back to his desk and took a file folder—this one green without any writing on the front—and handed it to Lee.

"This is your lawsuit settlement with Braxton & Braxton Law Offices. If you agree to it, I'll deposit the check in your account this morning."

A Strange Twist of Fate

Inside the folder were several documents and also a printed check. The amount quickly caught his attention, and he had to sit down. "Three hundred thousand dollars?" He looked up at Homer. The grin that had been on his attorney's lips had disappeared, along with several of the deeper lines around his mouth.

"I have a reputation of winning all my cases, and Seth Braxton knows it to be fact. I sued for one million dollars for breach of contract, on your behalf, but told them we'd settle for seven hundred and fifty thousand." Homer returned to his chair. "I said that we'd take half of that, three hundred seventy-five thousand dollars, if they cut a check by close of business Tuesday. They messengered the agreement and a check last night. I already took out my fee. Like I said, if we had more time, I wouldn't have settled for half, but I know you wanted your decree more than the money."

Lee put the folder on the desk. "Yes, yes, I want this divorce. I want it all just to be over with and done."

"Then sign that settlement agreement, and I'll deposit your check. I'll also file your divorce decree with Judge Abernathy this morning whether you agree with the lawsuit settlement or if you want to take this to court."

The $300,000 check persuaded Lee into signing without any hesitation. He'd never seen that amount before and probably never would again. Now, he'd be able to help Anna with her financial trouble. "After you take my divorce papers to the judge, then my divorce will be official?"

"Yes, it will. And Anna will let you kiss her," Homer said with a chuckle.

Lee quickly looked up at the old man's smiling face. "How did you know about that?"

Homer leaned back in his chair and produced a cackling laugh before he said, "I've known Julianna Wright since she was in grade school, and her high standards would never let her even kiss you as long as you were married." He sat forward and put his elbows on the desk. "But I want you to know this, I'll take it very personally if you hurt her."

Debra Erfert

Lee lost any good humor he'd had the moment before, not only at the seriousness of his feelings for Anna but also at the heavy tone of the attorney. "I care too much for Anna to ever hurt her. But I'm not so sure about her father. Did you know about her car crash?"

Homer nodded. "Candice told me yesterday. I made a few calls to see how she was doing. What's the judge up to?"

"He booted me out of the hospital before she woke up from surgery, and he took her home a few hours after she was transferred from the ICU. I haven't been able to see her since her car crash."

Some of Homer's wrinkles reformed on his face as he frowned. "I suspect Jackson doesn't think you're good enough for Anna. He's always steered her toward attorneys. I like you better than those farts she dated before Greg." His gray eyes glanced toward the window again. "Get Candy to sneak you into the Wrights' fortress, and see how Anna's doing."

The tightness in Lee's chest lessened. "Is Candice experienced at breaking into houses?" Now he knew why the old man had so many wrinkles—he was either giving it his all, smiling, or they were from seriously frowning.

"Ask her about the times she ran away from her grandfather's home that first year she went to live with him," Homer said, nodding, his lips stretched apart in a wide smile, showing his not-so-straight teeth.

"I'll make a point of it." Lee stood up, exhilarated at the way the morning had gone. "Thank you for your hard work, Homer. I'm in your debt," he said, holding out his hand across the desk.

Homer laughed again, reaching out to shake Lee's hand. "You've paid me, son. You owe me nothing." Before the old man let go, his eyebrows pinched together. "Let Candy take the lead today—she knows what she's doing. Trust her. She'll pull the clues together for Anna. She's a very smart young lady."

"Hey, I'm just going along for the ride." Lee didn't exactly mean what he said. True, he was invited to go with Candice, but he didn't plan on standing idly by while she asked all the questions. "Thank you again, sir."

A Strange Twist of Fate

When Lee got outside, Candice had the looped handhold of Rusty's leash cleverly threaded through his collar, and the middle seat belt secured the shortened leash to the back seat. Rusty sat ready to go, while Candice placed a silk scarf over her hair, tying it under her chin.

"I guess we're taking your car," Lee said, opening the passenger door to get inside.

The engine roared to life. "You're good!" Candice said with a big smile on her lips. Lee noticed that she was a lot like her granduncle in respect to her facial expressions—no halfways in showing her feelings. After she slipped on a big pair of white-framed sunglasses, she shifted into reverse and backed out.

She had the right idea, Lee found out. Even with the visor up, he had wind blowing his hair around. Rusty enjoyed the air. His nose bobbed up and down, with his mouth slightly open. Lee figured the dog tasted every new scent that passed his face. And he swore it looked like Rusty was smiling.

It'd been a long time since Lee had been a passenger on a trip out of town—and in such a fine car. He found the electric button on the side of the seat, reclining the back a touch, and got comfortable while Candice expertly maneuvered out of the city. Traffic was heavy during morning rush hour, but she didn't so much as swear when avoiding cars cutting into their lane. As far as Lee could tell, she didn't have a panic button.

Lee checked his phone again. Still no message from Anna, but considering it was the judge who took her home, realistically, Lee didn't expect her to call now.

"You're checking your phone a lot," Candace said, glancing at Lee, "yet you're not sending a text or making a call. What's going on?"

Homer Peabody obviously had a high regard for his grandniece. "Did you really run away from home a lot when you were a kid?"

Candice bobbed back her head once. "What?" She held out her hand, wriggling her fingers. "Give me your phone!"

Lee stuffed it back into his pocket. "I don't think so."

With her lips in a pout, she said, "You had no right to research my past."

While Candice might not panic easily, she did have a temper. "*You* did research on Anna's past."

"It's my job!"

Yep—by the hardened tone in her voice, he'd ticked Candice off. "Your granduncle told me you might be able to help me break into Anna's parents' home."

Candice opened her mouth and then closed it, then opened it again. "What? Why?"

Lee went through the same explanation he'd given Homer about Anna's dad taking her home early and not telling Anna that Lee wanted to see her, with a little more detail.

"That's so not right."

"Yeah, that's what I think," Lee said. "Can you get into their house without being caught?"

"Of course." She hadn't even hesitated with her answer.

"How can you be so sure?" he asked.

Candice tilted her head toward him and glanced at him over the rim of her sunglasses. "I went to live with my mother's parents when I was eight, after my parents were killed. It was an incredibly difficult first year, and I'm afraid I didn't help things by running away too many times to remember. Anyway, when night came around, I would find a house, one where the owners were gone, and get inside to sleep. I never broke a window, and twice it was on the second floor." She glanced at Lee again. "I believe that was what Uncle Homer was alluding to."

"I'm sure it was," Lee told her. "So you'll help me?"

She shrugged. "Let's see what today brings, OK?"

Lee leaned against the headrest. That answer wasn't encouraging. "How did you get caught—assuming you did?" A dimple appeared in her right cheek, next to the corner of her mouth, when she smiled.

A Strange Twist of Fate

"I was only eight back then, and I didn't appreciate the need to cover my tracks." When Lee stayed quiet, she added, "I would forget to close the windows, and the next time Grandfather would call in my running away, they would look for an empty house with an open window." Candice laughed. "I didn't catch on until nearly a year later when one of the officers lectured me and let it slip about the window."

"Did the lecture change your ways?"

"You bet! The next time I ran away, I made sure I closed the window."

Lee chuckled at her matter-of-fact attitude.

"But"—Candice lifted a shoulder—"I did learn that being by myself for three days felt lonelier than I ever imagined. I went back home on my own and never ran away again. So, yeah, I guess you could say that lecture did end up doing me some good."

"And now you're an expert at breaking and entering."

"I never broke anything. The windows were left open."

Lee chuckled at her response. She sounded like Anna.

"Your granduncle has a lot of faith in your skills as an investigator."

That made her smile again. "He's had to have a lot of patience with me since my grandfather died. I'd like to think I finally earned his respect." She shook her head. "I would've bet a good chunk of my trust fund that he'd given up on me long ago."

He stared at her. "Trust fund? I thought you're working for Homer."

Candice adjusted her sunglasses higher on her nose. "I am. I just would be bored out of my skull if I didn't work, and Uncle Homer understands that."

"Does he pay you?"

Candice glanced at Lee. "Does that matter to you?"

"It might. Mrs. Eddington's financial situation is getting pretty desperate. Maybe you could send your bill to me?"

Grinning, she said, "I could. You do know Uncle Homer isn't going to charge her, right?"

215

Debra Erfert

Anna would be so relieved knowing a huge bill wouldn't be in the mail after everything was over. He'd tell her the first chance he got—if he ever saw her again. "I'm glad."

The drive was quiet for the next hour until they neared the Tucson city limits. "Do you have a plan?" Lee asked.

"Yes, I do. Remember the drugstore number on the back of the photographs you gave me?"

"Uh-huh."

"They were each developed at the same Walgreens drugstore, only we don't know where that store is exactly, but we can assume it's in Tucson because of Mount Lemon being in the picture."

"I agree, but how are you going to find the exact Walgreens drugstore they were developed in twenty-five years ago?"

Candice smiled again. "Did you know that Walgreens has a main business office on East Speedway and North Knob Road?"

Lee looked at the GPS unit on the dashboard. The next turn would be on East Speedway. "I take it that's where we're headed?"

"It is. And after we get a store location, then . . ." Candice sighed.

"Then comes the hard work," Lee finished for her.

"Yeah." She glanced at him. "I hope you have on a pair of good walking shoes because sometimes the only way to find answers is to knock on doors. I'm hoping that Margo Wright used the closest, most convenient place to have her photos developed, but I'm also counting on her having had her prescriptions filled there. It's possible we'll find a longtime, dedicated employee."

~*~

The district office was snuggled into a strip mall that stretched across a long block. Candice parked near the front doors, but before getting out, she reached back and unbuckled Rusty's collar, let his leash loose, and then buckled it again. "Come on, pretty boy."

Lee ended up standing outside the office, impatiently waiting while Candice took his dog for a necessary walk. But the lead the pictures gave them was too good to wait on, and Lee decided to go inside alone.

A Strange Twist of Fate

A long, elbow-height laminate counter bisected the small office, where two women sat behind matching desks on opposite sides of the room. Both women looked up from their computers, and it was then Lee figured that not many people walked in off the street. Just as he fingered the button of his jacket to open it and expose his detective's badge pinned to his belt, Lee thought about the consequences of bringing in his police authority. Truthfully, he didn't know if Anna's birth mother willingly gave her up or if a large amount of money exchanged hands first.

The information they could get out of their files was important enough that maybe Lee should bring in a search warrant, but that would take time and enough probable cause for a judge to grant that warrant. The little evidence Lee had didn't meet even the lowest standards he'd need to talk to a Tucson detective to fill out the paperwork.

One woman stood up just as the front door opened. Candice rushed in, with Rusty next to her. He knew she wasn't happy the instant he saw her frowning face and squinting eyes staring at him. She passed him the leash handle.

In a fast whisper, she asked, "Did you talk to anyone yet?"

Lee shook his head as Rusty softly whined.

"May I help you?" the woman asked, coming to the counter.

"We hope you can," Candice said, moving closer to the woman and taking out the three photographs from her messenger bag. "I'm Candice Shane, and this is Lee Adams, and we're trying to find the store in which these were developed twenty-five years ago." She handed one to the woman and turned over one of the pictures still in her hand. "They each have the same store location number on them."

"I'm sure I can find it." The woman went to her desk and picked up her laptop before returning to the counter. "Now, let's see . . ." It took her a few moments, but a satisfied grin spread on her lips. "Here we go. The store you're looking for is at East Tanque Verde Road and North Sabino Canyon Road. It's in a small shopping center."

Debra Erfert

She then turned her computer around to show an aerial view of a map showing all the Walgreens locations in Tucson.

"Look how close that is to the Tucson Country Club." Lee touched the screen. "The judge"—his gaze momentarily flicked to the clerk—"Anna's dad plays golf every Sunday, like clockwork. It would make sense that he might live near a golf course back then. He does now."

"And Sabino Canyon and Mount Lemon are in the distance," Candice said.

Lee picked up the third picture. "This was taken on the edge of a desert. Twenty-five years ago, that probably was as far away from the city as you could get."

Candice caught the gaze of the woman helping them. "What's your name?"

"Salina Davies."

"Ms. Davies, it's very important that we find someone who worked at that store in 1992. Do you have access to the employee records from twenty-five years ago?"

The other clerk stood and said, "We're not allowed to give out personal information."

The helpful smile that Salina wore faded, and she stood up straighter.

Lee moved closer, ready to argue with the women, but Candice clamped her hand on his arm, effectively quieting him before he said a word.

"Salina," Candice began softly, "could you at least look and see if your computer even holds that information—so we'll know what our next step should be?"

Salina pulled in her lip and chewed on it for a bit. "Why do you need to know?"

"I have a client looking for her birth mother," Candice told her. It was a simple statement and true, just more complicated than she let on.

"A client?" Salina asked, her brows sliding up higher on her forehead.

A Strange Twist of Fate

"Yes." Candice retrieved a thin wallet from her bag and opened it, setting it on the counter in front of the woman. "I'm a private investigator, and it's very important we get at least one name. We can take it from there."

Salina closed the laptop. "I'm sorry. I don't think I should."

"Please," Lee pleaded, "just give us one name, someone who might remember a customer." He reached to open his jacket again.

"It's OK. We'll find another way." Candice stuffed her ID back in her bag. "Let's go do some legwork." She took Rusty's leash from his hand and led the way out the door.

Lee didn't want to give up so easily. He had a strong suspicion that what he needed sat less than ten feet away, yet it might as well have been in the next county. He felt defeated.

When he stepped outside, Candice had Rusty jumping in the back seat. By the time Lee got inside, she had Rusty buckled. She wasn't wasting any time. He snapped his seat belt into place while Candice turned over the Beemer's engine, but before they moved, she touched the GPS and inputted the address of the target Walgreens. As she pulled out of the parking spot, she touched another button, and the ragtop began to close over their heads. He hadn't noticed the dark clouds that had gathered. It was a little early in the year for a monsoon storm, but a spring rain could happen without much warning.

She hadn't spoken a word to him since they'd left the office. He'd gaze at her every so often, but she had a determined look on her face that could be interpreted as concentration or irritation—at him, probably. He'd stayed quiet, like she told him to—almost. It was difficult being shut down like that. No discussion, no debate. Lee slumped in his seat and stewed about the loss. If he could contact a local detective, he could still salvage that lead. Salina might not be cooperative with a private investigator, but if speaking to an official from the City of Tucson, with or without a search warrant, she may be more inclined to help.

Debra Erfert

Twenty-Two

Anna sat on her bed, clamped down on the pillow in her hand, and closed her eyes against the stinging discomfort of the medical tape being stripped off her back. This morning, Vicky, her mother's housekeeper and secret nurse, had covered Anna's bandages with plastic sheeting and then helped her take a warm shower. Without having any painkillers in her body to take the edge off, the whole agonizing process had drained her of what little energy she had. Last night had passed in short, unrestful naps as intense pulses of pain would yank her up through the fog of the Valium-induced sleep. The doctor had also given her a supply of Vicodin. It was a futile gesture on his part, after she told him her reaction to narcotics, but she had a feeling he felt better knowing she had an option—just in case she couldn't tolerate the pain any longer.

But Anna felt more than beat down from her wounds—she felt abandoned. The depression spurred by Lee not contacting her seemed to intensify the physical ache she felt. She left the hospital yesterday, and not once had he tried to call her. He knew where her parents lived—he'd driven Anna here just last week. She just couldn't understand why he didn't come by to check on her. She truly thought they'd had a connection, something deeper than just friendship. But even a friend would come to visit, to see how she was getting along.

"Are you ready to take a pain pill yet?" Vicky asked. "I need to change your dressing."

Anna let her head hang. "I don't want to argue about this anymore." She opened her eyes enough to see the nurse's white athletic shoes as she stood next to her bed. Adidas. Vickie always wore the same brand—she was so predictable, so reliable. "I'd rather endure the pain than the vomiting."

A Strange Twist of Fate

"The doctor prescribed an antinausea med for that," Vicky told her as she began to take the tape off the bandage from her shoulder.

"It doesn't work well enough. I still get sick."

"Your parents can't stand seeing you in so much pain," she said, peeling off a strip of tape.

Anna saw her mother step into the bedroom—and stop—again. She would hover near the door for a while before disappearing, never saying anything, just watching her.

"Where's my dad? I haven't seen him all morning."

"He went to talk with Greg," Margo said, finally coming into the room. Her arms were wrapped around her middle like she was cold even though the room was warm. Anna hadn't noticed how similar their postures were before then. Lee had called it a learned gesture. A pang of loneliness pulsed through her heart. What could he be doing? "He must be worried about where you are," Margo added.

"What?" Anna looked over her shoulder at Vicky.

"Judge Wright went to your home to meet with a glass repairman earlier this morning, Mrs. Eddington."

"The broken window. I forgot about that. How did he know about it?"

"He talked with the police lieutenant yesterday," Vicky said.

Anna inhaled sharply when the nurse tore up another length of tape, this one from the tender part of her arm. She blew out a couple of breaths, letting the sting pass.

"Don't hurt her, you stupid woman!" Margo snapped, her face distorted and pinked. The unexpected outburst surprised Anna, as did the anger showing on her face. In the next moment, her mother turned and rushed from the room.

Vicky spent a minute or so gently rubbing Anna's tender skin. "I'm sorry," she said. "I really wish you'd take something for the pain."

"I'm sorry, too," Anna said tiredly as the nurse peeled off another piece of tape. "You must have a lot of patience, taking that from Mother."

Debra Erfert

"It's OK. I'm used to her ups and downs."

She would have to be, Anna thought. "Vicky, how long have you worked for my parents?"

"Hmm . . . your father hired me about fifteen years ago, but I wasn't a live-in nurse then. I came in on weekdays while you were at school."

Anna grinned, remembering catching Vicky driving away when she came home. Anna would stay as late after school as she could, not wanting to deal with her mother any more than she had to. On the weekends, Vicky's absence was noticeable. "When did you make the transition to live-in nurse?"

Vicky reached for a large piece of gauze on the side table next to the bed and opened it before she answered. "It was after my youngest son entered college. His father and I divorced when both of my sons were still in grade school, and, well, quite frankly, I needed the money this full-time job gave me to put them through the university. Your father has been very generous to me."

"Don't you ever get tired of being treated like a housekeeper?"

While Vicky taped down the clean bandage, she said, "I would have to clean my own house anyway. Like I said, your father pays me very well for the nursing duties. And he has another housekeeper come in three times a week to help. I even have a retirement account. What more could I ask for in a job?"

"Vacations would be nice." Anna sighed as she watched Vicky work in the reflection in the panels of the French doors. The drapes had been pulled back, filling the room with warm light. That could be the reason her mother didn't stay and why she had been so irritated—her reflection in each little pane distorted her image slightly in different directions. The sky had a few clouds bumping into one another. Anna wouldn't mind some rain.

Being her mother's nurse, and possibly being close when a lot of personal conversations might've been going on, Anna wondered what Vicky knew about her birth. "Did you know I was adopted?"

Vicky stilled her hands for a moment and then stepped to the side, staring intensely into Anna's face, scouring each of her

A Strange Twist of Fate

features. It seemed like she was trying to discover an answer without ever asking a single question. Finally, in a quiet voice that only carried across the short distance to Anna, she asked, "Did you steal the vial of blood from my bag?"

Anna glanced at the door. Her mother wasn't there. She nodded and said, "I had to know for sure."

"And?"

"Mother has blood type O—I'm type AB."

Vicky gasped softly.

"You didn't know?" Anna whispered.

She touched Anna's hair. "I'd noticed the physical differences years ago—your eyes, your hair—but it wasn't my place to ask about that part of your life. If you're adopted, then, you're still their daughter. You didn't know?"

"No. They never told me." Anna needed to take a chance that she could trust the nurse about what she saw in one of the pictures. "Did you know that Mother had a miscarriage the same month they got me?"

Vicky puckered her lips, like she had eaten something bitter and extremely sour at the same time. "That's impossible."

"Not probable," Anna said, "but not impossible, right?"

The nurse's eyes darted to the door, and Anna thought she saw the shadow of a figure disappearing.

~*~

The instant Candice killed the engine in front of the Walgreens, she pulled off her sunglasses and turned to Lee with one brow lifted higher than the other. Her pointed stare worried him more than the silent drive across town did. "When we go inside, who are you going to be?"

Like he had a choice? "I'm . . ." Lee shook his head, not understanding.

"Are you Phoenix Police Detective Adams, or Lee Adams, Anna Eddington's boyfriend?"

"Is there a problem with my being both?"

Debra Erfert

"There might be if you pull your badge at an inconvenient time and we lose this lead, setting my investigation back to the beginning. So—if you're going in with me, I need you to unclip the badge from your belt and put it under your car seat."

"No." Lee went to open his door but heard the locks click before he could pull the handle. "Candice!"

"Stay in the car with Rusty, and let me take this one, solo," Candice told him, tossing her sunglasses on the dashboard.

"I'm coming in with you."

"Then leave your badge and your official attitude out here. Don't make me regret having you along." Candice lowered the car windows an inch before climbing out.

For all her bluster, Lee knew she was right. One little indication that he was a cop searching for answers and the whole thing might become an official investigation. If he had to resort to getting a search warrant, then he could screw up Candice's search for Anna's birth mother, and not only would he have Candice angry with him, but he also would disappoint Anna. And who knew how long it would take Candice to undo the damage. Lee unclipped his badge and placed it under the seat. If he needed a badge, he had his off-duty one in his wallet.

"Back in a few minutes, Rusty." Lee rubbed his dog's neck and then followed Candice in through the automatic front doors onto the faded-blue linoleum floor. Immediately inside and to the left, shelves of glass liquor bottles were stacked on circular displays, and to the right, three checkout counters had closed signs on their revolving belts, with the fourth one being open. Candice didn't waste any time. She strode confidently down the main aisle, parallel to the front of the store, to the photo department, where the male clerk stood staring at her from behind the counter. Now Lee understood why she wore such a powerful, eye-catching outfit. It did what she intended it to do—it got her attention.

Deciding to hang back, Lee stayed within earshot of their conversation and let her do the job she was hired to do.

"Hello, Salina Davies from corporate sent me."

A Strange Twist of Fate

That wasn't exactly accurate, Lee thought, amused.

"I need to talk to someone who has been working at this store for at least twenty-five years. Would you happen to know who I can speak with?" Candice asked sweetly.

Lee suppressed a grin at the sugary tone in her voice. He watched the clerk's face. The man had to be in his late forties, maybe early fifties, and he wore a wedding ring, but that didn't stop a smile from forming or prevent his eyes from taking another look at Candice's figure.

"I'm Ralph Castillo, the assistant manager. How can I help you?"

"Have you been working here since 1992?"

"I was hired last year." His smile wavered some.

Candice glanced at Lee. Even in that brief eye contact, he could see puzzlement in her face. The man didn't seem to understand the question she'd asked. "Do you know of an employee who worked here in '92, possibly in the photo department?"

"Can't say that I do," Ralph told her. "But we have a high turnover rate. I seriously doubt anybody still works here after, you know, that long."

"OK, I understand. Is the store manager here?" Candice looked around, briefly catching Lee's gaze again.

"Sure, I'll call her, but she was only recently promoted."

While Ralph took out his cell phone, Lee stepped next to Candice, keeping his back to the clerk. "You're not discouraged?" She gave her head a single shake and moved to the sunglasses display on the end of an aisle, where she used the time to try on several pairs. Lee went to the opposite side of the circular rack and looked for a pretty pair for Anna. "Do you have any other leads if this doesn't pan out?"

"One I'd rather not follow," Candice said quietly, putting a rhinestone-studded pair of sunglasses back onto its post. "Last night, during an Internet search, I discovered Judge Wright spent his first years practicing here in Tucson. Gately, Taylor, & Haws, Attorneys at Law is still a thriving firm, but trying to get private information out of a lawyer is next to impossible, with or without a warrant."

"Are you saying you couldn't do it?" he asked in a teasing tone.

Candice glared at him. "Oh, I can do it! It would just cost me some bribery money." Then she smiled. "Or rather, it would cost *you* some bribery money."

She was right, of course, about lawyers not being a cooperative sort of people. An older woman approached Candice, and then Lee paid closer attention to their conversation than Candice's smug look.

"I'm Diane Marie, the manager—were you looking for me?" the woman asked Candice. With the amount of gray she had at the untouched roots of her dark hair, she had to be as old as the assistant manager was, maybe midfifties.

Turning to the woman, Candice smiled. "Yes, ma'am. Do you have an office where we can talk in private?"

Lee panicked. Was he going to be left out? He had to do something quick.

"What is this about?"

"My girlfriend is trying to find her birth mother," Lee said, stepping closer and getting the manager's attention. From the squinted stare Candice gave him, he knew he'd catch her wrath later, but he'd handle it. He just didn't want to be left standing alone while they went behind closed doors.

The woman turned to Candice again. "You're looking for your birth mother? How do you think I can help?"

With a tentative smile on her face, Candice didn't immediately correct the misunderstanding. "I'd much rather talk to you about this in private if we could."

"Sure, follow me." After Lee gave the manager an appreciative look, she led them to the back of the store and through a door into a good-size room where a large glass-topped wooden desk sat tucked in the corner. She dropped into a chair behind it while motioning toward a couple of armless chairs in front of it. "Please, sit down."

A Strange Twist of Fate

Lee's jacket opened as he sat, and Candice noticed the badge missing from his belt. If she approved of it being gone, she didn't give him even a hint of it before turning to the manager.

"So you're adopted. What led you to our store?" Ms. Marie asked as she leaned her elbows on her desk. She wore a touch of a sympathetic smile while she stared at Candice with companionate deep brown eyes. They were darker than Anna's. He wondered what Anna was doing now. It was closing in on noon. Would she be eating lunch alone? Who would make it for her?

"My name is Candice Shane, and this is Lee Adams, but I'm not the woman Lee is speaking of." The woman's smile faded and was replaced by a guarded near-frown. "We're here trying to find someone who might remember seeing this woman"—Candice handed her one of the pictures—"coming into this store on a regular basis twenty-five years ago, to fill her prescriptions or to develop her photographs."

"She looks pregnant. Is this the birth mother? You're looking for her name?" Ms. Marie asked, studying the picture.

"No, ma'am," Candice said. "This is the adoptive mother. We're trying to find someone who remembers her and can give us more information about her time here, such as where she lived, a name of a friend, where she might've worked. Were you here in 1992?"

"I was hired on in 1991, in this store, actually. Stayed for three years before spending the next twenty years opening new stores around the state. I only came back here when I heard Rodney was retiring." She lifted the picture. "Can't you just ask her?"

"No. The adoptive mother isn't mentally able to discuss this," Lee told her.

Ms. Marie looked up with a surprised look in her wide brown eyes. "Not mentally able . . ." After she took a pair of half-glasses out of the desk's top drawer, she slipped them on and held the picture closer. The frown grew more pronounced even as her brow wrinkled.

Debra Erfert

"You recognize her, don't you?" Candice said, leaning forward.

"I"—Ms. Marie shook her head—"I'm not sure."

"Or is it that you remember a customer who looked similar to her who might've had a"—Lee tried to remember the term **David Curtis**, his ex-cop assistant prosecutor friend, had used about Anna—"a psychotic breakdown?"

The manager's stunned gaze jumped to Lee's. "I think you need to talk to Rodney Jones. I took his place as store manager nine months ago. He may know the woman in this picture."

A Strange Twist of Fate

Twenty-Three

Vicky had pulled the drapes closed across the French doors before she went downstairs. It darkened the room enough that Anna should've been able to nap. As hard as she tried, sleep eluded her. The constant pain just wouldn't let her relax enough to drift off. The ice pack she'd had balanced on the back of her shoulder slipped every time she moved. Frankly, it wasn't worth the trouble of her having to sit up, find it, and then put it in place again for the minimum relief it gave her.

Lying in the darkness, knowing she would have nothing to do for weeks while she healed, Anna let her thoughts float to Lee. His strong embrace held her when she needed comfort, and his tender kisses had made her feel loved. She wanted to feel his lips on hers, although that didn't seem likely since he hadn't bothered to even send her flowers. That, at least, would've told her he hadn't completely forgotten about her.

~*~

The store manager made a phone call, finding out if Rodney Jones was home, before Lee and Candice followed her south to his condo. It seemed like a lot of trouble for her, but Lee wasn't going to argue about it. Timing was everything. Tomorrow, Jones and his wife were leaving for a ten-day Mediterranean cruise, and this would be their only chance to get information out of him—if he remembered anything.

"What made you think I would've left you out, Detective Adams?" Candice sped after Diane Marie's silver Toyota Prius after hanging a right on East Tanque Verde Road. From the aggressive way she changed lanes, she telegraphed her anger with every sharp movement. "Just what made you think I would do something so low?"

Debra Erfert

"I'm sorry, Candice," Lee told her in a pleading voice, trying to calm her. "I lost my head. I panicked."

The dimple below her right cheek appeared when she frowned. "That's redundant."

"I mean it. For a split second there, I thought I'd be left stuck out by that rack of cheap sunglasses while you asked all the questions. I'm sorry I didn't trust you enough to wait and find out."

Candice chewed on her lip in contemplation, and Lee hoped she was thinking about forgiving him and not figuring out a way to conveniently ditch him at the next corner. When she released her lip, she said, "You owe me, Detective."

"I know I do—"

"And you can bet I won't forget it," she told him.

Lee sat back. He suddenly sensed he'd been manipulated into feeling that way. When Lee gazed closer at her, he was positive he could see the corner of her lips tipped upward a bit, and the dimple dipped deeper into her skin.

They drove the rest of the way to Green Valley, a growing bedroom community south of Tucson, in relative silence. Candice had turned on the radio and sang along to some country music, and at that point, Lee figured she wasn't angry any longer—if she truly had been to begin with. When they pulled up behind Diane's Prius parked by the curb, a balding man was standing on the front porch. He waved as the manager climbed out of her car.

"Rod"—Diane Marie gave a generous hug to the man as Candice, Lee, and Rusty approached—"these are the two people who need to talk with you about the old days at the pharmacy."

Candice reached out her hand to the man. "My name is Candice Shane, Mr. Jones." After he shook her hand, she motioned to Lee. "This is Lee Adams, and his pup, Rusty."

Lee shook his extended hand. "Thank you for meeting with us, sir."

"We don't have much time, young man. We have to be at Sky Harbor at five tomorrow morning. Please, come in," Rod said as he opened the front door and stepped inside.

A Strange Twist of Fate

Lee motioned for Diane and Candice to go in first, and then he followed them into a bright living room, keeping Rusty at his heel. Four partially filled suitcases were open on the sofa and two chairs. Obviously they had interrupted their packing. Rod took them through to the dining room, where a pitcher of what looked like iced lemonade sat on the table, surrounded by five tall glasses with tiny red apples painted around the outside. A plate of blueberry muffins sat next to them. Lee's stomach quietly rumbled. It was almost one, and they hadn't eaten lunch. The blueberries smelled deliciously sweet.

"Please, have a muffin," a woman's voice said from behind Lee. He turned to see who he assumed was Mrs. Jones, carrying a plate of sandwiches. The scent of peanut butter and strawberries wafted in the air as she walked by. Since it was close to one already, Lee sat down and picked up a muffin. Rusty sat by his leg. Candice, on the other hand, stayed standing and took out a picture from her bag.

"Mr. Jones, I understand you worked at the Walgreens on East Tanque Verde Road and North Sabino Canyon Road."

"Yes, I retired from that location a few months ago," Rod said as he sat in the chair next to Lee.

"Were you working there in 1992?" Candice asked.

"I was. That was the year my daughter was born."

Diane said, "That's right. Nancy's twenty-five now."

"And married to a Phoenix city police officer," Rod added.

"What's his name?" Lee asked, curious if he knew him.

"Graham Dawson," Mrs. Jones told him, handing him a cold glass of lemonade.

"Thank you." Lee smiled up at her. "I know your son-in-law. He's on the sergeant's promotion list. He's a good guy!"

"Oh, small world. How do you know him?" Rod asked, lifting a sandwich to his mouth.

Lee looked up at Candice, and she rolled her eyes. He'd made a mistake in mentioning his profession. Hopefully, it wouldn't stop their cooperation.

Debra Erfert

"I work with him, but I'm on a different shift."

"You're a police officer too?" Rod asked just before he took a bite.

"I am," Lee told him.

"Is this an official investigation, officer?" Mrs. Jones asked.

"Lee's helping his girlfriend find her birth mother," Diane told her. She motioned toward Candice with a wave of a hand. "Show Rod the picture."

Candice handed it to him. Rod dusted the crumbs off his hands before taking it. Lee assumed it was the one of Anna's mother sitting on the wall, the one without the stroller and with her shirt pulled across her bulging stomach. Candice didn't offer any other information about it while he held it an arm's length away from his eyes.

"Do you remember this woman coming into your store—picking up prescriptions or developing photographs?" Candice asked.

"I don't think so."

Diane moved behind him and looked over his shoulder at the picture. "During a morning employees' meeting, you told me about an incident where a pregnant woman went ballistic at the photo counter, breaking the swivel mirror that used to sit next to the small rack of Ray-Ban sunglasses. Remember? How many times has that happened?"

Rod looked up at his wife. "Bea, find my reading glasses."

"OK, sure," she said, turning around and heading for the kitchen.

"Then you remember that incident?" Candice asked.

"Clearly," Rod said.

"Here you go." Bea hurried around the table and handed Rod the plastic-framed glasses. He quickly slipped them on. It didn't take a moment before he looked up at Lee.

"This is the woman who went nuts on that mirror. She broke the glass countertop, too, before the police got there."

A Strange Twist of Fate

"The police were called?" Candice asked quickly. Lee knew what that meant. A report would have her address.

"Yes, but I'm pretty sure they took her to the hospital and not to jail. She'd cut herself on the glass," Rod said. "I'm sorry, but I don't remember this woman's name."

"We know her name," Lee said.

Rod's gray brows pinched together. "Then why did you need me to tell you if you already knew your girlfriend's birth mother's name?"

"She's the adoptive mother," Candice told him as she took out another picture from her messenger bag. "We're hoping to find their old home, maybe talk to old neighbors who could give us some more information about the adoption of Julianna." She held out the close-up picture of Anna smiling.

"Holy crap!" Rod whispered. "I remember *her*."

Lee's heart thumped against his ribs. Anna must look very similar to her natural mother or Rod wouldn't have had such a reaction. "Do you remember her name?"

Rod shook his head. "No . . . no, but she was German. She used to come into the store on a regular basis. Peter was heartbroken when she just left. We didn't know for sure, but we thought he was the father of the young woman's baby."

"Who's Peter?" Lee asked.

Rod took the picture from Candice. "He worked part time at the store, under me, stocking shelves while attending the University of Tucson. I think she was going there, too."

"Do you remember Peter's last name?" Candice asked, taking out her smartphone.

He shook his head. "It's been a long time, but I can find out." He set Anna's picture down and took out a cell phone from his pocket. The ringing was audible through the earpiece he didn't quite hold against his head. So was the woman's voice when she answered, "Walgreens main office, how may I help you?"

"Hello, Salina. Rodney Jones here. Could you look up an old associate's name for me, please?"

Debra Erfert

"Sure, Rod."

"His first name is Peter, but I can't remember his last name. We worked together back in 1992 at the Tanque Verde Road store." After several seconds of silence, Rod lifted his gaze from Anna's picture and stared at Lee. "Salina, are you there?"

"Why do you want to know? Did a woman and a man tell you to ask me?"

Rod shrugged, looking between Lee and Candice. "Does it make a difference?"

"You know I can't—"

"Salina, the man's a police officer, like my son-in-law. You know how I feel about cooperating with the law. Just do as I ask and find Peter's last name for me, and I'll bring you back a little something from Greece."

"Rod," Bea whispered sharply. He waved back her objection with his free hand.

"Well, OK. Give me a minute."

Rod grinned as he touched the speaker button. He set it down on the table and then picked up his sandwich. Lee stayed very quiet and ate his muffin, while Candice took out her phone, probably preparing to research the name the second they had one.

"OK, I found it, Rod. Peter's last name is Carpenter."

"Does he have a middle name?" Candice asked.

There was a hesitation again, but after a long moment, Salina said, "Peter is his middle name. His full name is Alfred Peter Carpenter."

"Do you have a current phone number or address for him?" Candice asked.

"No, we don't keep track of ex-employees," Salina told her.

"A date of birth?" Lee asked quickly, leaning closer to the phone.

"1971, and that's all the information I can give you. I'm sorry."

The phone made three beeping tones. Salina had hung up.

Lee looked up at Candice to ask if she would use one of her contacts to track down the name, but he didn't need to worry. Her

A Strange Twist of Fate

fingers were already tapping on her phone. Before Lee could finish drinking his glass of lemonade, a broad smile graced Candice's lips.

"There's only one Alfred Peter Carpenter. He has a 2014 Chevrolet Tahoe and a 1997 Honda Valkyrie registered in Arizona. He's the right age."

"Where is he?" Rod asked, standing up.

"You aren't going," Bea told him. "We still have packing to finish."

"That depends." He looked at Candice and asked again, "Where is he?"

"He registered his vehicles in Yuma."

"Rod—no!" Bea pleaded. "That's over four hours from here, one way."

Rod's shoulders fell, and he noticeably exhaled. "You're right, sweetheart." He turned to Lee. "Do me a favor and let me know how things go."

"Yes, sir, I will." Lee shook the man's hand as Candice gathered the pictures.

~*~

The trip to Yuma took longer than the estimated four hours. The highway patrol officer delayed them by twenty minutes when he gave Candice a speeding ticket outside Wellton. Lee briefly wondered if he'd have to foot the cost of that ticket, but in the end, finding Anna's birth father seemed more important than a couple of hundred dollars in a fine. Oddly enough, before the officer left, Candice had his business card and an invitation from him for a ride-along. Lee guessed she would have another well-positioned contact before that afternoon was over.

Lee had agreed that the trip west to contact the possible father was a better idea than going to the Tucson police station for the old report on Margo Wright. While they would get Margo's old address, finding a neighbor who knew the Wrights back then wasn't guaranteed. If he wasn't any closer to finding Anna's mother after talking with Peter Carpenter, then finding that report would take priority.

"Your granduncle told me you had multiple degrees." Lee watched her face as he spoke, in case he had touched a nerve. "I would guess one of them is in criminal justice?"

The dimple in Candice's cheek dipped as she grinned. "That wasn't a hard guess."

"So you do have more than one degree?"

She nodded but otherwise stayed quiet.

"OK, then . . . do you have a law degree?"

"No offense to Uncle Homer, but I'd rather clean horse stalls than be an attorney." She fell quiet again.

"NASCAR driving?"

She laughed. "You can't get a degree in that."

Lee laughed along with her. "But if you could, you'd have your master's."

Rusty whined and poked his nose into Lee's shoulder. He got the hint.

"You better pull over," Lee said. "Rusty needs to go."

"Yuma is just over Telegraph Pass. We're only fifteen minutes away from our destination." Candice reached up and rubbed Rusty's muzzle. "Your boy *will* hold it."

"You have a lot of faith in my dog."

"I know animals. You have a well-trained canine."

"Ah, you have a degree in veterinary medicine."

"Wrong again. I volunteered in an animal shelter during the summer for a couple of years. Let me know when you give up guessing."

Lee sat quietly, watching the small city coming into view as they rounded the curve at the peak of the pass. He'd gone through Yuma twice on his way to the beach in San Diego, but the time he spent there could be measured in buying Thirst Buster sodas and taking bathroom breaks.

When they were within a mile of their exit, the GPS reminded them about the turnoff.

A Strange Twist of Fate

"Just so I'm not confused, do I get to be Anna's boyfriend and a detective too? Or what?"

"I doubt that the subject of your employment will come up."

"You mean, again?"

Candice tilted her head and glanced at him. "We were lucky. Why don't you try being Anna's boyfriend for a while?"

Lee would love to do just that. He had four weeks of vacation coming to him, time that he'd avoided taking. Why vacation during the throes of a divorce? But he could now, and he could take care of Anna—if she wanted him. Seeing her through her recuperation would bring them even closer.

He watched the sandy desert landscape pass by, thinking of Anna and of how he might get inside her parents' home or at least contact her. He could send flowers and see if they were accepted. On the note, he could write his phone number with a pleading message: I miss you. Please call me.

Driving down the short cul-de-sac toward the Santa Fe–style ranch house in a subdivision filled with like homes snapped Lee back to their investigation. He could be minutes away from meeting Anna's natural father. He looked at his watch. It was after five. If the man had a regular working schedule, then he most likely should be home. But Lee hadn't had shift work for years. Why should he assume the man did?

At the end of the street, a pregnant woman stood on the sidewalk while a young boy and older girl rode their bikes in the road. Candice pulled the car over and stopped several houses away. "That woman is standing in front of Carpenter's house."

"Peter's married."

"And has young children," Candice added.

The rumbling of a loud motor came from behind them. Lee turned around in time to see a man dressed in dark blue uniform pants and a matching shirt with patches on the sleeves riding past them on a big turquoise and black motorcycle. He wore an obvious wide smile. And even though he had a pair of dark sunglasses on, Lee figured he had his eyes on either the woman or the children.

237

Debra Erfert

Lee had a momentary pang of envy at the man's apparent happiness. He wanted that, too.

"It looks like my occupation may come up again," Lee said. "He's a firefighter."

Candice grinned over at him. "Sometimes you guys don't get along too well." She rubbed Rusty's face. "Let's get out here and walk up."

It seemed like a good idea. It also gave Rusty a chance to relieve his bladder, away from the family they were going to grill about their father's past romance. It would've been so much easier if the man they were searching for had been . . . what? Divorced? Alone and pining away since Anna's birth mother left him more than two decades ago? Lee knew the man was allowed to get a life. What were the chances that Peter knew where Anna's mother was right now? All they really needed was a name, and Lee had no doubt Candice could find her even if she was currently living under a rock in the Grand Canyon.

The firefighter had parked his motorcycle in the driveway next to a minivan as Candice, Lee, and Rusty stopped on the sidewalk. They were quickly noticed. The two children had dropped their bikes on the curb a few feet away from them. Rusty tugged at his leash, wriggling and whining toward the kids.

"Does he bite?" the mother asked as she headed for her small son.

"No, ma'am." Lee knelt down and looped his arm around Rusty's neck. "He's gentle."

"Can I pet him?" the girl asked with her hand out. She looked around eight years old. Lee stared into familiar wide brown eyes. Her light brown hair was pulled back into a ponytail—like how Anna usually wore it.

"Chief Carpenter, may we speak with you in private?" Candice asked.

Lee looked up at the man taking off his helmet, curious how Candice knew how to address him. It was then he saw the insignia on the shirt collar.

A Strange Twist of Fate

"What's this about?" Carpenter asked as he stored the helmet on the side of his bike's saddlebag.

Candice moved close enough to hold out a picture for him to see. Lee couldn't see which one she showed him from his point of view, but after the man looked at it for a few seconds, he blinked, and his head jerked.

"Gisela," Carpenter said. But then he took the picture from Candice and held it closer to his face. "No, she isn't . . ." His stare shot up to Candice. "Who is this?"

"Gisela's daughter," Candice told him. That wasn't such a far leap to make, not after what the man had said.

It was as if an unseen force punched the air out of the man's chest—he exhaled so fast. His wife took the picture from him, and after she stared at it for a short time, she looked up at her husband. "I'll take the kids inside," she told him softly and gave him back the picture.

After both of the children had petted Rusty, the mother took their hands and led them inside the house, leaving the three adults alone.

Candice moved next to the quiet man, who still gazed at Anna's picture like he couldn't get enough of her. "Chief, I'm sorry we had to break the news like this, but Anna Eddington is looking for her birth mother, and you're our only lead."

That wasn't exactly true, Lee knew. But he was the best lead they had at the moment.

"How did you know about me?"

"Your old boss at Walgreens, Rodney Jones, gave us your name after he remembered a pregnant woman who went crazy and bashed a mirror at the photo counter."

"And she smashed the glass counter pretty good, too," he told them. The chief finally looked up from Anna's picture. "I was working that day, and I had to clean up the mess she left behind after the police put her in handcuffs. I knew her, sort of. Not enough to get her to stop her tantrum. She just"—he shrugged—

"went off the deep end, completely nuts. But Gisela worked part time cleaning her house while going to the university."

Lee pointed at the picture. He needed to know the truth right now. "Are you Anna's birth father?"

"I don't know!" Carpenter scrubbed his hand over his jaw, eliciting a soft sandpaper sound. "I didn't know then—how could I possibly know now?"

"I can rule you out," Lee told him, although all he had to do was look into the man's brown eyes and he could see Anna.

"How?" Carpenter asked, keeping a hard stare on Lee.

"Anna's blood type is very rare, AB. Her parents can only have AB, A, or B, all of which only a small percentage of the population have. What's your blood type?"

With as slow as the man moved, taking out his wallet from his back pocket, Lee had a feeling he already knew the answer. Carpenter took out a Red Cross blood donor's card, and after he gazed at it for several moments, he passed it to Lee.

"A positive." Lee handed it back to him. "Anna has your eyes."

"What is Gisela's last name?" Candice asked. She took Anna's picture out of the chief's hand. For a brief moment, Lee thought he would ask for it back.

"Sommer, with an O," he said, still with his eyes on the picture in Candice's hand. Lee reached over and took it from Candice and gave it back to the fire chief, freeing her to take out her phone. She immediately started a search on the name.

"Did you know about Gisela being pregnant?" Lee asked.

Carpenter's demeanor changed. He seemed upset. "I knew. I just didn't believe . . . I thought if she slept with me, then she might've slept with other guys, too. I"—he swallowed hard, staring at Anna's face—"I was going to the university, planning my career. Getting saddled with a wife and baby . . ." he trailed off, shaking his head. "I was only a kid."

He looked up at Lee. "You said she's looking for her birth mother? That means Gisela gave her up for adoption. I don't

A Strange Twist of Fate

understand that. She was so determined to raise her baby. Who adopted her? Can I meet Anna?"

"Margo Wright—the woman who smashed the mirror at the photo counter—adopted her."

"No, no, she couldn't have! That woman was pregnant—she had her own baby! And she was crazy! Why would Gisela do something like that?"

"How would you know if she gave her up for adoption or not?" Candice snapped the question, with irritation in her voice. "You didn't care what happened to her."

"I did care about Gisela." Carpenter glanced over his shoulder at the house before he spoke again. "I thought I was in love with her. And as she neared full term, I thought we might've worked things out. I even checked into family housing on campus. But she left without saying good-bye."

"When was the last time you saw her?" Lee asked. Candice seemed to be having trouble with her phone. She kept stabbing at the keypad.

Carpenter rubbed his hand slowly across his mouth while staring off down the street. Lee doubted he was looking at anything in particular. Then Carpenter's gaze returned to the picture, and his face softened. "It must've been the day before she had the baby. It was a Friday, and I had a couple of tests before work that day. I saw her between classes like I normally did, and she told me she wasn't feeling well and that she was going home. She asked me if I'd drive her, but I still had another test. I didn't think taking the bus would hurt her. She'd done it most every day. Some days I'd drive her. But then the next night she called me from the hospital. She'd had a baby girl. Anya."

"Anna," Lee whispered.

He smiled at Lee. "Gisela's German. She came over from Heidelberg to study in America for a year. I think she had a scholarship." The smiled dissolved from his mouth. "But when I went to the hospital on Sunday morning, she had been discharged.

Debra Erfert

I went to the apartment she was renting, but she wasn't there. I left the flowers with the landlady and a note asking Gisela to call me."

The hairs on Lee's arms stood up as gooseflesh prickled his skin. "Did you ever hear from her again?"

"I went back the next day. She still hadn't come home."

"Maybe she went to stay with a girlfriend," Candice said, still with an edge in her voice. "Since she didn't have a husband to take care of her."

"Can you remember the date she gave birth?" Lee asked, not giving the man time to respond to Candice's terse statement.

"Not exactly, but it was at the beginning of October."

"Candice, find a birth certificate for Anya," Lee said. She still hadn't lifted her worried stare away from her phone.

"Phillip's on it. I'm waiting for his text. But Gisela Sommer hasn't registered a vehicle in the state of Arizona, ever. That's not a common name—if that's her name any longer." Candice looked up at the chief. "She probably married and moved on as well."

Carpenter swung his gaze back at the house again.

"If she hasn't returned to Germany," Lee said.

"I discovered something interesting." Candice tapped a few keys and then held out her phone close enough for Lee to see. It was a picture of a certificate.

"A stillbirth certificate issued for a baby girl Wright?"

"Yes, I should've looked for this last night. It lists Margo Wright as the mother and Jackson Wright as the father, dated October 1, 1992, issued from the University of Arizona Medical Center."

"That was around the time Anya was born," Carpenter said softly.

Lee's chest hurt when a sick thought entered his mind. "What if Gisela went to the Wrights' house after she left the hospital?"

A Strange Twist of Fate

Twenty-Four

"Phillip just returned my text. He found a registered copy of Anya Sommer's birth certificate, born October third." Candice gazed up at the chief and told him without any censure in her voice, "She has you listed as the father, and she named her Anya Sommer Carpenter."

Carpenter blew out a heavy breath, then another. Lee could see him trying to keep his emotions in check, but the sudden sheen in his brown eyes said everything about how he felt.

"I need to go to my office and see if we can find a missing person report for Gisela Sommer," Lee said, looking away from the emotional man.

"Did you file one, Chief?" Candice asked.

"I thought she ran away from me, not anything worse than that. I, uh, I need to talk to my wife first, but I want to go with you. I'd like to meet my, my daughter."

"We'll wait in my car." Candice pointed to her Beemer. "Take your time."

It didn't seem like the chief would take her advice. He rushed inside his front door before Lee had Rusty to the sidewalk. "That's going to be an interesting conversation."

"I don't think it's going to be difficult. The wife already knew—at least she did after she saw Anna's picture. She looks so much like their little girl."

"They have the same eyes. I noticed that immediately. But their faces are shaped differently. When he first saw Anna's picture, he thought it was Gisela. Anna must look a lot like her to get that kind of reaction." Lee opened the passenger side door, and Rusty jumped in. They only had to wait fifteen minutes before Peter Carpenter came back outside, wearing blue jeans and a dark polo shirt, carrying a duffel bag. "He must be planning on a longer visit with Anna."

"He doesn't even know about her being shot."

"He doesn't know a lot of things."

"Like how he's going to get past Judge Wright."

Candice pushed the start button on the dash, bringing the powerful engine to life. "We'll need to bring him up to speed." She pressed another button, and the trunk opened for the chief to put his bags into.

"We have three hours to Phoenix," Lee said. "Not much time to talk."

After Chief Carpenter sat in back next to Rusty, he asked, "Who's the medic?"

"What?" Lee asked, looking back.

"There's a jump bag—a medic's bag—in the trunk."

"I'm not a medic. I'm a police detective with the city of Phoenix." Lee turned his attention to Candice and ventured another guess. "Did you get a degree in fire science?"

Candice nodded once before shifting gears. As she turned the car around, they could see the chief's family standing in their doorway, waving. "I graduated from the University of Arizona with a degree in fire science and then went through the Tucson Fire Academy, believing I could be a firefighter."

"Yet you're a private investigator. Why's that?" Lee had to ask.

Candice sighed exceptionally loudly. "I have a little problem with seeing blood, and you can't be a firefighter without actively being an EMT."

"You pass out?" Carpenter asked.

"That's about it."

"That's not so uncommon," he told her. "It happens more often than you think. And you can get by it with some therapy."

"Yeah, well"—Candice shrugged—"maybe sometime I'll try it, but right now, I'm having fun playing detective."

A Strange Twist of Fate

"You play very well," Lee muttered under his breath. Her cheek dimpled. She must've heard him.

"Why the bag, Chief?" Candice asked.

"Well, I don't know where I'm going or how long I'll be gone, exactly. I like being prepared."

"And your wife is OK with this?" Lee asked.

"Kayla . . . understands. We'd talked about our old romances while we were dating, so she knew about Gisela."

Candice couldn't let it be. "But she didn't know about Anya—did she?"

It took a few moments before the chief murmured, "No."

Lee's phone vibrated. He quickly took it out of its holder as it vibrated again. His heart jumped, thinking it was Anna. The number was from the police department, though. Hopefully, she'd left a message. "Adams."

"Detective Adams, this is Officer Spencer. We just arrested Harold Bivens, a.k.a. Razor, for strong-armed robbery. I saw that you put out a warrant, and I thought I'd let you know he's in custody."

"Thank you, Officer Spencer. I appreciate the call. I'll let the victim know." *If I ever get to see her again*, Lee thought as he touched off his phone, wishing more than ever Anna would get in touch with him.

~*~

It was nearly ten before Candice pulled into the back lot of the police department. She parked in Lee's usual spot. During the drive, he'd told Peter everything he knew about Anna, about her deceased husband, her investigation, and about her being shot. It didn't make things easier on Peter when he found out about her adopted father being an overprotective judge who wouldn't let Lee in to see her. The chances of Peter getting inside to meet his daughter by knocking on the front door were zero, and they all knew it. Lee's only hope of seeing Anna was Candice's ability to sneak him inside to see if her lack of communication was because she didn't want to talk with him or if there had been some misunderstanding.

But there could be another reason she hadn't called Lee: Judge Jackson Wright intentionally running interference between them because he didn't think Lee was good enough to love his daughter, like Homer said. Adopted or natural, the judge's feelings for her ran deep.

"It'll take me a minute to boot up my computer." Lee dropped down onto his office chair and pushed the Power button. He never felt time drag as much as then. Neither Candice nor Peter sat. Pacing the small office seemed to be their choice in keeping their nerves steady. Rusty lay near the door, watching them.

"OK, here we go." Lee logged in and opened the National Crime Information Center, or NCIC, database. "Pete, do you remember Gisela's birth date?"

"April Fools' Day, and she's my age, so 1971."

"OK, I'll input her name and birth date in the search box." At that point, Candice and Pete moved around behind Lee to watch the screen change.

Peter moaned softly. "There's a report."

Lee leaned his elbow on the desk while keeping a hand on the wireless mouse. "On October 6, 1992, Mrs. Ethel Meyer reported Gisela Sommer missing."

"Yes, that was Gisela's landlady. She was a nice woman."

"She said Gisela left without paying her October's rent or taking her belongings." Lee scrolled through the report to see what the detectives did. "Paperwork found in Gisela's room led Detective Clarence Black to contact her parents in Heidelberg, Germany. He called them every week for a month, then"—Lee sat back, with his heart beating irrationally fast—"once a month for the next year, updating them on the case."

"The case is still open." Candice crossed her arms and paced around the small room. "She never made it home, either."

"We know where her baby is," Lee said, hitting Print. He wanted a physical copy to take with him. He didn't really know

A Strange Twist of Fate

why. Maybe to use as leverage to see Anna if he was caught sneaking in. "This doesn't prove anything sinister happened to Gisela," Lee went on to say. "But I'd rather talk with Anna now and see that she's safe before we start an in-depth search—"

"For Jane Does?" Candice asked, interrupting him.

Lee got up and went over to the printer. He couldn't think the worst of two people who raised Anna for the past twenty-five years. Gisela could be one of the many homeless Anna came in contact with on a weekly basis, and Anna wouldn't even know it was the woman who gave her up as an infant. "We don't know if Gisela had postpartum depression and took a walk after giving up Anna to the Wrights."

"You really believe that?" Candice asked.

Lee picked up the three-page report from the printer bin. "Jackson Wright is a highly respected judge. He didn't get that way by being dishonest. We need to give him the benefit of the doubt."

"Even though he doesn't think a police detective is good enough to date Anna?" Candice asked, digging into that already sore spot of needless insecurity.

"I want to speak with her." Lee headed for the door. "Candice, get me inside the judge's house."

~*~

"Julianna?"

Anna woke to her mother's voice, shocked that she was in her room so late at night and just as surprised at actually being in a deep sleep. The light was on, and the drapes were pulled closed across the French doors again. She glanced at the bedside clock. It was nearing eleven. "Mother," Anna groaned, "what is it?"

"I want you to feel better." She held out a paper cup and an amber prescription bottle. Anna couldn't focus enough to read the label; her head hurt too badly from the concussion. But she could see her mother's dark hair was a mess hanging around her face, as if she'd been sleeping. And the fact that she was in her favorite flannel nightgown affirmed that she'd risen from her bed to tend Anna. While endearing, it was very frustrating.

Debra Erfert

"I was sleeping."

"You're in pain. I can stop your pain, Julianna." Margo held the cup closer. "Please, let me help you."

Sitting up was too difficult, and the ice pack Vicky brought the last time she came in had slid off her shoulder again. "I can't take pain pills, Mother. They make me throw up." Anna held back the rebuking "I told you that already," knowing it would hurt her feelings.

Margo put the cup and bottle down on the side table next to the clock, surprising Anna again that she'd cooperated so quickly. Without moving, she studied her mother's placid face. It showed no emotion while she picked up an extra pillow from the chair next to the bed and gently fluffed it. Anna couldn't remember the last time she saw her mother smile or look happy. Was Anna to blame for her mother's misery? Or was it the miscarriage she'd suffered? Anna was a replacement for a child she'd lost. That might've played into her mother's mental deterioration, which seemed to have spiraled down faster over the past few months. She still didn't remember about Greg being killed. If only they could talk openly, honestly. Anna was tired and in pain and quite possibly wasn't thinking too clearly about the consequences of her next words.

"I know your baby died," Anna whispered, wanting to share with her about her own miscarriage. Her mother's hands froze in midfluff, but her head turned until their stare met. Anna recoiled at the instant hatred seething in her mother's green eyes. That emotional abhorrence visibly moved through her mother's body, stiffening her back as she clutched the pillow tighter and tighter until she was wringing the edges with bloodless fingers.

In a low voice, one that was deep and threatening, and holding the pillow in front of her, Margo stepped closer. "You can't have her back, Gisela. She's my baby. *My baby!* Why are you here?" Even lower, she ground her teeth and growled the words, "I killed you! You're buried under the water! Why can't you stay dead?"

Terrified, Anna's pulse raced with a horrifying thought—she was being mistaken for another woman—quite probably the

A Strange Twist of Fate

woman who had given birth to her. She had to figure out a way to bring her mother back to the present if she was lost in the past—one that was filled with a dreadful, mind-crippling secret. "Mother! Mother, my arm hurts. May I have some ice cream, please?"

Margo blinked again and again, and then that missing spark of recognition brightened her eyes. Her shoulders relaxed. "Yes—yes, I'll go get your favorite." She dropped the pillow on the floor and walked passed Vicky, who was standing in the doorway, on her way out of the room.

"Are you hurt?" Vicky asked, rushing to Anna's bedside as she sat up.

"You need to do me a favor." Anna held her elbow, trembling as adrenaline coursed through her body. She gasped at the surge of pain the sudden movement caused. "Go to Lee's apartment and bring him back. Tell him what just happened and that I need him. If Dad sees you leaving . . . make any excuse for going out this late." Anna told her Lee's address in Phoenix.

"What just happened?" Vicky asked in a softened voice.

"I think Mother confessed to killing my birth mother. I don't think I'm really adopted," Anna told her quietly. "Please"—she grasped Vicky's arm—"go find Lee for me. Tell him I may be in danger."

"Should I get you out? I could take you—"

"No. You aren't strong enough to carry me down the stairs. I need Lee."

Vicky leaned closer to Anna's face. "Should I call the police? They can help you quicker."

"What could they do? Mother's mentally ill, and Dad would probably cover for her." Anna's heart sank, breaking, as another thought pushed into her mind. Her dad must've known what Mother had done—if her mother actually *did* anything. Could what she said be another part of her illness? How could Anna take the chance? No, she had to leave quickly, and Lee was her only way without unnecessarily dragging other police officers into it.

Debra Erfert

"I can get around your father. Don't worry." Vicky fished the ice pack from under the cover and gave it back to her before turning and leaving the room. She closed the door behind her.

It took a great deal of energy and caused Anna significant pain to get up off her bed, but she needed to clear her head and think about what her mother had said. With the help of a cane to support her injured leg as she walked, she went to the French doors and opened the curtains. Now the reflection of the glass would discourage her mother from coming into the room, or at least from staying very long if she actually made it downstairs for the ice cream. Suffocated by being confined to her room, Anna unlatched the deadbolt and opened the doors. Standing out on the balcony, taking in a few deep breaths of the cool night air, gave her the illusion of being free even though she was trapped in a house with a woman who just confessed to killing her real mother.

How could that have happened? Surely, her dad would've known about it, yet he stayed quiet? That would've made him an accessory to the major crime. That didn't make sense. He was a judge who put criminals in prison, and justly so. But he was always fair and had a good reputation with everyone, including defense attorneys. Greg had admired him. A man didn't get that kind of standing in his community by being a criminal. The only logical, rational thing Anna could think of was that her mother was delusional about it, but that didn't make Anna any safer being around her.

The bedroom door opened. Anna's dad came into the room carrying a bowl. Her mother wasn't with him.

"Julianna, come back inside, or you'll get sick. I have your ice cream."

On the way back to her bed, Anna walked with as much difficulty as she did getting to the balcony, and her dad watched her take every pain-filled step with a frown on his lips. He set the bowl on the end table.

"Where's Mother?" Anna asked as he helped her sit on the edge of the bed.

A Strange Twist of Fate

"I put her to bed after I promised to bring you your ice cream." He picked up the pillow from the floor and tossed it on the chair. "Why are you eating ice cream this late at night?"

"I was asleep, but Mother woke me up. Dad, who's Gisela?" Anna kept a close watch on his reaction to the name, but all he did was blink a couple of times. Which could've meant anything, considering how late it was. He might just be as tired as Anna.

"Your mother is mixed up." He held the bowl and dipped the spoon into the strawberry ice cream. She hated strawberry ice cream. That was her mother's favorite flavor.

Anna held out her right hand, stopping the spoon from leaving the bowl. "I'm not hungry. I only asked for this to stop Mother from smothering me with a pillow when she thought I was Gisela. She asked me why I wouldn't stay dead."

He blinked twice again.

"Your mother's medication is out of balance, and her worrying about you isn't helping any." He set the bowl back on the end table. "I'll leave this here in case you want it later, but I think you need to take some pain medication." The bottle that was on the table must've been the Vicodin.

"Dad, I can't. It'll make me sick—you know that. I'd rather have the pain than have to throw up for the next twelve hours."

He went to the dresser and brought back another prescription bottle. "That's why the doctor gave you the antinausea medication."

"It doesn't work well enough," Anna told him.

"Julianna, either you do as I say, or I'll get a court order to be your guardian, and you won't have a choice."

Taking in a full breath became hard. He'd threatened to take away her freedom. And he could do it, too. Anna held out her hand, and he put a big antinausea pill on her palm. She swallowed it with the water from the paper cup as tears filled her eyes.

When he gave her the pain pill, he said, "This is for your own good."

251

Debra Erfert

Anna put the pill in her mouth and quickly used her tongue to push it between her gum and cheek before drinking down the last of the water. The tears spilled down her cheek, and she threw the empty cup across the room, angry at her dad for making her take something he knew would sicken her. It didn't make sense. Nothing seemed to be making sense. Anna leaned sideways, and he lifted her feet up on the bed before putting the ice pack on her shoulder and covering her up. After he closed the French doors and the curtain, he turned off the light and left the room.

In the dark, Anna lay quietly for a minute or so to make sure her dad didn't come back in. The pill tucked in her cheek had already begun to soften. She focused on the anger with her dad to help her make it to the bathroom sink, where she spat it out. The bitter taste was enough to make her stomach clench into a sickening knot. It took two full times of brushing her teeth before she'd cleaned any residual medication out of her mouth.

Leaning her fist on the edge of the vanity, she let her head hang. "Oh, Lee, where are you?"

Being a stubborn woman, probably a learned trait from her dad, Anna hobbled over to the French doors. She wanted the curtains open to keep her mother out and fresh air coming inside to breathe. As she stood at the threshold, feeling a cool breeze touch her skin—a rustling sound from below the balcony caught her attention. It didn't really alarm her. They'd had plenty of stray cats climb the olive tree planted right outside. Sometimes they'd jumped onto her balcony and peeked into her door. But cats were never allowed inside the house while Anna was growing up. Her mother never could tolerate pets.

What Anna didn't expect to see was a hand reaching up on top of the stucco-covered wall—and then the other hand appeared. Anna carefully lifted the lightweight metal cane above her shoulder, readying to swing it, to take down the intruder. A head and broad shoulders pushed up above the wall. She'd need to take her shot now.

"Anna?"

A Strange Twist of Fate

"Lee?"

He climbed over the railing and stood in front of Anna as relief cooled her body.

"Oh, Lee! Where've you been?" She dropped the cane in time for him to wrap his arms around her. She clutched tightly to his shirt with her good hand, pulling him that much closer.

"I've missed you," Lee said with his lips on her neck. His warm breath sent a rush of goose bumps down her skin. But Anna wanted more—and she didn't want to wait any longer. He may have started at her neck, but Lee's lips kept moving upward with a trail of plentiful soft kisses. When he finally lifted his head, Anna pushed her mouth against his and kissed him with fierce intensity. The feelings she thought he might've had for her came alive in the next moment. Long-awaited passion pushed aside the pain she'd been in since her accident, sending fire roiling down inside her body. With his arm still around her, he held her face with one hand. She felt safe in his embrace, and he seemed to know where not to touch her, like he'd been briefed on her injuries. Soon, too soon, he softened the pressure until he released her lips.

"You wouldn't wake up," Lee whispered as he repeatedly stroked the round of her cheek with his thumb. "And I was afraid."

"Wake up?" Anna closed her eyes, enjoying the sensation his touch produced. "When?"

"In the hospital, after you were brought into the ICU." Lee brushed her hair back from her ear. "I talked to you, but you wouldn't wake up."

Anna leaned back to look at him. There was enough ambient light to see the outline of his handsome face. "You didn't forget me?"

His dark brows lowered. "Anna—don't you remember Rusty and me finding you after the crash?"

"I don't remember anything from the time I was shot until waking up in the hospital. And even now, I get confused. They tell me it's my concussion."

Debra Erfert

Lee lifted her chin and pressed another tender kiss on her mouth again and then said, "I would've been with you every minute if your dad would've let me."

"My dad?" Anna's heart flipped again.

"Yeah, he made me leave, but he told me you'd call if you wanted me to visit you. And I waited. You didn't call me."

"Yet you're here. Why?"

"After what we've learned about your birth parents, I needed to know you're safe."

"Oh, Lee! Mother said she killed a woman named Gisela."

"Gisela Sommer is your real mother," Lee told her quickly. "She went missing right after you were born." He held her closer. "I need to get you out of here." Lee was looking out toward the balcony.

"I can't climb. I can barely walk."

"I know, honey. I can have a friend meet us out in front. Let me send her a text." Lee used one hand, and without letting Anna loose, he took out his phone. In a few moments, he smiled. "OK, it's all set. Candice, your private investigator, is waiting for us at the curb. She'll take us to my car, and I'll take you absolutely anywhere you want me to—I will take care of you."

Anna leaned her head on his shoulder, relieved. "OK. Let's go."

Lee reached under her legs and lifted her. She looped her right arm around his neck, holding on tightly while he moved toward the bedroom door. Her dad had left it open. "Be very quiet," Anna whispered into Lee's ear. "I don't want to see my dad before we get out."

"I don't either," Lee said, whispering just as softly. "Are you warm enough?"

"I'm fine. I'll use your blanket."

Lee smiled; he seemingly enjoyed her voice in his ear. "We're going to my place?" He began to descend the stairs. They were carpeted, and his footsteps were nearly silent.

A Strange Twist of Fate

"I'm looking forward to sleeping on your couch, although I may need a few more pillows."

"I have several extras on my bed. You might be more comfortable there."

Anna grinned. "We'll see."

"Can you get the door?" Lee bent down enough for Anna to reach the deadbolt. She got it unlocked, and just as she opened the door, a sharp metallic click echoed through the foyer that had nothing to do with the knob.

"Close the door, Julianna. You're not leaving."

Lee stiffened. When Anna looked over his shoulder at her dad standing in the den's doorway, his usual pinkish face was even more ruddy, and his eyes looked glassy and a little red around the edges. At best, he seemed shaky. And then she saw the gun in his hand, pointed at them, and it had an extra-long barrel. No—it was tipped with a silencer. She'd almost missed it—her dad holding a weapon, of any kind, was so incongruent it was hard to fathom. Lee turned around, facing him—and the gun.

"What are you doing?" Anna asked, shrieking her question, panicking.

Jackson Wright, a judge who she'd thought was of upstanding character, was someone who loved her, motioned down the hallway with the barrel of the gun—the gun that he had pointed at her. "Carry her to the dining room." Anna heard the uncharacteristic stress in his voice. "Do it *now*!"

"Lee?" Anna cried, clutching at his shirt.

"It'll be all right, honey." Lee's breathing came heavy and fast as he carried her through the living room and into the kitchen. They didn't make it past the breakfast bar before her dad spoke again.

"Hold it—stop right there."

Lee held very still, but Anna watched her dad from over Lee's shoulder as he stepped close enough to tug the gun from his holster clipped in the back of his waistband. The thick odor of alcohol drifted off her dad. She rarely saw him drink. He'd always liked to keep a clear head. But tonight, he must've needed the liquid courage to do whatever he had planned. Or maybe it was just clouding his good judgment. Lee's gun made a loud clink as he set it on the granite countertop.

"What are you doing?" Anna shouted, nearly hysterical, still not believing her dad could aim a gun at her—at them.

"That's a good question," Lee said, much calmer than Anna could've ever been, as he put a little more distance between them by moving into the dining room, then gently put her feet on the tile floor. He kept one arm around her to keep her from falling, yet Lee stood in such a way he put his body between her and the business end of the gun that was now aimed at his heart. Anna didn't know what scared her more—the thought of her dad shooting someone or of her and Lee being shot.

The normally reserved Judge Jack Wright seemed to be breaking down in front of Anna's eyes. His gun hand shook—slightly, but it was enough she could see it. He breathed in and out too quickly.

"Dad, please, put down the gun. Don't!" Anna held out her hand, begging for him to stop aiming it at them. She'd been shot, nearly killed, and knew how very painful it was. More than that—she didn't want to die.

"I . . . I'm sorry, Julianna, but you know the secret."

"About what? Mother? What she told me is true? She killed my birth mother?" Anna glanced up at the ceiling as tears flooded her eyes. Her anger swelled, and she yelled again. "She must've had a mental breakdown when she had her miscarriage—she didn't know what she was doing! No one would've put her in jail for what she did!"

"But they would've put her away." Her dad's voice had weakened. In that instant, Anna hoped his resolve had, too. But then he straightened his arm and pointed the gun at her, and Lee could only do so much to block her from the bullet's path. "I won't let Margo be locked away, be treated like an animal. She'd—she'd die!"

A Strange Twist of Fate

"So you're going to kill me?" Anna cried the words. "How can you do that? Don't you love me?" If the tears in his eyes were any indication, yes, he loved her, too.

He started shaking, and the gun lowered a little.

"Where's Mother?"

"She's asleep."

"How are you going to explain it when she finds me gone?"

He motioned to Lee. "You ran off with your boyfriend, just like you were doing tonight."

"Judge Wright—this could end now and still be OK. You haven't done anything to us." Lee held out his free hand, palm up. "Just put the gun down."

Jack moved closer to them, and Anna was terrified by the man who'd raised her—who'd loved her all her life. He wasn't thinking rationally—he couldn't be.

"I can't go to jail!" His voice was stronger, with a hardened edge to it. "I put too many evil men behind bars." He shook his head. "I wouldn't live out the first day."

"You helped Mother bury Gisela, didn't you?" Anna whispered.

"I . . . when Gisela came over to the house, Margo saw you in her arms, and she must've thought you were her baby. I came home and found Gisela strangled, I assumed, and Margo in the nursery, rocking you, singing . . . It was over, and I had to deal with it."

"So you're going to get rid of us?" Lee asked, moving Anna a little farther behind him. "You don't think anyone will miss us?" When her dad blinked a couple of times, Lee told him, "I'm an officer of the law. There will be an investigation when I don't show up to work in the morning. You can be assured, a detective will be at your door to speak to Anna, at least."

"You're an unexpected complication, Detective, but that can't be helped now—I'll deal with it."

The gun suddenly pointed directly at them. Lee pivoted, turning his back to her dad, and took Anna down to the tile floor as muted pops from the gun's silencer sounded like hot light bulbs bursting. Her dad had shot. She landed on her back as Lee fell on top of her, pinning her down and groaning. Pain jolted her shoulder like lightning striking, searing through her body. Anna screamed as her dad stepped closer. He wasn't done. "Dad, *please*, no!"

"I'm sorry," he whispered hoarsely.

"My baby! *My baby!*" Loud gunshots blasted, reverberating throughout the house. Jack Wright's eyes went wide, and his mouth popped open as he slumped to his knees before falling on his face near Anna's feet. "My baby! My baby! My baby!" Margo screamed over and over.

A Strange Twist of Fate

Twenty-Five

Anna saw a woman grab Margo and bend her facedown over the breakfast bar, taking Lee's gun from her hand. The woman looked as pale as Anna felt. Sirens were growing in the distance, and a man with brown eyes, carrying a medical bag, checked her dad with a touch to his neck. He caught Anna's gaze and frowned. "He's dead." The man then quickly moved to Anna's and Lee's side.

"Candice, get on the phone and dial 911. We need rescue," the man said. His voice was calm, unhurried—professional.

"On it," Candice said, still holding Mother down on the counter. At least now Mother had stopped screaming, but the way she stared openmouthed at the man pressing thick bandages on Lee's back told Anna that she recognized him or was trying to remember who he was.

"Sirens?" Anna asked.

"We called the police when we heard you screaming," Candice told her.

"Lee?" Anna couldn't move with his body lying halfway on top of hers, but she could talk to him. And with the way Lee's hand squeezed her arm, pulling at her, she knew he was still alive and mostly conscious. "Hold still, sweetheart. Let this man help you." She looked up into his dark eyes. "Are you a paramedic?"

"Yes, Anya, I am."

"Anya?" Anna whispered.

Her mother started screaming again and struggled to get away from Candice's hold. "She's my baby—*my* baby! Get away from her!"

"Don't hurt her," Anna said, feeling her strength draining with every passing moment. "She didn't know what she was doing."

Debra Erfert

"We know," the man told her. "Are you shot?"

Anna closed her eyes and nodded.

"Candice, I need your help here!" His voice had broken out of the professional-sounding mode.

Anna looked up at the man after he'd raised his voice. "No. I was shot a few days ago. Lee protected me from my dad after he went . . . crazy." She couldn't touch his face with her good arm pinned under his body, but she could return his distraught gaze. "Stay with me, Lee."

"I need to turn your boyfriend over onto his back." His dark eyes held a mass of confusing emotions.

"Who are you?"

"My name is Peter Carpenter—your father."

Anna gasped. "My father . . . how?" She looked across the floor at her dad, the man she thought was her father—the only father she ever had—and groaned.

Peter positioned himself into a high squat and then gently muscled Lee onto his back, freeing Anna in the process.

"Oh, Lee!" The front of his shirt was soaked in blood, which had transferred onto hers.

"I'm OK," Lee whispered, clutching her hand. He was visually scouring her shirt. "Peter—check your daughter. There's a hole . . ."

His daughter? It's true? Anna looked closer at Peter. He was her birth father? When he cut off Lee's shirt, it revealed a single wound through his left shoulder. It confused her. How'd he get shot from the front when he'd turned around and shielded her from her dad, taking shots to his back? Unless . . . Anna pulled at her T-shirt's collar, revealing her right shoulder—and a new bloody hole in her skin.

~*~

Anna sat on a chair next to Lee's bed in the ICU. No one told her she needed to leave. In fact, her presence was never even questioned. The paramedics had arrived within two minutes of being called. Anna was numb. She'd seen her mother shoot her dad

A Strange Twist of Fate

dead while he'd tried his best to kill Anna in order to keep a decades-old secret from coming to light. A killing committed by an insane woman who'd just lost her baby.

The chances of the esteemed Judge Jackson Wright ever seeing the inside of a prison cell hadn't been likely, Anna was sure of it, no matter what he did to cover it up. It all came down to his unwavering love for Margo Wright. A woman who, in her confused way, believed that Anna was her own blood daughter. She believed it so much that she'd killed the man who had taken care of her in order to save that child.

In a strange twist of fate, the man who'd saved Lee from bleeding to death was Anna's birth father. Candice Shane, a private investigator, found him in under a day. She was good. Her keen investigative skills probably saved Anna's life. If she hadn't brought Lee back when she did, along with Peter, last night would've ended very differently.

The window was growing lighter, suggesting dawn was minutes away. Anna had spent most of the night in the surgical waiting room while Lee had two bullets removed from his back. The third bullet went through low on his left shoulder and high into Anna's right shoulder. The ER doctor removed that one bullet from Anna without bothering with anesthesia; it'd been so shallow—barely under her skin. Lee wasn't so lucky. One of his lungs had been punctured. He'd come too close to dying, all because of a sick woman's secret.

"Anya?"

Peter Carpenter, her birth father, stood in the doorway, holding a large soda he'd specifically gone to buy for her. But then he lifted a bag, and the scent of bacon and eggs drifted across the small room. Breakfast had arrived.

"How ironic that Mother named me Julianna," Anna said, slowly reaching for the cane leaning against the bed.

"Don't get up." Peter walked around the bed and set the soda on the table next to Anna's elbow. "I don't think it was a coincidence. Gisela probably told her your name, and it sounded so much like Anna that it stuck. How's Lee doing? Any changes?" He pulled an upholstered chair next to her and sat before taking out a breakfast sandwich from the bag. He took a moment to unwrap it for her.

"He woke up about an hour ago but fell back asleep after I gave him a real kiss."

Peter laughed. "Yeah, Lee told me all about that on our drive up from Yuma."

"What else did you discuss about me?" Anna asked, taking Lee's warm hand in hers.

"Lee is so proud of your investigation that he told Candice and me about basically every step you took trying to find the dark truck that killed your husband."

Anna looked at Lee's quiet face. "Yet he was the one who put everything together, not me." She turned to her newly found father. "I highway patrol lieutenant stopped in while you were getting our breakfast."

"What did he want?"

Anna sighed. "He said that Jeremy and Wade Gaines's mother called him last night. She wanted to apologize to me for the grief and pain her sons caused me. He'd promised to give me the message."

"What do you think about that?" Peter held out her sandwich. "Can you find forgiveness for them?"

Anna ignored the breakfast and leaned a little closer to Lee, studying his eyes. They flickered a little. He must've been dreaming. Of her? She could only hope. "Peter, over the past year, I've had so much anger inside me. Sometimes it was aimed at the driver who left Greg at the bottom of that canyon. And other times I'd be irrationally furious with Greg for being dead."

"That's not so unreasonable," Peter told her, setting her sandwich on the table next to her soda.

Anna moved the rest of the way and pressed a gentle kiss to Lee's cheek. "I want to be happy, and holding on to that negative

A Strange Twist of Fate

emotion won't let me feel that way." She sat back down and gave her attention to her father.

"Have you heard anything about my mother? I mean, about Margo?"

"Your mother saved your life, Anya. She loves you. And she always will."

Anna had doubts about that. "Except when she sees my birth mother in me, like she did yesterday. She came close to smothering me when she thought I was Gisela."

Peter paused from unwrapping his sandwich to gaze a little more intently into Anna's face. "There's a remarkable resemblance between you and Gisela. She had the clearest blue eyes I'd ever seen, though. You inherited her blonde hair and her beautiful face. I guess it was only a matter of time before your mother saw in you the woman she'd killed."

~*~

Ten months later
Phoenix, Arizona

Lee had a front-row seat for Anna's police academy graduation. Her hiring process with the Phoenix department took place only a month after her doctor had told her she was healthy enough to do push-ups and run a mile. That was all she needed to hear. From that moment on, all her energy had been devoted to getting stronger, and Lee was there for her every step of the way, helping her exercise, even though his wounds took a little longer to heal. At the end of the day, when his back pain had him just this side of pathetic, Anna would use Swedish massage techniques taught to her by their visiting home nurse, Vicky, the same woman who had taken care of Margo Wright for so many years.

Lee knew it was hard on Anna when she went to see her mother at the mental hospital in Phoenix, where Margo had been placed after being found incompetent to stand trial for killing the judge. Sometimes they would have a pleasant visit, but other times her mother would regress and ask about Jack. That was when things would flip for the worse. Margo would turn violent, attacking not only Anna but Lee, too.

Jeremy Gaines had pleaded guilty to killing Greg Eddington, keeping the death penalty off the table. His sentence of life without parole came with a price—he had to recount what had happened on the highway that day to everyone in the courtroom, to Anna. He even apologized to her for what he'd done. He said it was a terrible, spur-of-the-moment decision, and he regretted it. Lee believed he was only sorry about getting caught.

It had taken Candice Shane one week to find Gisela's remains. Lee was impressed. Once she found Margo Wright's arrest report, she quickly got permission from the landlord to look around the Wrights' old home. The owner and her husband, who was alive and healthy at that time, had taken possession of the big house, excited about the newly installed luxury swimming pool and spa with a lovely waterfall streaming down stacked natural slate rocks. The company that built the pool was still in business and had a good record-keeping system. The Wrights contracted the builder on October 5, 1992, and building began the same day. That was two days after Gisela Sommer gave birth. A coincidence? Candice didn't think so, and through Granduncle Homer, she got a court order to dig up all of it, using Margo's confession that Gisela was "buried under the water." It took three crews of FBI-supervised, around-the-clock, delicate excavating to find her bones beneath the pool. Anna and Peter Carpenter had been able to give Gisela a proper burial. Gisela's parents—Anna's grandparents in Germany—attended the private ceremony via Skype.

Candice sent Lee a bill for $214. She made him pay for her speeding ticket. She'd yet to call in the favor he owed her.

Carolyn never made a counteroffer on their house, so now Anna lived in it, and thanks to her Realtor friend, her home sold quickly and without any problems. She moved with the help of an amusing assortment of characters ranging from highway patrol officers to tattooed bikers wearing black leather vests with white

A Strange Twist of Fate

angel wings embroidered near their shoulders. Lee had been well enough to carry light items while the parade of people carried in furniture and boxes. Anna also inherited her father's estate. He must've known that if anything happened to him, Margo couldn't have taken care of herself. He was a smart man. The inheritance had strings attached. Anna had to take guardianship of Margo in order to receive his estate, but he had no way of knowing she would be confined to a state mental facility for the rest of her life for killing him. It was irony at its darkest.

Anna wasn't criminally charged in the death of Mrs. McCarthy's grandson, although his mother filed a wrongful death civil lawsuit, which she promptly dropped once Homer Peabody had a heart-to-heart talk with her about how much publicity there would be with that kind of a trial. Turned out, the threat of airing Travis's criminal history and their family problems left a bad taste in her mouth. Homer also might've mentioned something about a countersuit for not warning the neighbors about her son being a sexual predator before he went to live with his grandmother.

Lee tugged on the end of his white glove, tucking it under the sleeve of his jacket, and made sure his Purple Heart and Lifesaving pins he'd been awarded for saving Anna were hanging straight below his badge. He wanted his Class A uniform to look as crisp as possible. Anna had asked him to pin on her badge, and he hadn't hesitated in accepting that honor. For the past sixteen weeks, she'd gone through extensive academic and physical training, and she came out second in her class. She was bummed a little at not being first. It turned out she and another student named Bryan Cavanaugh had been competing against each other. While she couldn't beat him on any physical course, although Lee heard she'd tried her best, Anna repeatedly came in five to ten points above him on every written test at the end of each week. Their shooting competition seesawed back and forth, but in the end, Bryan got that coveted overall number one slot.

Sitting behind Lee was Peter Carpenter and his wife. They'd had their third child six months ago—another girl. They made a special trip to Phoenix to watch Peter's oldest daughter graduate. Lee smiled. Anna thought she was an only child. Now she had a father, a stepmother, and three half siblings in Yuma, plus grandparents living in Tucson and Germany. Her German grandparents were planning a trip to Arizona within the next year.

Sitting next to Anna's new parents were Lee's mom and dad. Next to them were Candice Shane and her granduncle Homer, and tonight Candice had auburn hair and no piercings, and she wore a nice knee-length dress. Behind the Carpenters and Candice were ex-marine-turned-bread-baker Caesar Aguirre and his wife, Colleen. Lee had doubted the marine would miss such a huge event in Anna's life.

Rodney and Beatrice Jones sat next to the Aguirres. After they had returned from their cruise, they drove up to Phoenix to meet Anna. Since then, they'd stayed in close contact, becoming surrogate grandparents. Anna had her own cheering section. And she deserved it. She threw herself into the academy life like she had the investigation of her husband's crash—with her whole heart. Lee knew she was going to be a first-rate officer. No doubt.

The program started, and Lee sat quietly, paying attention to every aspect of the graduation. The speeches, the awards—each moment brought back memories of the day ten years ago when Lee received his own badge. His father, a retired cop from Salt Lake, had pinned his badge on, while his mother watched from the audience. Their thirty-seventh wedding anniversary was next month. That was a long time to be married. Lee wanted that, too.

He considered his options as he fingered the small velvet box in his jacket pocket that contained the diamond ring. He could leave the proposal for later tonight when they were alone, keeping her answer their secret for as long as she wanted. Or he could ask Anna to marry him in front of hundreds of people, ensuring the start of a unique engagement with a woman he knew was exceptional.

They'd talked about their future enough to know they would be spending it together. They even speculated on what the wedding

A Strange Twist of Fate

might be like, although he never exactly asked her to marry him—yet. Tonight would change things—if everything went as he planned.

~*~

Anna's heart quickened. Her name was called, along with those of the other nine cadets in her group. They were the top ten in the class and the first ones to go up on stage to get their badges pinned. She kept her eyes locked on the back of Officer Cavanaugh's collar as she made her way up the stairs. She knew there were three different cameras positioned around the auditorium taking video of the event, and each cadet would get a copy after graduation. Maintaining composure during the ceremony was important to the cadets, but she was positive Lee had a surprise for her that might make her break her concentration, and she had a feeling she knew what it was.

Standing in line, facing forward with her shoulders back and her eyes looking out over the auditorium, Anna listened as Police Chief Arnold McArthur called Cavanaugh forward. Captain Rose, assisted by Chief McArthur, pinned on Cavanaugh's badge, and her competitor took a step back, falling in line next to Anna again.

"Officer Julianna Sommer Eddington," Chief McArthur said. With her pulse steamrolling through her body, Anna moved one step forward and tried to keep her breathing even. "Presenting the badge will be Senior Detective Lee Adams. Assisting will be Deputy Chief Rick Stevens."

Big monitors positioned around the room allowed those on stage to watch everything without looking like they were watching. Anna stared at the screen straight across the room while tamping down the overwhelming urge to smile as Lee marched up on stage, his shoulders straight and his chin up. Every couple of steps or so, he'd tap the lower edge of his jacket with his thumb. He probably didn't even know he was doing it. Anna almost sighed—he looked terribly handsome in his uniform.

Debra Erfert

When Lee met the deputy chief in front of her, his beautiful face blocked her view of the screen, and she had to stare through his head instead.

"Officer Eddington"—Lee lifted the shiny badge from its case being held by the deputy chief, calmly unhooked the latch, and opened the pin—"congratulations on your graduation." Anna didn't blink but kept staring ahead. He slid the pin in through a reinforced patch above her shirt's left pocket and secured the tiny swivel lock. "You know, J. S. Eddington is a long name to have to sign when you're filling out your reports." He ran his gloved finger across the brass nameplate pinned just above her right pocket. "And it's a tight fit here."

Lee reached into his pocket and lifted up a small card with a shiny new nameplate. He held it high enough for her to see it had *J. S. Adams* engraved on it—and Anna's heart thudded with expectation. While it wasn't exactly a marriage proposal, it came close. She briefly lifted a single brow. With that tiny gesture, she acknowledged his attempt to distract her but otherwise stayed mute. She'd successfully maintained her composure. Lee grinned widely as he placed the card in her shirt pocket.

"You could wear that nameplate if . . ." Lee let that sentence hang in the air while he reached into his pocket again. She looked down to see him taking out a black velvet box and opening it up, revealing a brilliant diamond solitaire that Anna couldn't tear her eyes away from—she could barely breathe. A low rumbling of voices waved through the audience. The bright stage lights added an extra burst of sparkle to the beautiful diamond. With her gaze on the ring, she parted her lips and struggled to draw in a breath, waiting in anticipation of what would come next, not just with his words but in their future together.

"Julianna Sommer Eddington," Lee said, taking out the ring and handing the empty box to Cavanaugh. Lifting her hand, he said, "Please marry me."

Anna gave him a smile that reflected how hard her heart was pounding, and he slid the ring onto her finger. At that point,

A Strange Twist of Fate

happiness was a dramatic understatement. She felt an overwhelming love for him, an emotion she thought she'd never truly have again.

"Oh, Lee! What took you so long?" Going against every suggested protocol, she reached out and looped her arms around his neck and gave him a real kiss, in front of her superiors, coworkers, family, friends, and three different cameras that caught every romantic detail.

Note from the author

I am grateful that you chose to spend time in a world I created. I love Anna and Lee, and I hope you do, too.

Would you like to hear about upcoming releases? I'm sure Candice Shane would love to have you tag along as she solves one of her more interesting cases. She might even run into an old love. Be sure to sign up for my mailing list on my website:

http://www.debraerfert.com/contact.html

You can also like me on Facebook or catch up with me on Twitter:

https://www.facebook.com/AuthorDJErfert/
https://twitter.com/debraerfert

And if you enjoyed this book, I would be completely grateful if you would leave a review on sites like Amazon and Goodreads.

Thank you so much!

Debra Erfert

Acknowledgments

I'd like to give a big *thank you* to everyone who nominated this book in Amazon's Kindle Scout program, helping me achieve this dream. I deeply appreciate every one of you!

I'd like to thank Amazon and Kindle Press for selecting my book. D. Robert Pease of http://www.walking-stick.com is responsible for the awesomely beautiful cover. I want to give an extra thanks to my technical advisors, Mike Erfert and Adam Erfert, who helped me better understand police procedures, and to Ryan Erfert for giving me a better understanding of the medic side of public service. They helped me understand the sometimes strange world in which they work.

I also need to thank my many beta readers who encouraged me and helped make this story the best it can be—Janine Christensen, Christina Tarbet, Carol Daut, Ellen Cay Havlik, Diane Patmore, Sara Werra, Danyelle Ferguson, and MJ Ferguson—and give a special thanks to Andrea Pearson. She's a ninja editor.

I want to express my everlasting love and personal gratitude to my children, who had to put up with a great many fast-food dinners and inattention while I wrote, and to my husband, Mike, for supporting me and for believing I could achieve my dreams.

A Strange Twist of Fate

About the Author

Debra Erfert has always loved reading. While growing up, going to libraries felt like an adventure filled with mystery and wonder. The hushed tones invoked secrets, and the dusty, sometimes moldy scent of paper smelled like expensive perfume. Leaving the library with just a single book never happened. Years later, her love of reading turned into a passion for writing.

Debra grew up in dozens of cities in the Southwest, sometimes moving twice in one year. She attended thirteen different schools before finally graduating from high school. Soon after, she met Mike, the love of her life. Once she earned her degree in drafting from Arizona Western College, she started writing full-time.

Debra's an award-winning artist who lives in southern Arizona, where the average summer temperatures are truly hot enough to fry an egg on the sidewalk.

Her website is http://www.debraerfert.com.

Made in the USA
Middletown, DE
16 August 2018